PAINT A MURDER

Paint a Murder

Lily Ashton

An
Alice Haydon
Mystery

Published by Magenta Lily Publishing 2019
London, Great Britain

ISBN 978-1-9161062-0-8

Cover design by Design for Writers

Chapter 1

THE ONLY TIME ALICE Haydon saw Jason Marley in real life, he was floating face down in the River Nare.

She had taken a shortcut to work along the river path, intending to sneak in the back door and give herself half a chance of making her meeting on time. Haring round the bend, she had nearly slammed into a policeman standing in the centre of the path.

"Steady now." He took a step back, his arms stretched out in front of him. "The path is closed this morning, you'll have to go back to Albany Street."

Alice teetered on the balls of her feet, craning her neck over the officer's shoulder and squinting through the glare. Two men in suits were standing on the river's edge, peering at a little raft of clothes in the shallows.

A police launch was pulling up, slapping water against the bank, redefining the clothes into arms and legs. The body shifted on the wash, splaying into a cross, then pulling itself back into an indeterminate heap, as if it was ashamed of being dead. Alice could not take her eyes off it, despite the nausea creeping through her stomach. "Is that a …?"

The policeman nodded. "Here, I'll take you back to the road. There's no need to worry; everything's in hand." He cupped her elbow, turned her around and walked her back along the path. "I'm sorry," he said. "Must have been a bit of a shock."

Once on the street, her feet pulled her along the pavement as she stole backward glances. She nearly tripped into a line of protestors handing out leaflets urging her to 'Support Nature not Profit'. Alice stopped at a green painted door with 'Gregory's House Art Gallery' engraved on a polished brass plate. As she stared, the words morphed into a blurry face, framed with long, messy hair.

Alice rested her forehead and both hands against the door and closed her eyes for a moment. Clang! St Edmund's chime reverberated through her head. She shoved the door open, half-ran across the entrance lobby and took the stairs two at a time. At the top, she stumbled across the reception area, putting a hand on the visitors' sofa to prevent her crashing into the receptionist's desk. Heading into the open plan office, she threw her bag on the desk, rushed to the window and looked down at the Nare. She was just in time to see the police boat, with the suited men and their deathly companion, chug away.

"Morning, Alice," said Tommy Norton, the gallery's technician, as he rolled his chair back from his desk. "You're late today. Heavy night?"

A sly smile lifted his sharp cheekbones.

"There's … a dead man. In the river!"

"I know. Duncan saw him earlier and called the police."

"They've just taken him away. Poor man."

Alice sat down. She put both elbows on the desk and her chin in her hands. She drew a couple of deep breaths, though her heart ignored her and galloped on. Pulling open a drawer, she took out a paper napkin and mopped a mist of sweat from her forehead, gathered her hair into a ponytail, securing it with a scrunchie.

"Well, a dead man and a late start were not part of my Tuesday schedule. Especially not before my big pitch to Jenna." Alice scanned the empty desks to her left. "I suppose Control Freak is in the meeting room already."

"No." Tommy peered over his computer screen. "She's not here."

"Why? Where is she?"

"How should I know, nobody tells me anything? By the way, Duncan wants to see you – you can ask him."

Poppy Lee, the receptionist, plopped down a brown envelope with Alice's name handwritten in capitals. "This came for you."

"Thanks."

She made a circle on the desktop with the palm of one hand, digesting her boss' absence. One good thing, she had avoided a reprimand for being late. But after a year of trying to convince Jenna Farling that she could curate an exhibition herself, she may have missed the opportunity to present her own ideas. It could be ages before she got another chance; at this rate, she would be assistant curator forever.

Alice found the chief executive in his corner office, gazing out of the window, throwing a squash ball from one hand to the other.

"Morning, Duncan. You wanted to see me?" Alice pulled out the plastic bucket chair on the opposite side of the desk. "I've spoken to Tommy; that was a terrible thing."

"Morning, Alice. Yes, it was a painful incident."

"Huh! Death is more than painful, I think."

Duncan snatched the ball from the air and stared at her. "Oh no, not him. I mean Jenna." He rubbed his bald head. "She fell down some stairs last night and they think she has broken her leg and pelvis. She's in hospital now, waiting for a consultant's assessment." He looked over Alice's head, his brown eyes narrowing. "She'll probably need surgery, so she's likely to be away for some time."

Duncan seemed to shrink, as though his already lean body had lost mass and part-melted, soaking into the chair. The toes of his polished black-laced shoes protruded from under the desk, one foot balanced atop the other. The effect was of a nervous schoolboy, covertly crossing his feet because it was too obvious to cross his fingers.

"Oh no! That sounds horrible – and painful. Send her my best wishes when you speak to her again."

Duncan nodded. He placed the ball on the desktop and rolled it beneath his fingertips. "Someone has to do Jenna's work while she's away," he said to the ball. "So, I need you to look after things until she gets back."

"Hold on. What?" Alice lay a hand on her fluttering stomach. A late night curry and two morning shocks were playing havoc with her internal plumbing. "You mean, you want *me* to do Jenna's job? I get to be the senior curator?" The words came out loud and shrill, prompting a stony glare from Duncan. She tucked her exhilaration away.

"The role is temporary; you will only be covering Jenna while she's away." He stilled the ball with his palm. "You'll report to me. Don't make any decisions until you've run them by me first. Is that clear?"

"Hundred percent. I wouldn't dream of making an important decision without consulting you first." She knew she was gushing. "I suppose the centenary is a priority. But we should also plan for the group exhibition after that. I've got some ideas for artists."

"The centenary exhibition is your only priority, Alice. It's got to be an outstanding show, with a really good catalogue. We have six weeks to pull it all together and there's a lot of work to do." Duncan ran a hand over his unshaven chin. "I'll sort out items for the shop, but do you think you can manage everything else on your own?"

"Yes, I can. And I really appreciate you putting your trust in me. I won't let you down."

Duncan picked up a bulging green folder. "Jenna told me that everything you need to know is in here. I keep telling her to put her work on the network, so everyone can access it and save all this paper."

Alice took the folder and thumbed through the pages.

"As you can see, there's everything on the project, but all you need is the timetable and the list of loans." Duncan rolled the ball across the desk and into his waiting hand. "I suggest you start by bringing in the artworks as quickly as you can. This is a big show."

"So, I see. Eighty pieces." Gathering up that many pictures would be an admin nightmare, as they would all be on loan from different people. Perhaps agreeing to do it all by herself had been a bit rash.

"Are any of the paintings here already?"

"Yep, over there. Arrived this morning from the council." He pointed to a package wrapped in brown paper, propped up against the wall behind her. 'Great Wheaton District Council.' She ran her eye down the lenders' list in Jenna's folder. "Here we are. It's a seascape called *Beach*. Jenna's written, 'Brilliant work, star of the show, never been seen in public before'. Wow, that sounds amazing."

Duncan put down the ball. "It's the best piece on the list. Make sure it's in the most prominent position when you plan the hang."

"Sure, no problem."

"And put it on the front of the catalogue."

Alice closed the folder. "About publicity. I think we should do something different to really sell this show. Like produce leaflets and distribute them around the town."

"That's not in the marketing plan and there's no money for any extras."

"But we want the show to be successful. Can't we run to a few leaflets?"

"Just concentrate on collecting the artworks and producing the catalogue. Leave the marketing to Rosie."

The desk phone rang and Duncan snatched it up. "I've got to take this, we'll talk later."

Alice tucked the folder under her arm, took hold of the council's painting and went back to her desk.

"I just heard about Jenna's accident," said Tommy. "Sounds bad."

Alice cleared a space on the desk and put the painting down. "Yes, nasty. I'll pop out later and buy her a card. Are you allowed to send flowers to hospitals these days?"

"Perhaps you should send flowers to Duncan – I don't know how he'll cope without his prop."

"That's harsh, Tommy."

Alice sat down and leant back, her arms dangling at her sides. She swung around and faced the wall. *Senior curator!* She screamed a silent scream. It was the role she had coveted since the first time she set foot in an art gallery eight years before, the role she had worked so hard for. The last thing she wanted was to get the job at Jenna's expense

– and the centenary exhibition was hardly the one she'd choose by way of introduction – but on with the show!

Duncan had decided to celebrate the gallery's one hundredth birthday by inviting local residents to lend an artwork from their own homes. He reckoned that giving people the rare opportunity to display their favourite artworks in a public gallery would attract attention and a bumper crop of visitors.

Alice heaved Jenna's folder into her lap and read through the list of proposed works, with accompanying snaps. A boring landscape, a dull flower arrangement, an uninspiring portrait, ditto, ditto.

Alice grabbed a pair of scissors and cut the binding on the package from the council. Removing several layers of brown paper and bubble wrap, she picked up the painting. A still life of pink flowers.

"Interesting," said Tommy from over her shoulder.

"It's…" She turned the painting over and read the back of the canvas. "*Peonies* by Jane Kenton Hills, whoever she is. But it's supposed to be *Beach*."

Alice patted the abandoned wrapping paper, lifting it up and looking underneath.

"Hang on, I'll just check my drawer and see if it's in there." Tommy laughed, spilling coffee onto the floor. "To be honest, it's not my sort of thing. But it's not bad as floral paintings go."

The arrangement itself was unremarkable. A bunch of pink peonies, placed casually in a plain white jug on top of a polished hardwood table. Blushing spheres fought for space with green shoots of rosemary in the packed receptacle. One stem, fatigued with the weight of its flower, bowed deeply, discarding a couple of petals on the shiny surface.

"The flowers are exquisite, but it's supposed to be a beach."

Alice searched Jenna's folder for the council's contact details and dialled the number for the cabinet support officer, Helen Yardley. When she reached Helen's voicemail, Alice explained that there was a mix-up with the paintings.

"Tommy." Alice gathered up the painting. "I'm just popping round to the town hall to swap this."

"You can't take it like that. Here, let me wrap it properly."

While Alice waited for Tommy, her eye fell on the envelope Poppy had given her. She picked it up and opened it. Inside was a piece of paper, one side jagged and a rip down the middle. In scrawly handwriting a note read:

'*We need to talk about* Beach. *Meet me on the bridge – tonight at 10.30. JM*'

Alice read it again. She had no idea who JM was, or why they could not talk to her at a more sociable time of day.

Tommy returned with the painting, now beautifully wrapped, and Alice folded the note and slid it into her jeans pocket.

She was still thinking about the dead body and the strange letter as she left the office and made for the staircase. She hummed an upbeat tune as she started down the stairs, but the song's pep failed to break an unfriendly and strangely foreboding silence. When a floorboard creaked behind her, her skin pricked and she was filled with a sudden and unaccountable feeling of unease.

Chapter 2

The town hall's high ceiling and thick stone walls should have kept the building cool, but the sweltering air that swept across the lobby wilted flower arrangements and doorman alike. Alice wiped her forehead with her shirt cuff and pushed both sleeves up her arms as she sat on a faded wooden bench.

An elfin woman with thick brown spectacles appeared, introducing herself as Helen Yardley. She marched Alice along a corridor lined with austere portraits of former council leaders who glowered at each other as they passed.

In her office, Helen stood behind a tidy desk and pointed to a chair piled with folders and loose papers. "You can sit there. Just plonk all that stuff on the floor."

"I really appreciate you seeing me at such short notice." Alice shifted the pile and sat down. "So, you're the lucky person who looks after the council's art collection." She took a notebook from her bag and felt around for a pen.

"No, someone else does that on a day-to-day basis. I look after Councillor Vivien Taylor and her portfolio includes culture – and your gallery among others. I was just given a painting and asked to send it to you." Hands on hips, she fixed Alice a defensive stare. "Though you say it's not the right one?"

"No, it isn't. I'd like to swap you the flowers for the sea."

Helen tucked a stray russet curl behind her ear.

"Where is the collection kept?" said Alice. "Is it here in the building?"

"Most of it is stored down in the basement, but we lend artworks to local residents and businesses, so some of the pieces are scattered around the district."

"You lend the paintings out? Like a library?"

"Yes, sort of. The collection belongs to the taxpayer and the councillors thought it only right they get some benefit. And people do borrow them, even the councillors."

"Lending an artwork to a company I can understand, but people, councillors?"

"Why not?" Helen sat down and rolled her chair towards the desk. "Councillors, at least, are responsible people and this way the paintings get to be seen by a wider audience. Otherwise they would just stay in the storeroom."

Alice spied some pens in an organiser, but as she leant across the desk she knocked over a framed photo, sending it tumbling to the floor. She reached down for it and a middle-aged man with thinning brown hair and soft hazel eyes looked up at her.

"I'm sorry." She wiped the glass with her sleeve. "I'm so clumsy." Alice placed the frame back on the desk, fiddling until it was in its original position. "Your husband? Partner?"

Helen glared at Alice, unconsciously caressing the ringless third finger of her left hand.

"Councillor Taylor." Alice bent over her pad to test the pen, but mostly to hide her flaming cheeks. "Does she have a personal interest in art?"

"Yes, she has a fine collection, or so I'm told, I haven't seen it myself." Helen swung around to face a computer screen on the desk extension to her right. "Councillor Taylor will be here in a minute, she can tell you more."

As she spoke, the door opened and a tall slender woman paused in the doorway. She wore a peacock-blue tailored dress and a patterned silk scarf was slung with apparent carelessness around her neck.

"Hello," she said. "I'm Vivien Taylor. It's Alice, isn't it? So nice to meet you." A sunny smile exposed a dimple in Vivien's cheek. She shook Alice's hand, laying a maternal second hand on top. "I understand you're holding the fort while Jenna's away. I'm sure you'll do splendidly." She indicated a sofa on the other side of the office. "Let's make ourselves comfortable."

Vivien sat down and crossed her shapely legs. Alice sat beside her.

"Duncan told me all about Jenna's accident. That poor girl, how dreadful." Vivien leant close enough to Alice to exude a waft of Chanel N° 5.

"Now, you've come about *Beach*."

"Yes, that's the painting Jenna was promised."

Vivien folded her hands in her lap. "This is a bit embarrassing, Alice, but I'm afraid there's been a tiny mix-up." Vivien dropped her chin to her chest. "When I told Jenna she could have *Beach,* I didn't realise it had already been promised to someone else. Easy mistake to make. You can vouch for that Helen, can't you?"

Helen threw the councillor a hostile stare that made

Alice wince, though it appeared to pass over Vivien's head.

"Unfortunately, it means the painting is no longer available for you. I know that's a nuisance, I'm really sorry." Vivien patted Alice's hand. "However, I do want you to have a piece from the council's collection for your exhibition, so I sent *Peonies* over. I realise it's not what you expected, but I hope you understand."

Beach was the centenary exhibition's star painting, and Alice was not going to face Duncan Jones without it.

"That is unfortunate, Councillor Taylor …"

"Call me Vivien, please."

"Vivien. But I'm keen to have *Beach*. Jenna was very excited about it, Duncan too. Actually, I don't need it right now, the show doesn't open until September. When do you expect it back?"

"It's a sweet suggestion, Alice, but it's unlikely to be available before the exhibition opening. I can't apologise enough. I would hate to let you down again, so I think it's best if you take another piece. And *Peonies* is a delightful painting. Or, if you prefer, you can pick out something else?" Vivien uncrossed her legs and folded one ankle behind the other. "Monica Streatham looks after the administrative side of the collection, so make an appointment with her for a viewing and you can choose something else. I want you to be happy, Alice."

"That's kind of you, Vivien, but *Beach* is the painting we want, it's the best piece in the exhibition."

"I can see that you want to follow your boss' instructions Alice. And believe me, I have tried to find a way around it, but I just can't see an alternative." Vivien clutched Alice's arm. "I hope you can help me out on this Alice, we girls need to stick together."

Helen clacked at her keyboard, filling the silence.

"Where is the painting now, may I ask?"

Vivien's lips pursed and a wrinkle broke her smooth brow. "Well, I'm not supposed to tell you, data protection and all that, but because I know I can trust you to keep it to yourself, I will. One of the council's benefactors has the painting at their office. If it were anyone else, I would ask for it back straight away, but he has been so generous to us over the years and *Beach* is his favourite painting. He borrows it every year."

Finally, Alice felt defeated. "Well, thank you for explaining, though I'm really disappointed not to have this special work. I'll take up your offer to see the collection though, perhaps I'll find something similar."

She knew it was unlikely, but it would be fun to nose through an art collection that was hidden away most of the time.

"Of course. Thank you for being so understanding. And to make up for letting you down, I have a surprise. I'm lending a painting from my own collection and I'm holding a kind of unveiling at my house tomorrow. I've invited the media too. It's at twelve o'clock, I hope you'll be there." Vivien paused and arched her eyebrows, as if waiting to be congratulated.

"That sounds … fun."

"I thought it would generate a bit of drama and give you some advance publicity for the exhibition." Vivien lifted her hand, but Alice moved her own away just in time. "I've invited some friends along and we'll have a drink to celebrate. It's the least I can do, to make up for welching on my promise to you and Jenna."

"It's good of you to go to all that trouble. By the way, what is the piece you're lending? It wasn't named on the list."

"When I met Jenna I hadn't decided which one to lend and now it's going to be a surprise! You'll find out tomorrow."

Vivien stood up and ironed out a couple of creases in her dress. "It's been lovely meeting you, Alice, thank you for coming over. Now you'll have to excuse me as I've got another meeting. I'll see you tomorrow." And with that, she disappeared.

Alice stared after her. She wasn't sure what just happened, but she was clear on one thing – she did not have *Beach.*

"So, that's sorted then." Helen carried on typing, her eyes glued to her screen. "You can remember the way out, can't you?"

As she walked home, Alice played over the conversation with Vivien. The explanation for the missing painting seemed plausible enough – it could have been a genuine mistake. But if this generous benefactor borrowed *Beach* every year, surely Vivien would have remembered that when she promised it to Jenna? And who was this mysterious benefactor anyway?

Now that the painting was unavailable, the letter Alice had received from 'JM' took on a whole new significance. Alice was dying to know what JM had to say about *Beach.* What could be so special about the painting that people were fighting over it?

Chapter 3

A FRAGILE RIVER BREEZE played with Alice's hair as she turned onto Sam's Lane. She tracked the path beside the River Nare, her long legs taking her swiftly past a line of barges. Great Wheaton's small water-based community may have embraced an alternative way of living, but they had conventional methods of paying the rent, so the barges were deserted this morning.

Except for one.

"Roddy Rafferty!" she yelled to a man lying, open-mouthed, on a faded sun lounger. "Did you go to sleep with a lit cigarette in your hand again?"

Alice crossed over the gangway to Roddy's battered barge and jumped down to the peeling deck. He opened his eyes and swung his legs around to the side. Taking off a frayed straw hat, he threw it onto a director's chair nearby.

"I wasn't asleep." Charcoal eyes twinkled above an impish smile. "I just had my eyes closed." Roddy threw his cigarette into the river.

"Anyway, what are you doing home, it's still morning? You didn't get fired, did you?" Roddy prised his stocky frame off the lounger and put his hands on his hips, stretching his back. His paint-splattered t-shirt rose up, exposing more midriff than necessary. A mop of unruly curly hair and a bushy beard stuck out at odd angles, framing his sunburnt face with a grey halo.

"Actually, I got promoted." She stuck out her chin and raised a smug eyebrow. "To senior curator."

"Dear girl, that's marvellous. Did you push the other girl down the stairs?"

"Bad joke – she actually did fall down the stairs!" Alice lifted a hand against the sun. "So, I'm only filling in until she's back. But I still get to be top curator for a while."

"And you thought you'd impress your new boss by skiving off down here!"

"I've only come back to get changed into something cooler. I'm baked."

"It's a scorcher okay, even the paint is melting." He indicated a canvas propped against an easel at the other side of the deck.

"Hey, you didn't tell me you were painting again."

"I don't have to tell you everything I do, Miss Haydon." Roddy's velvet voice boomed through the air.

"I'm a bit surprised, that's all. Though I'm delighted you've started a new piece. Is it going well?"

"It's a decent start," he said cheerfully, though without conviction.

Alice took in the pencil outline of a river and fields beyond, overlaid here and there with broad brushstrokes of green and blue. A few drips streaked the canvas.

"A landscape! And quite figurative. What happened to the abstracts?"

"I'm all out of ideas, so I thought I'd borrow someone else's – nature's."

Alice rested a finger on her lip. The painting was barely there, though the pencil sketch was sound.

"I see you've moved the big willow to the right, it works well there, I like it."

"Well even Mother Nature can't escape improvement! And thanks, I'm pleased you like it." Roddy grinned as he tugged at his beard.

It would be a pity, she thought, if it ended up on the rubbish pile with all the other paintings he'd started. But a landscape? She wasn't sure how that would turn out.

"Well, good luck with the rest of it. Can't stand here nattering, I need to get on."

"Pop over when you're free and we'll have a celebratory drink. I've got a nice bottle of red below."

"You're on." Alice waved as she headed back over the gangway and towards *Daisy Dawn*, the next barge along. Not for the first time, she was struck by the contrast between Roddy's midden and *Daisy*, resplendent and pristine.

She saw it as soon as she stepped onto the deck. The familiar black rucksack, plonked by the side of the saloon hatch, a navy blue helmet with a white stripe perched on top.

"Crapola!" Alice threw hands to her mouth and looked up to the sky.

She tiptoed down the companionway and into the saloon, where she found Joe Buchanan sitting on her sofa, reading a magazine.

"Hey, I wasn't expecting to see you so early. Did Duncan give you the day off after all?" Joe smiled and rubbed his cheek, reddening the scar that ran temple to chin. He put the magazine down and bounced over to her, putting both hands on her shoulders. "That's grand. Grab your bag, we need to make a move now or we'll miss the flight."

Alice's throat cramped and she struggled to swallow.

"Is something wrong?" He ran a soft finger down her nose. "Don't look so worried, we can stick to the original plan. Anyway, it'll cause a stink if you change your flight now."

She tore her eyes away from him, from the open face and the kind smile.

"I can't come with you, Joe, I'm so sorry." It came out before Alice could stop it. "I got promoted this morning to senior curator." The words flew out in a torrent, as arms flapped. "I can't go away, not on the same day, I've got so much to do."

Joe's hands dropped from her shoulders. He pulled his body up to its full height and glared down at her, his blue eyes darkening. "We'll only be away one night; you can get the early morning flight and still be here for starting time. And there's internet in Galway you know, you can still get your emails." His melodious Irish voice had a hardness that surprised her.

Tears gathered. Cheeks burned. She turned away. "I have to stay, Joe. I'm sorry."

"Damn it, Alice!" Joe's voice echoed around the saloon. "You promised Patrick you'd be there for his birthday. You promised me. And look at me when I'm talking to you."

She half-turned towards him.

"You're always complaining about your job." He was almost shouting. "How they treat you so badly. But now you're telling me you'd rather do something for them, than be with me. I—"

Joe's cheeks cherried. He stared at her, fists clenched. Then he thundered across the saloon, took the steps in two bounds and disappeared through the hatch door. The barge shuddered as he slammed the door behind him.

Chapter 4

WHEN ALICE ARRIVED AT The Coffee Pot, Livvie Manners was wiping chocolate splashes off a white wall.

"Hey, you look frazzled. There's some iced water on the counter. Help yourself."

Alice poured a large glass, dragged a bar stool underneath an air conditioning vent and bathed in its icy blast.

Livvie threw a cleaning rag under the counter and wiped her hands on a paper towel. "So, how's that gorgeous man of yours?"

"Busy." Alice squirmed as Joe's angry face floated into her head. She should send him an apology text, but she was struggling to come up with the handful of words to say what needed to be said.

"Hey, isn't it Uncle Patrick's party tonight? So, you should be in Galway now."

Alice related her row with Joe. "I messed up big this time, Livvie. But what do I do now? Joe and I have never fought like this." She folded her arms on the counter and dropped her forehead onto them.

"Get down on your knees and beg his forgiveness, is what you should do, Alice Haydon. That was bad, letting him down at the last minute like that. And for what? It's just a job you know. But Joe ..." She flicked a long black plait over her shoulder. "Well, you don't find men like him every day, that's all I'm saying."

"Ouch. Don't hold back, will you?"

Livvie meant Joe or the job. It hardly seemed a fair choice. Joe left her all the time, travelling across the world for work. He was a war photographer when they first met and he would be away for weeks at a time. She accepted that went with the job. It was only recently, after he had given up war reporting, that she saw him for more than a few days at a time. She felt sure that he would have done the same thing in her position. But that did not stop the acrobats in her stomach.

"And what about you and Steve? You work long hours here, how would he feel if you missed out on a family party?"

"Steve is so absent-minded he wouldn't notice if I had two heads. Remember the time we stopped at a garage for petrol and while I was in the shop he got in the car and drove off without me?"

Alice laughed. "Okay, I get it. And that wasn't even my first row today, I'd already had a spat with the council." She repeated the episode with Vivien Taylor at the town hall.

"So, why don't you just take the flower painting she offered?"

"Jenna picked out *Beach* because it's an exciting painting and she planned the exhibition around it. When she comes back and finds that I haven't got her showstopper, she'll think I'm completely useless. I'm not blowing my promotion on day one by taking the understudy instead of the star."

Alice lifted up a plastic cake cover and helped herself to a chocolate brownie. "Put this on my tab, Livvie." She bit into the crumbly square and closed her eyes, rolling the gooey, fudgy sumptuousness around her mouth. She opened her eyes to find Livvie staring at her.

"Feel better?"

"Much better. You know, it was that dead man in the river. Gave me the evil eye and brought me bad luck all day."

"You didn't see his eye, he was floating face down. And don't be disrespectful."

"Point taken, I apologise." She swallowed the last piece of brownie. "Who was he, anyway? You hear everything."

"I don't know, he hasn't been identified apparently." Livvie wiped crumbs off the wooden counter top. "But back to you, what are you going to do about your missing painting?"

"I'll find out who has it, then I'll ring them up and get them to bring it back."

"Good luck with that, I've been arguing with the council for years. If it's not business rates or hygiene conditions, it's some other petty regulation they get heavy about. I've yet to meet anyone at Town Hall I would trust to run a bath." Livvie reached beneath the counter and pulled out a bunch of papers.

"I completed their tortuous tender process for a catering contract – at their invitation I might add – and this is my letter of rejection. I run the most successful café in town, with the highest Trip Advisor rating, but I'm not good enough for them." Livvie's dark eyes flashed as she tossed the letter into a bin.

"Hey, I think you nearly lost your cool there, Miss Manners!"

"I'm sorry, but the words Great, Wheaton and District Council are enough to bring me out in blue spots. And the new shopping centre they're going to build on Dunn Road will be full of cafés – that's even more competition."

"What can you do? Join the protest group and leaflet everyone in town? I saw them out this morning."

"Why not? I've already signed the petition. I catered for a meeting of theirs yesterday and caught some of the conversation, but next time I'm going as a fully fledged member."

"Well, I hope you enjoy it." Alice picked up her bag from the floor. "I'd better get going. Duncan agreed that I could work from *Daisy* most of the time. Makes sense as I've got all Jenna's work as well as my own and I'll be free from office distractions."

"Now, if you want something for dinner, I've got one piece of spinach quiche left."

"I'll have it, thanks. And a portion of potato salad please, if you can spare it."

Livvie packed up the food, handing it to Alice in a paper carrier bag. "Hey, stay cool now. And apologise to that man."

Alice walked through the café, turning right at the end of the courtyard and following Sam's Lane along the river. A team of rowers powered through the water, sending ripples across the surface and ducks scurrying for the reeds. Caught in the sway, an aluminium boat rocked, stretching its occupant's fishing line across the swell.

At the end of the path, Alice came to a wooden fence marking the corner of Farrell's field, where half a dozen ponies swished tails and chewed grass. The farmer ran riding stables and often turned out the ponies in the riverside paddock. At her whistle, a black and white skewbald pony pricked up its ears, trotted over and took a Polo from her flat palm.

"What am I going to do, Patches?" She rubbed the pony's face. "Joe is furious with me and I need to make it right."

The pony pulled at her jeans pocket with his lips.

"There's no point looking there." She lifted the pony's head. "I've given you my last Polo. But seriously, Patches. You know how much I like Joe but he wants me to move in and … well, I'm not sure I can do it. Not yet anyway. At the same time, I don't want to lose him – that is, in a definitely maybe kind of way."

Patches muzzled her arm, then caught her bag strap with his teeth and jerked it towards him.

"Hey, stop!" She laughed, and with a lighter tread she retraced her footsteps, back along the river and over *Daisy Dawn's* gangway. She opened the hatch door and stepped down the companionway into the saloon, still heavy with the smell of a smouldering Joe.

With dinner safely stored in the fridge, Alice moved through *Daisy*'s sparsely furnished open plan living space, opening the windows to catch any breeze that might break the humid air. Each of the barge's large windows framed a view of the river – a constantly changing exhibition – and she looked out, thinking of the long, fretful day a year ago that she spent viewing rental properties. Stopping for a drink at The Coffee Pot, she had seen a postcard advertising *Daisy Dawn* on Livvie's notice board. A phone call later and she was standing in the same spot in the saloon, taking in the stylish modern furniture, the elegant oatmeal walls and carpets. She had already decided to take the barge.

It ranked as one of the best decisions she'd ever made.

In the cabin, she closed the pale wood wardrobe door and picked a pillow from the floor, brushing off the cover and returning it to the bed.

Alice changed into a pair of casual shorts and as she threw her jeans onto a wicker chair, the envelope with JM's note fluttered out of the pocket. She read it again, but she was still thinking of Joe. She put the note back in the envelope and shoved it in a drawer under a pile of underwear.

She settled down on the bamboo sofa facing the windows that looked over the river. With her laptop on her knees, she typed Joe's email address.

'*Hi Joe,*' she wrote. Then she stared at the screen.

Unable to come up with anything else, she sent an email to her local Member of Parliament about releasing his painting from the clutches of Westminster instead. She received a picture of a smiley MP in response, with a promise to answer her question within five working days.

An email asking Monica Streatham for an appointment to view the council's art collection drew a similar response, but without the customer-friendly smile. Alice dialled Monica's number. There was no reply, so she left a message asking her to call back.

She leant over to the wooden coffee table, removed the lid of a half-filled glass jar and foraged through the sweets inside. She singled out a pear drop and popped it in her mouth. Back to Joe's email, she wrote a few lines, read them over and made changes. She wrote another paragraph, signing off with an extra 'x'. A reading from beginning to end resulted in a punch to the sofa and she deleted the whole thing.

She picked up her phone and hit Joe's name. As it rang, she leant back against the sofa and gulped for breath. She was unprepared for his voicemail, and muttered a quick, "Hey it's me, I'll call you later," and hung up. Not what she had planned.

About to open the fridge for an evening glass of wine, she remembered Roddy Rafferty's earlier offer and headed back through the hatch door for a glass of red with her neighbour.

Chapter 5

"COME ON OVER, ALICE Haydon, Senior Curator, come on over!" Roddy boomed from the bottom of the gangway.

Alice crossed the creaking plank and fell into his embrace, the older man's scraggy beard tickling her cheek as he crushed her in a bear hug.

"Dear girl, I'm delighted about your new job. I think a little drink is required to celebrate."

He rolled across the deck to a rusting, metal table, where he poured wine into two large glasses. "I thought we'd start with a little Rioja … I've tested it already and it's very good. Here's to your well-deserved promotion to the exalted heights of senior curating. *Salut*!" Roddy raised his glass above his head before taking a hearty gulp.

Alice settled into a faded deckchair and sipped her wine.

"Now, tell me more about this centenary show of yours." Roddy took the director's chair. "It strikes me that asking Great Wheaton's esteemed residents to pick out artworks is the recipe for a jumble sale, not a professional art exhibition."

"My thoughts too, at least at first, but there's one exception." Alice told him about *Beach* and her encounter with

Vivien Taylor. "But the odd thing is, somebody wants to meet me later tonight, to talk about *Beach*. The very same painting."

"Who wants to meet you?"

"I've no idea, they just sent a note to my office this morning, asking me to meet them on the bridge."

"Dearie me, sounds like a silly prank. You're not going to go are you?"

"I haven't decided yet. But they obviously know something about *Beach* and, hopefully, where I can find it, so I'm tempted to go."

"Well, if you want to waste your time, that's up to you." Roddy slapped a mosquito against his thigh.

"Anyway, I still have to organise a good show. Duncan thinks that involving local people will drive up the gallery's flagging visitor numbers."

"No doubt he's right. But doesn't that make the curator's role redundant?"

"I thought I would visit some of the lenders in their homes and have a nose around, see if I can find something better. Then I would be picking the work. But there are eighty pieces in the exhibition and I can't get around that many houses."

"Isn't there someone at the gallery who can help you?"

"Not really, everyone is stretched enough already. I can't ask them to take on something that's not strictly required." Alice beamed. "Hey, what about you? You know more about art than anyone I know. If there's a masterpiece to be sniffed out in this town, you're just the person to do it."

"Dear girl, you're flattering me. Though I do have a good eye, if I say so myself!"

Alice jumped out of the deckchair, rushed over to Roddy and went down on one knee. "Will you be my exhibition partner, Roddy? Please?"

He put a hand on his chin and raised an eyebrow. "Hmm … let me see."

"It'll be fun working together. You'll be paid, of course."

Where the money would come from, she had no idea. Duncan wouldn't approve the expenditure, especially after knocking back her leaflet suggestion. He probably wouldn't like Roddy working for him either. But he did say he wanted a high-quality exhibition, and Roddy's experience would be invaluable.

"Ah well," said Roddy, "now you've mentioned money, I don't see how I can refuse!"

"You already know some of the lenders, so if their original choice is not up to par, you can persuade them to swap it for something else. They'd be thrilled to have a famous artist pick out one of their artworks for an exhibition."

"Getting paid to visit my friends, that's my kind of job."

Alice picked up her glass from the deck.

"Then there's the catalogue. I want to do something different for a change. A bit about each lender and how they acquired their painting, with some good photos too. But it should be fun and entertaining."

"So, you want a gossip and picture book. A hardback version of *Hello!*?"

"Roddy, you read my mind!" Alice giggled. "Though, we'll have to take some of the pieces whether we like them or not – Vivien Taylor's for starters. She won't tell me which painting she's lending. She's being a bit cloak and dagger. This sudden unveiling and then there's her mad security instructions."

"Oh?" Roddy kicked off his flip-flops.

"She doesn't want anyone to know when the painting is being delivered to the gallery. She'll send Duncan some cryptic text message telling him it's on its way. Poor Tommy will have to be on call at all times, so he can take immediate delivery."

"Dearie, me, the woman is a shameless exhibitionist."

"Oh, I don't know, I think she's trying to be helpful. The unveiling event will be good publicity for the gallery."

"Vivien will always try to be helpful. The point is, who is she trying to help?"

Roddy topped up their glasses.

"You should come with me to Vivien's, after all you're going to help me with the exhibition and it'll be the perfect time to get some gossip from lenders."

"I wouldn't miss it for the world."

"And then there's the *Beach* situation. Though, I'm sure that's just a misunderstanding."

Roddy stroked his beard. "I'm sure it's not. Where Vivien goes, confusion generally follows."

"Oh, surely not. You know how often the council makes mistakes, it's taken you forever to sort out your council tax." Alice crossed the deck, leaning against the side. "By the way Roddy, I'm pleased you're painting again. A landscape too, something completely different. What made you decide to do that?"

"These days, I find abstracts too emotionally draining, which is probably why I've made such a hash of them since Elisabeth died. Landscapes are the antidote to all that, they're civilised and harmonious and they make me feel peaceful. And I don't even mind that they're not cool."

"A landscape of yours would be amazingly cool. Please, carry on. I can't wait to see it finished."

"As you're flattering me so sweetly, I will dab a little more and see how it turns out." A shadow crossed his eyes despite the words of optimism.

"Promise?"

"I promise, on one condition. Whilst I think that your occasional impulsive outbursts are charming, not everyone is as good-natured as me. So perhaps you should limit your spontaneity to one dose a day. You don't have to become all tick boxy, just don't do anything silly."

"Outbursts? Me? Don't know where that came from but okay." Alice looked across the river. A pair of ducks clambered out of the water and waddled up the bank, settling in the grass for the night.

"I saw Joe this morning." Alice heard behind her. "What did he have to say about your new role? He must be delighted for you."

"Yeah. He is."

"He was off to his uncle's birthday do, he was saying. Weren't you supposed to go too?"

Alice spun around and was met with a Roddy Rafferty poker face special.

"I wanted to go, but I didn't have any holiday left."

Roddy's usually animated face and body stiffened. Alice fiddled with her shorts pocket, her gaze darting away from his face, then back.

"Has he asked you to move in with him again?"

"It sort of came up recently."

"You know it would make life simpler if you both lived at the same place."

"I don't want to live with Joe. Besides, I love *Daisy* and living here on the river."

"Of course you do and you could still keep *Daisy*, use her as an office or something."

"I like my independence and I'm not ready to give it up."

"Independence is overrated, Alice. I've lived with it a long time and it's not good company."

Alice rubbed sweaty palms against her shorts. Taking a sip of wine, she rolled the rich fruity liquid around her mouth, before gulping it down.

"Do you think about Elisabeth often?"

"It's been twenty-four years, but there still isn't a day I don't think of her." He contemplated the deck before fixing Alice with a doe-eyed frown. "After she went, life became so complicated. There was nothing I could have done to stop the idiot driver who took her away from me; but you can stop Joe walking away from you."

Alice sighed away a tear before it formed. "I couldn't go to Galway today, Roddy. I'm sure Joe understands."

"I know you're thinking of your father, but not every man is like him. Joe cares for you, he's a good man and sometimes he needs all of your attention."

The sun ended its slow fall into the fields, flaming the willow branches on the opposite bank. Alice shivered and rubbed her bare arms.

"I think I can do without the fortune cookie philosophy tonight, so I'll call it a day."

"I'm just giving you some friendly advice …"

But Alice was already halfway across the gangway and the rest of Roddy's advice stayed on the barge's deck.

There was nobody on the bridge when she arrived, so with five minutes to spare, Alice ambled to the central hump and stood beneath a lamppost.

From the waterside terrace of Jerry's Bar, music played for the few remaining customers. Alice rested her forearms on the bridge's parapet and gazed into the inky pool beneath. Reflections from a string of coloured lights played on the surface, and traces of steak dinners permeated the air.

Despite searching her contacts list for anyone who could conceivably sign off 'JM', the identity of the note's sender was still a mystery to Alice. At first, she had worried about meeting a stranger alone and late at night. But she figured that this part of town was well lit and Jerry's was close by. Besides, she was dying to know what JM had to say about *Beach*.

The musicians began to pack up and Alice watched the last punters leave the bar, just as St Edmunds's clock struck eleven. A stubby man approached the bridge, short bandy legs driving him towards her until they were level. His bowed head obscured his features, though tufts of amber curls rimming his peaked cap glimmered under the lamplight. Alice's knees weakened and her shoulders hunched as she leant against the lamppost's reassuring bulk.

The man passed without a glance and once he had disappeared into the darkness, Alice breathed again.

She scanned the surrounding roads and paths. There were the odd few people on their way home from the pub and a couple of dog walkers, but nobody was coming in her direction. JM was already half an hour late.

One last glance over her shoulder, then she strode off the bridge and home.

Alice lay on the sofa in *Daisy*'s saloon. Visions of dead bodies, upset boyfriends, missing paintings and empty bridges swirled around her mind. She felt exhausted. But she would never get to sleep with her mind in such a spin. There was only one thing for it.

She jumped up, closed the curtains tight and pushed the coffee table to the wall. She opened a drawer in the sideboard and took out a CD she kept specially for these occasions. She put the disc into the player, skipped to track five and turned the volume up. Alice was ready when Van Morrison's *Brown Eyed Girl* began. She punched the air and danced until her feet ached.

Chapter 6

THE NEXT MORNING ALICE walked into Great Wheaton's heart, past thin buildings – pink, yellow and more – lining narrow streets. At the corner of Bull's Passage she ducked by a triangular window protruding from the side of The Bull Hotel. Crossing the road, she felt spherical stones beneath her Vans, the same stones trod by medieval merchants with leather shoes and turned up toes.

She swung her bag by her side as she weaved between the stalls on Market Square, where sultry air was trapped beneath striped awnings. A musty, piquant aroma drew her to the cheese stall, but it was too hot to have smelly cheese in her bag. It was always a sweet day, though.

"Hey Marilyn! Anything new?" Alice tripped light fingers along the edge of Marilyn's stall.

"It just so happens I do have something today. Try this." Marilyn held out a saucer of jade blobs. "See if you can guess what it is."

Alice placed one on her tongue. "Wow, oh, wow." She giggled, wiping a tear from her cheek. "That's seriously sharp lime fizz! There's something else too, though I can't quite place it."

"Would you think lavender?"

"No way? There's a definite floral hint, but I would never have guessed it was lavender. I'll have to have some." Alice placed the sweets in her pocket and wandered on.

Crimson, peacock, peach and banana shades burst from Tilda's flower stall as Alice passed, pondering her next meeting. Nicholas Waites had no reputation for collecting art, so his contribution to the centenary exhibition was unlikely to be noteworthy, but Jenna had promised to collect his contribution personally. A nuisance, but she resolved to grab the painting and go.

A Grecian-style fountain tinkled through the market-day buzz. Alice walked by St Edmund's, its towering clock tower alone in the sapphire sky, as she threaded her way through the crowd to Rowley Way, and Nicholas Waites' townhouse.

A rotund Nicholas Waites led Alice into a small room choked with furniture and smothered with knick-knacks. "Have a seat in here, Alice, and I'll get you a cup of tea. Or maybe you'd like a cold drink?"

He swept cushions aside, clearing a space on a sagging sofa.

"No, thanks. I'll just take the painting and get going if you don't mind."

Nicholas's crestfallen face brought a little heat to her cheeks. "Well, perhaps I could squeeze in a quick drink. Something cold please, but only if it's not too much trouble."

"It's no trouble at all. I won't be a minute." Nicholas shuffled off to the kitchen.

She tried to guess what sort of painting he would lend. Something similar to the pair of hackneyed landscapes fighting with the rose-patterned wallpaper probably. Her heart sank at a rectangular-shaped patch of brighter roses where she assumed a similar landscape had hung. Judging from the neatly wrapped package resting on the table, it was waiting for her. She glared at the package as she ambled over to a glass-fronted display case against the far wall.

Inside, a collection of small figurines of white clay, with brightly coloured features, was crammed onto glass shelves. There were a jumble of different tableaux. A man, a woman and two children sat on a checked cloth around a little wicker hamper filled with tiny sausage rolls, fizzy drinks and a pineapple cake. A white dog sat between the children, a yellow and red ball by its side.

They were utterly delightful, Alice thought, and much more engaging than the paintings. She pulled the phone from her pocket and snapped a few photos.

"Here we are." Nicholas returned with a tray of refreshments. "I've got some lime cordial, I hope you like lime." He set the tray down on a coffee table. "Do help yourself. Would you like a biscuit? It's shortbread." He gave a shy smile. "Homemade."

"I will, thank you." She bit into the biscuit, putting out a hand to catch the crumbs. "Yum, these are *so* good."

"That's kind of you. There's some chocolate-covered ones too, if you'd like."

Alice's stomach rumbled in response; she had skipped breakfast.

She demolished the biscuit and took a chocolate one too.

"I was looking at your figurines. They're gorgeous and so beautifully made. Where did you get them?"

"Margaret, my wife, made them. She used our conservatory out the back as a workshop. Her paints are still there, just where she left them ..." Nicholas looked at the floor.

"Oh, I'm sorry for your loss." Alice reached over and touched his arm. "Your wife was very talented. The figurines have such vitality and the detailing is amazing." She went back to the cabinet and rested on her haunches. "This picnic scene here, you can almost feel how happy the people are, it looks just like a real family."

"It is a real family, it's us. That's me and there's Margaret." Nicholas crouched down beside her. "And there's our children, George and Catherine, they would have been about nine and seven. Margaret would pack a picnic and we'd go and sit by the river just along from the cricket pavilion. We'd take our dog too, Tuppence, that's him there. He was only a puppy when Margaret made this figure. The children would play with Tuppence and Margaret would sketch."

Nicholas winced as he wound himself up. "My knees are not what they used to be. Anyway, I'm lucky I had such a wonderful family, and seeing them so full of life and enjoying themselves, it made me burst with pride." He wiped his eye, brushing away a tear before it fell. "Don't take any notice of me, I'm a silly old fool."

"It sounds like you had a lovely life together. It must be a comfort for you to have those memories."

A picture of her absent father and distracted mother blew into Alice's mind. Her mother had been too busy working or lying down in her bedroom to cook a proper dinner for her and her brother, let alone plan a picnic. Usually, she let the picture linger, desperate to cling onto any memory of her parents. But it also made her sad and she did not need another day of emotions and stress. Not after yesterday. She blinked the image away.

"So, Margaret made all of these ..." Alice swept her arm the width of the cabinet.

"She did." There's my niece, Anna, with her husband, on their wedding day. That's our Catherine, she was one of the bridesmaids. The girls were given baskets of flowers, but Catherine lost most of hers before she got to the church, that's why her basket is nearly empty."

Nicholas indicated figures at the bottom of the cabinet. "This is George's graduation from Trinity College." A young man wearing a black gown and a mortar board was flanked by his beaming and very recognisable father and a pretty, smiling lady wearing a pink hat.

"This is our family album. Memories of clay."

Alice did a quick calculation.

"These are remarkable, and with the stories attached to them, they're enchanting. I would love to show some of them as part of the exhibition, they are exactly the sort of original local artwork I was hoping to find. Would you be willing to lend me a few pieces?"

"But what about the painting? Jenna Farling told me there was only one entry per person and I did particularly want to lend you the painting."

"Well, we can always make exceptions and these figures are exceptional. What do you think?"

Nicholas put his hands in his pockets and stared out the window.

She could see the figures were precious to him, clearly more important than the painting, and she realised she could not push him.

"Look, there's no rush. Have a think about it, I'll call back in a few days and we'll chat again. How does that sound?"

Nicholas brightened. "Okay. You'll take the painting in the meantime though, won't you?"

"Of course I will."

"Here it is, all packed and ready to go. You will look after it won't you? It was Margaret's special painting, she bought it on holiday in Mallorca."

"Don't worry about it. Me and Tommy Norton will look after it for you. We handle valuable paintings all the time, it'll be safe in our storeroom."

Alice was delighted with her discovery. The visit had turned out to be more productive than she could have imagined – potentially a better artwork than the one offered. There was no telling what might turn up when she visited other lenders.

Alice would get around Jenna's dismal list of pieces and put her own stamp on the exhibition. It would not please her boss, but if Duncan Jones wanted a high-quality exhibition, sacrifices had to be made!

Chapter 7

BACK ON BOARD *DAISY*, Alice stood in the shower, reflecting on Joe's text response.

'*Speak later.*'

She had not heard from him since and it was nearly lunchtime. She hoped it was because the Buchanan family was still sleeping off the effects of Uncle Patrick's party.

Earlier in the year, Joe had mentioned that he might take up his cousin's offer to work in his photography business. Joe could commute to Galway and spend some time with his family. Alice worried that he might be taking the opportunity to discuss it.

Alice longed to speak to him. The shower's watery rods pounded her shoulders and she twisted her long hair around her finger.

In the meantime, there was no more news about the dead body, though there would be plenty of people at Vivien Taylor's unveiling party. She might hear more then.

Alice dressed in a pink shift dress, rolled her hair into a bun and secured it with a pink scrunchie. She laced up a pair of white Vans, picked up a pair of large, round sunglasses from the kitchen counter and stepped into bright sunlight.

She walked along Sam's Lane and almost straight past the dashing gentleman wearing a cream linen suit and crisp white shirt, standing beside Roddy's barge. His shoulder-length curly hair was neatly combed and brushed off his face.

"Gosh, you look smart. I didn't know you even owned a suit."

"I don't. Stanley lent it to me, the shirt and shoes too." Roddy winked and popped on a white fedora at a rakish angle.

"You look like an Italian movie star. I bet someone will ask you about your latest film."

"Rather that than they ask me about my work. I couldn't even remember what my last painting was called."

"Just make something up, no one will know the difference."

"Dear girl, titles of paintings are to artists what lines of *Hamlet* are to an actor. The audience knows them better than you do, you daren't get them wrong."

They wandered along Sam's Lane and stopped at the car park, where Alice unlocked her navy blue Defender, its white roof grey from dusty idleness. She got in and opened the passenger door for Roddy.

"I forgot you have to climb up into this thing," he said. "Don't you ever feel the urge to drive a car rather than a tank?"

"You can stop being rude about my car or I'll make you walk to Vivien's," said Alice. "I love my Defender, he never lets me down."

She started up the car and let it run for a while, before driving out and onto River Street.

"Now, what do you want me to do at this party, other than charm and imbibe?"

"I'd like you to get some material for the exhibition catalogue, from the lenders. Find out what attracted them to the work and how they came by it. There's a list of them in my bag there, along with the name of the painting they're lending."

"Okay then, let's see who you've got." Roddy unfolded the list. "The Lincolns. They're lending one of their dreary landscapes – only to be expected. The Shorts. No imagination those people, but *River at Sunset* is a respectable painting. Ah, Lady Esther Graydon," he said to Alice's profile. "I've never been to her house, I hear it's lovely, but she, dear girl, has a Picasso. An early one, not one of his best, but a Picasso nonetheless."

"And she fobbed us off with a portrait of her grandfather. I'm beginning to wonder whether Jenna put any real effort into this exhibition at all."

Alice stopped at the Narebridge road T-junction and let a crocodile of school children cross the road.

"Would you mind writing that down please? The bit about the Picasso. There's a pen in the glove box."

"Who's next? Ah, Sean Cummings. He's as rich as Croesus, but he's the sort of man who wears baseball caps in public! I had dinner at his house, which is full of appalling paintings. The dining room was covered with gaudy burgundy wallpaper, there were long velvet curtains at the windows and a huge chandelier with tassels dangled over the table. I felt as if I was eating in a bordello!"

"Perfect! That's exactly the sort of story I'm looking for. I knew you were just the man for this job."

"I fear I've set the bar too high already!" Roddy laughed. "OK, I shall drag a bunch of entertaining stories out of these lenders. By the way, there is going to be food at Vivien's isn't there? I didn't have any breakfast."

"I'm sure there'll be food and champagne. But you, sir, are working, so a little restraint if you don't mind."

"I think I can manage a *little* restraint!"

"Good. Right, we're here."

Larchdale lay in the middle of lush farmland, tucked away at the bottom of a dusty, pot-holed dirt road. The Defender snaked along the track until it broadened out into a tear-drop shingle driveway. A substantial, ivy-covered house stood at the far end.

A man in khaki shorts and matching shirt directed Alice to a paddock on the left. She pulled up at the end of a row.

She followed Roddy around the side of the house to the back and onto a large patio. A wide, sloping lawn ran down to the River Nare, and beyond, a patchwork of coloured fields ran to the horizon. To the east lay a small village with a massive church, the colours from its stained-glass windows dancing in the sunlight.

Guests engaged in mellow conversation and sipped glasses filled with bubbles. Alice edged between delicate petunias bursting from terracotta pots and mouthed greetings to people she knew and a couple she did not.

Vivien waved from across the paving, hastening over to join her. "I saw you looking at the view, it's glorious, isn't it? It was this beautiful scene that sold me the house."

"Yes, it's stunning. As is the house."

"Thank you. The house and its grounds were wrecks when I bought them. It's taken a lot of work to get everything looking this way, but I'm very pleased with how the old girl turned out." Vivien beamed, as if she were describing a daughter rather than a house.

"Anyway, welcome. I'm delighted you could be here, Alice. You too, Roddy. We—"

"Roddy!" The bellow came from a squat, plump lady careering towards them, wearing a smart, if snug, peach-coloured suit. She flung an arm around Roddy's neck and pushed her reddened, sweaty face into his, kissing him on both cheeks. "Roddy, how marvellous to see you, it's been ages. You look wonderful."

"Marjorie, my dear, what a lovely surprise. How the devil are you?"

"Getting older and more decrepit, bits keep seizing up. But I can still quaff a good bottle of red, so I can't complain."

"I didn't realise you two knew each other." Vivien's rounded vowels flattened as she glanced between Roddy and Marjorie.

"Roddy and I go back decades. We bump into each other every few years and keep promising to meet up properly, but it never happens."

"This time, we'll make an arrangement and stick to it." Roddy pointed between Marjorie and Vivien. "And how do *you* two know each other? Through your interest in art or your council work?"

"Both," said Marjorie. "We meet now and again at charity fundraisers. The last time we met, I sold Vivien a marvellous painting. I must show it to you, Roddy, it's in her study."

"Roddy has very discerning taste, Marjorie. I doubt a professional artist like him would be impressed with that little painting." Vivien tossed Roddy a teasing grin.

"Don't I know it. But I think you'll find this one interesting, Roddy."

Vivien rolled her bottom lip. "Oh dear! And I had hoped that people would be talking about my special artwork today. That's why we're here after all. I won't apologise for hogging the limelight to promote the centenary exhibition."

"Of course, how inconsiderate of me," said Marjorie. "I'm dying to see which piece in your fabulous collection you're unveiling." She turned to Alice. "And who are you, my dear? I don't think we've met."

"Allow me." Roddy grasped Alice's arm. "My dear friend Marjorie Cavendish, please meet my dear friend and neighbour Alice Haydon."

"It's good to meet you." Alice shook Marjorie's clammy hand.

"It's lovely to meet you too, dear. Now, don't tell me you live on one of those gloomy barge thingies like Roddy?"

"Alice lives in a nice new and clean barge thingy," said Roddy. "Even you would approve!"

Vivien signalled to a waiter carrying a tray of drinks.

"You'll have a glass of champagne, won't you?" she said, handing Alice a glass. "I'll do the unveiling in about half an hour and in the meantime, please make yourselves at home. There's plenty more champagne, or soft drinks if you prefer, and a buffet table in the dining room." She headed off, spreading bonhomie amongst her other guests.

Marjorie and Roddy meandered towards the house, presumably in search of a quiet corner for a catch-up. Left alone, Alice took the opportunity to look over Vivien's famed art collection. She found a large sitting room with high ceilings and mustard-coloured walls. Above a wooden mantelpiece hung a portrait of a thin, severe woman dressed in black, with a white ruffle collar. Her skin was chalky and the whites around her cold, dark eyes were tinged with yellow. It was hard to tell whether the woman had been alive or dead when it was painted.

"Miserable cow, isn't she." Alice jumped at the gravelly voice, which came from a man tucked into the corner of the room, nursing a plaster-encased leg. "No accounting for taste is there?"

"She is a bit stern." Alice shuffled towards the open door, fortuitously situated between the miserable cow and the incapacitated man.

"Still, the little bird watercolours over there are easier on the emotions. But don't let me detain you. I expect you've got some friends inside." He thumbed towards the door.

"Thanks," Alice mumbled before slipping into the hall, where she found Claudia Rowan, the arts writer for the local newspaper.

"Hello Alice, I was just talking to Finn about you." Claudia threw a multi-braceleted arm at the good-looking man beside her. "About our plans to promote the exhibition for you and Vivien. We've got a big spread planned for next week's issue and Finn's going to take pictures to go with it. He could take some for you too if you like."

"What sort of shots do you want me to take?"

Alice couldn't miss the American accent.

"That's really good of you, Finn. Could you take some pictures of Vivien with her painting and then the painting by itself, please? Also, some shots of the house and grounds, seeing as we're here. Is that alright?"

"Yeah, that's cool. I'm enjoying shooting this wonderful house and all the art. The grounds too."

"Are you interested in art?"

"All I know is what I learnt when I covered an art theft case at the Old Bailey a few years ago – does that count?"

"Well I'm guessing it sparked an interest." Alice laughed.

"I've done some kayaking up this way, so I've been by the house before. I'll get some shots outside now while there are still people out there."

Finn picked up a camera bag from the table beside him and headed towards the sitting room.

"Well Claudia, I like Finn – he looks … athletic! Where did you meet him?"

"Ex-California junior tennis champ!" Claudia stuck out her chin. "We met at a friend's party ages ago, but he was travelling so much I hardly saw him. Until recently that is, when he moved up here to be near his mother. She owns Ellie's in the high street."

"I love that shop. I bought this dress there." Alice waited while Vivien passed by them. "Originally, I thought this event was a bit over the top. But it's drumming up interest in the exhibition, judging from the people here."

"And what a crowd. All the movers and shakers in our little town have turned out. Not that they would dream of ignoring Vivien's summons!" Claudia's green eyes shone. "No doubt they'll be suitably appreciative of Vivien Taylor's selfless generosity to the community." She roared with laughter, turning the heads of a couple nearby. "What will you do if you don't like her painting? Shove it in a corner somewhere?"

"Probably, though I'm crossing my fingers that won't be necessary. Not that I've seen anything here to rave about."

"That's probably because you haven't seen the best stuff. There are a few expensive, if ordinary, paintings in the formal dining room over there. But for the real show, you need to see the bedrooms."

"And how, may I ask, are you familiar with Vivien's bedrooms?"

"I came here for a drinks reception once and I was talking to Walker Hampton, Vivien's husband, who offered to give me a tour of the collection. I should say that we had had a few drinks by this point. I was so busy chatting away, I didn't notice that he'd led me into his bedroom and was showing me his Gauguin!"

They both screamed with laughter. Claudia adjusted a strap of her black dress and plonked her empty glass on a waiter's tray.

"A Gauguin, wow, that's quite something," said Alice. "What else was he hiding up there, or were you too distracted to notice the paintings?"

"I don't remember much about them. All I can say is that they were much better than the works down here."

"I'd love to see them." Alice looked up the staircase. "Which one is Walker's bedroom?"

"Turn left at the top of the stairs. It's one of the doors on the right, I'm not sure which one." Claudia raised an eyebrow. "Are you thinking what I think you're thinking?"

"I'm just going to run up and take a quick look." Alice threw a cursory glance behind her. No one was looking. "I won't be long."

She darted up the stairs and turned into a long corridor. The first door was closed, but the next two revealed bedrooms, comfortably but sparsely furnished. More bedrooms followed.

By the time she reached the end of the corridor, Alice had seen all the open rooms. It had to be the one with the closed door.

She retraced her steps, prised the door open a fraction, and peered in. A man's jacket lay casually across the bed. A double-check that she was still alone, then she slipped inside.

The room was enormous, much bigger than the others. It looked as if two rooms had been knocked together. Despite its size, it too was sparsely furnished. But the walls! The walls were crammed with paintings, end to end. What a feast! Alice spun around, her eyes seesawing over the canvases. She picked out a John Nash, a Dali.

Glorious artworks, each trying to out-sparkle the others. It was electrifying, hypnotic and a little mad.

Above the bedside table, a Degas caught her eye. She moved closer and stretched out a hand; a gentle touch on the frame just to make sure it was real.

If Walker was a collector too, he certainly had better taste than his wife.

Just along from the Degas was a Frida Kahlo. Alice had studied this beautiful painting as part of her art degree, but had never expected to see it in real life. She moved in front of it to get a better look.

"You little beauty."

"See anything you fancy?"

Alice jerked back and turned around, to find a tall, rangy man leaning against the doorframe, arms crossed.

"I'm so sorry, I was just …" she stuttered.

"A beautiful woman making herself at home in my bedroom! I can keep a secret like that; but you know people talk." He treated her to a Cheshire cat grin.

Alice walked towards him. His dark hair was shot with grey and as she got closer, the grin dropped from his long, tanned face. Close-up, his baggy, faded blue jeans were grubbier than had first appeared, and the sleeves of his white t-shirt were frayed. She stretched out her hand, but he moved off the doorframe and got his introduction in first.

"I'm Walker Hampton, and you are Alice."

She examined his face. Generously wrinkled but no less handsome for that. With unreasonably attractive chocolate eyes …

"How do you know my name?"

"I Googled you and found an old photo. I prefer your hair shorter."

"You've been stalking me? That's a little creepy, if I may say."

"Yes, isn't it? I heard you were in charge of the centenary exhibition, so I thought I'd better check you out. Could I trust you with one of our paintings, I asked myself?"

"And what did you decide?"

"You have relevant experience and you've done some interesting research. But poking around other people's bedrooms uninvited – you lose marks for that."

Alice smiled. "What else did you find out about me?"

"That you're very nosy and ask lots of boring questions. And you can fit thirty-nine Maltesers in your mouth at the same time."

Alice's mouth gaped open and a hand flew up to cover it. "That's not true."

"I'm joking." He sniggered.

She cast an arm around the room. "I was wondering how you managed to bag the best paintings for your bedroom."

"Just lucky I guess. We move the paintings around every now and again and at the last move, I landed this lot. Anyway, that's enough dull questioning. I've got work to do and I think Vivien has already started speaking. You don't want to miss the grand unveiling."

"No, I'm looking forward to it. And thank you."

As Alice ran along the corridor she could feel Walker's eyes on her back, as Vivien's voice rose up from downstairs.

Chapter 8

The conservatory was packed so Alice joined the back of the crowd, jockeying amongst the guests for a good position. Vivien was standing beside an easel, with a painting hidden by a paisley shawl. Finn was crouching off to the side, taking photos.

Alice hoped the piece was one of Walker's and she wondered how she could pretend to be delighted if it was not. Too late now. Vivien's speech was heading for the big reveal.

"You will have heard me beating the drum for Gregory's House many times before," she said. "The gallery has proved itself a valuable asset to Great Wheaton over the past century. Loved by local residents, it has also brought in visitors from outside the area and my council colleagues and I have been happy to support it." Vivien stood erect.

"But I'm particularly excited about the gallery's next show, the centenary exhibition. As soon as Duncan told me about it, I was sure it would be a winner. It's not every day that, as an amateur collector, you get the opportunity to contribute to a major exhibition. But in this show, local people will have the pleasure of seeing paintings from their own collections displayed in a public gallery. I'm sure you'll agree that's an exciting proposition."

She moved closer to the picture and took a teasing peak behind the shawl.

"I couldn't wait until opening day to show my own contribution, so I've invited you to see it today."

Alice wormed her way through the guests until she found a spot with a better view of the easel. Vivien reached for the shawl and whipped it away to reveal her picture. But it was not a painting.

"It's a drawing by Augustus John." Vivien ran a soft finger along its side. "It's one of my favourite pieces, so I hope you like it as much as I do."

The guests burst into applause and Vivien beamed, posing alongside the drawing as Finn stepped in to take photos. For a moment, Alice was rooted to the spot, then with mounting excitement she went to find Roddy. Together they studied the work.

Drawn with exquisite economy using just a few dark pencil lines, a young girl, about six years old, stared back at her.

In this setting, the girl looked different, but Alice knew her so well – she would recognise her anywhere. She had been six years old herself when she had first seen the drawing. The family was on holiday in Tenby, and her father had taken her to an art gallery to see an Augustus John exhibition. She was fascinated to find a picture of a girl the same age as herself. They looked at each other, and immediately Alice felt as if they had known each other for ever. Even when Alice backed away, the girl's eyes stayed on hers. She imagined the girl was speaking to her; so, she answered. Before they left, her father bought a postcard of the drawing from the gallery's shop, giving it to Alice as a memento.

When her father walked out of the family home just a few weeks later, the postcard took on a deep and powerful meaning. Over the years, she often looked at it, remembering that last outing to the gallery. The postcard was her only link to her father.

Augustus John became one of Alice's favourite artists, and she had even pitched the idea of an exhibition of his work to Jenna Farling. And now here was one of his most beautiful pieces, right in front of her.

"So, what do you think of my drawing?" Vivien's voice held a mixture of pride and swagger.

Alice decided to keep the connection to herself.

"I love it," she said. "It's ethereal and bewitching, though also a little sad, I think. She looks lonely. But the drawing is exquisite, Vivien."

"And Augustus John is a big name, so it should draw a lot of people into the gallery."

"I have no doubt it will attract a great deal of interest."

It occurred to Alice that Vivien might be planning to use the exhibition to promote herself in next year's council elections.

"How long have you had the drawing?"

"Not long. I bought it from a friend last year. He inherited it from an aunt, but he didn't particularly like it. I saw it when I visited him, loved it and made him an offer. He was only too happy to see it go to an appreciative home."

"That's a sweet story. Do you happen to know where your friend's aunt got it from?"

"I've no idea. One of those pieces that gets handed down, I expect."

"Trust Vivien to sniff out a bargain." A mellow voice cut through the surrounding chatter. "And in the unlikeliest of places."

The voice belonged to a grey-haired, middle-aged man dressed in a grey suit, whom Alice had not noticed before. His alert grey eyes darted between the two women.

Alice spoke first. "Vivien has picked up a fabulous artwork. And just finding it at a friend's house – that was an incredible piece of luck."

"I'm Councillor Julian de Havilland, by the way." He shook Alice's hand. "Are you one of the Gregory's House team?"

"Yes, I'm Alice Haydon and I'm curating the centenary exhibition. This beautiful drawing will form a central part of the show."

"It makes a change from the still lifes you usually see in people's homes. I suppose you've been offered plenty of those."

"We have indeed." Including one from his own council's collection, she thought.

"So, Vivien has everything in hand, as always." Julian rubbed his hands together. "I'm looking forward to seeing this exhibition, it should be popular. Ticks more boxes than some of your shows."

Alice scowled. What was it with funders and box-ticking? Couldn't they just enjoy art for its own sake?

"Though I brought my twin daughters to your Vanessa Bowman exhibition last year and they loved it. I rather enjoyed it myself."

"I plan to have some original and striking pieces in this exhibition. In fact, I've commissioned a painting specially for the show."

"How exciting," said Vivien. "Who from?"

"I'm not in a position to say. Not just yet anyway, the contract hasn't been finalised."

"You can tell me, Alice. I am one of the gallery's funders after all." Steely blue eyes glared out of a fixed face.

Alice regretted mentioning Roddy's painting. He had barely started it and he might not even finish it.

"There's plenty of time before the opening," said Julian. "I'm sure Alice will announce it at the appropriate time. Now, I think it's time for a drink. Vivien, are you going to give me a glass of your excellent champagne?"

Vivien softened, tore her eyes from Alice and steered Julian out to the patio.

Alice turned back to the drawing.

"That's what I was thinking too."

Alice jumped, forgetting that Roddy was still there. "And what was I thinking?"

"You were wondering whether this is a genuine Augustus John drawing."

Alice's lips parted and her chin jutted forward. She surveyed the drawing again.

"I'm doing no such thing. I've seen it before, in Tenby. I'm pretty sure it's the same drawing."

"Oh, Tenby! They thought one of my paintings was a Rothko." He laughed. "They wouldn't be able to tell a Constable from a Tracey Emin."

"But that's a recognisable Augustus John signature."

"It *is* a recognisable Augustus John signature. But is it a *real* Augustus John signature?"

"What *do* you mean?" Alice shifted closer to him and whispered, "Are you suggesting that someone forged the signature on this drawing, Mr Rafferty?"

"It has been known." Roddy twiddled a strand of grey beard. "That's all I'm saying."

"Even if that's true and I'm not saying it is, it doesn't mean the drawing itself is a fake."

"It does not, but it's best to err on the side of caution, wouldn't you agree? Things are not always what they appear to be. Now, I'm off to have a little chat with Vivien."

"Don't go accusing her of anything, Roddy." Alice grabbed his arm. "You don't know whether it's genuine or not."

"Dear girl, I'm only joking. I'm working, aren't I? Get some interesting stories from lenders on how they acquired their artworks, isn't that what you said? So, I'll ask Vivien about her lovely drawing." Roddy's eyes twinkled. "Like, can I see the receipt please?"

"I don't think that's funny." Alice put her hands on her hips. "And by the way, how much champagne have you had? You promised you would show some restraint."

"I've only had two glasses. Or is it three? But worry not, dear girl, I won't do anything to embarrass us. I don't want to get thrown out until I've had my fill of the buffet!"

Alice considered the drawing again, studying the lines, the shading, the composition. Was she allowing her treasured childhood memories to colour her judgement?

She ambled outside, across the patio and onto the grass. She mulled over the doubt that had shot through her mind after Roddy's comment. She tried to dismiss it as her usual perfectionist anxiety, but it persisted.

What had induced Roddy's doubt? The signature looked genuine enough, but could she be sure? Adding a perfect facsimile of an artist's signature to a fake painting, passing it off as an authentic work, was a well-known forger's trick.

Perhaps Vivien had been caught out by a clever faker who pretended to be her friend. It was possible.

But it could not happen to Alice. She could not afford to make such a big mistake. If she put a fake drawing in the exhibition she would never get a curating job again. Ever.

She had to find out for sure.

When she turned around, most of the guests had drifted away and the patio was almost empty. Roddy was sitting in a deckchair, soaking up the sun, an empty glass in his hand.

She stomped across the courtyard, fishing her car keys out of her bag. "Fill up your doggy bag, Rafferty, we're leaving."

Chapter 9

ALICE STOOD IN JULIA Marsh's airy, modern dining room, basking in its serenity after the excitement of Vivien Taylor's party.

"I just can't make up my mind." Julia put a hand on top of her head and a smile on her attractive face. "Help me out Alice – which painting do you prefer?"

"I like them both. Honestly."

When Alice first saw Julia's name on the lenders' list, with a blank space beside it, she was delighted. She thought she could persuade Julia to lend the swirly blue abstract painting that Alice liked so much. However, despite her best efforts, she had not been able to coax Julia into parting with it.

"Will there be other pieces hanging each side of the painting, when it's up on the gallery wall?"

"I don't know," said Alice. "I haven't seen most of the other paintings yet, let alone worked out a hanging scheme."

"I'm inclined to give you the Rowland Fisher, as I haven't seen any of his paintings displayed around here for ages. Though, in a way I would rather you had the Courtney

Slow watercolour. He painted it locally, so it's more appropriate for the exhibition, I feel." Julia played with the blue seahorse dangling from her left ear. "The Courtney Slow it is. Are you happy with that?"

"It's a good choice." She meant it, even though it was not the blue swirly number. "Now, I've got some paperwork for you to complete if you don't mind."

"I expected you would have a form. Why don't you sit outside and I'll make some coffee."

Alice shuffled through a wodge of papers, selecting a blank loan agreement. Julia's Jack Russell terriers rocketed around the tidy garden as Alice thought about JM's no show the previous evening.

She resolved to ring Poppy and find out if anyone saw JM when they dropped off the letter yesterday. Perhaps they left a phone number.

Julia put coffee and a selection of cakes on a low glass-topped table. Alice plumped for a slab of lemon drizzle despite still feeling full from Vivien's buffet table.

"Here's the form. Fill it in in your own time and drop it back to me next week. And thank you for the loan, Julia. Courtney is a fascinating artist and I'm pleased to have a young, emerging talent in the exhibition."

"I'm delighted the painting will be viewed by a bigger audience, as only me and Alistair see it here. I don't know if you know, Alice" – she crossed, then uncrossed her legs – "but Courtney is a friend of my brother Mark's, so I can find out if he would visit the exhibition. Perhaps he could give a talk or something. If that's alright with you, of course?"

"That would be amazing. Just let me know when he's available and I'll fix something up. Do you know him yourself?"

"Yes, a little. I met him at his degree show in London about ten years ago. Really good work, I thought. Afterwards, Mark brought him to stay with us and he did that watercolour here. He gave it to me and Alistair as a thank-you present, so sweet of him." Julia smiled and her small brown eyes almost disappeared under heavy lashes. "Alistair hung it, one of his fishing friends saw it and asked Courtney to paint something for his wife's birthday. Courtney got more commissions after that and he's since had exhibitions in Germany and Denmark. So, in a way, we helped to get him started."

"What a lovely story. I'd like to put it in the exhibition catalogue if you and Courtney don't mind." Alice licked lemony crumbs off her fingers. "Roddy Rafferty is helping me with research. He knows more about the local area than I do and he's good at picking up gossipy— I mean, interesting, stories."

Julia's face dropped. "I understand that you need to sell the things, Alice, and Roddy's early work was marvellous, But he's better known for his drinking now than his art. Which, sadly, is almost a good thing, as his recent work has been a bit shoddy." She threw a morsel of cake to one of the terriers. "Being part of this project though – do you really think that's wise?"

The words felt like a slap.

"Yes, I do think so. He's painting again, something completely different this time, which is a good sign. An artist of his stature has a great deal to contribute to this exhibition and to the gallery. I'm sure this job will keep him occupied and positive."

"I admire your thinking, but he's so unreliable. A pity as he's such a talented artist."

Alice followed her finger as she ran it around the rim of her empty coffee cup. She had expected some resistance to Roddy's involvement – from Duncan Jones for sure. But it was disappointing that normally warm-hearted Julia was not more supportive. Roddy had been through a tough patch after his girlfriend's death. But recently he had seemed more optimistic and Alice wanted to support him.

"If we can encourage him to finish the painting, a new work by Roddy would be front page news."

"Well it would certainly be better news than this morning's front page," said Julia. "That poor man. Drowned, they say."

"Yes, I saw him myself yesterday morning, in the river. So horrible. I don't know the details, though. What happened?"

Julia reached for a laptop on the table and spun it around. A photo of the River Nare was captioned, '*Man drowned in river*'.

"Nobody seems to know ..." Julia jerked around to face Alice. "He was just found in the river. As you know."

"Who was he?"

"His name was Jason Marley. Oddly enough I met him recently. He knocked on my door and asked me to sign a petition, opposing the new shopping centre on Dunn Road." Julia ran a blue pendant up and down a silver chain around her neck. "There'll be trucks going in and out all day, the traffic will be dreadful. And do we really need more shops? There's already everything you want on the high street."

Jason Marley; JM. Alice's heart sprinted. It had to be the same person. But no wonder JM hadn't turned up for their meeting. The man was dead! Blood rushed to her ears and she felt light-headed.

"The land is next door to Alistair's golf club." Julia rambled on, though Alice was only half-listening. "And the members are furious about it. So I was happy to sign Jason's petition. I wanted to know more about his opposition, so he invited me to a meeting at The Three Bells the night before last. I couldn't go, but I think Jason must have been on his way home from there when he died."

Alice grabbed the edge of the table.

"Are you alright, Alice? You look a bit pale. Would you like a glass of water?" Alice nodded and Julia disappeared inside the house.

Questions crowded her mind. What did JM know about *Beach*? Why did he arrange such a cloak-and-dagger way of telling her? And what did he want to tell Alice, anyway? What did he think she could do?

She took a deep breath, closed her eyes and waited for her heart to slow to something approaching normal.

"There you go." Julia handed her a glass of iced water. "Probably the heat, it's making me feel a bit woozy myself."

The water cleared her head. "Those demonstrators in town yesterday," Alice said. "They were opposing the shopping centre weren't they?"

"Yes they were. They caused chaos but I thought, good for them. If the councillors won't listen, you have to take things into your own hands."

"I know all about councillors that don't listen." Alice grimaced. "I wonder what will happen to the petition now?"

Alice could just see her friend Livvie relishing the opportunity to stick it to the council, and with more than just a petition.

"I hope it doesn't all fade away now that he's gone. I did admire his passion." Julia leant across the table and pulled over a pile of leaflets. "Actually, I've decided to get involved myself. Jason gave me these, so I could see what his group were doing. Perhaps you can take one back to the office and get the staff to sign the petition."

Julia handed over a leaflet and Alice took in the shouty SAVE OUR TOWN! headline. She tucked the leaflet in her bag, thanked Julia for her time, and left.

Joe had still not called, though she ignored that for the moment. She had questions that needed answers and she hoped to find them at the *Great Wheaton Courier*.

As Alice stumbled along the road, she revisited in her mind the scene from the previous evening. Alone on the bridge, waiting for the person she had seen floating in the river the same morning. She had been stood up by a dead man.

Chapter 10

ALICE EXPECTED THE NEWSPAPER office to be filled with buzz and urgency, but the *Great Wheaton Courier*'s buzz was inaudible. She followed Claudia Rowan through the main office, where staff at functional work stations sat seduced into silence by computer screens. Claudia had swapped her strappy dress for a pair of navy linen trousers and a white short-sleeved shirt. Her glossy chestnut hair pulled back into a ponytail, she looked younger than her thirty-five years.

In a small room at the back of the building, an open laptop lay on top of an uneven table.

"Here she is," said Claudia. "This little lady holds a copy of every weekly paper we've published over the past hundred and twenty years. You should find what you're looking for amongst that lot."

"That's brilliant, thank you, I've been looking forward to this." Alice pulled out a chair and sat down.

"So, what did you think of Vivien Taylor's little do earlier? Do you like her drawing?"

"I love it and I'm delighted to have it in the show." Alice settled in front of the laptop. "Everything else about Vivien was amazing too, including her house. That's some pile she has."

"Isn't it just? By the way, did you find Walker's bedroom?"

"I did. Unfortunately, he caught me red-handed before I had a chance to see the paintings properly." Alice's cheeks burned as she pictured Walker's grinning face.

"Well at least he let you out unscathed. Lucky for you it was broad daylight." Claudia winked.

"Even luckier, I didn't see him again. He said he had to work. What does he do anyway?"

"He used to work in the City, hedge funds or something, I gather he made a fortune. He used the money to fund his hobbies, and art dealing is one of them. He started by selling off some of his family's stuff, apparently. Now, let me show you how this works."

A folder with Alice's own name popped up in the middle of the screen.

"Are you keeping secret files on me?"

"Should I be?" Claudia giggled. "No, I dug out a few pieces to get you started." She clicked on the folder. "Though I wasn't sure what you were looking for."

"I'm not exactly sure myself. I want some quirky stories, on what's been going on at the gallery since it opened. But I haven't produced a catalogue from scratch before, so I was hoping that something would just leap out at me."

"Sometimes that's the best way to start. Anyway, it's all yours, shout if you need anything."

Alice sped through the first few documents, recently published stories about Gregory's House, written by Claudia. They were perfunctory pieces, though she did find some winning photos, capturing the gallery and its exhibitions over the last century.

She decided on an introduction that would include a piece on the Gregory family and Ann Gregory in particular, whose home became the art gallery bearing the family name. Alice found Ann's obituary in the 8 June 1915 edition of the *Courier* and read about the childless young widow who had died of tuberculosis, leaving her house and most of her possessions to the community she said had so warmly embraced her. Alice tagged the piece and jotted down notes about the councillors who had overseen the project that saw the residential home become an art gallery.

Alice wondered what the database held on Vivien Taylor, so she typed the name in the search box and a list of close on 1,500 entries appeared. The ubiquitous Vivien had been involved in a wealth of local organisations, from kindergartens to funeral parlours, in her twenty-five year career as a Great Wheaton district councillor. In the process, she had built up a prominent profile.

Alice scrolled through pictures of Vivien opening charity fetes and handing out prizes at school sports days. She noticed that Vivien was accompanied, if at all, by Julian de Havilland rather than her husband.

Eating scones at church fetes, Alice concluded, was not Walker Hampton's idea of a fun day out.

The councillor's ownership of the Augustus John drawing played on her mind. It would allay her doubts about its authenticity if Vivien could produce a credible provenance. In the past, Alice had seen beautifully bound provenance books; receipts for every time an artwork had changed hands, together with signed notes from previous owners stating how and when they bought it. A complete record that traced a line right back to the artist and definitively proved its legitimacy.

Alice was not expecting a detailed provenance, but she needed to see a record of how the drawing came into the possession of Vivien's friend and his aunt.

She tapped away, exploring every variation of the words 'Vivien Taylor' and 'Augustus John' she could think of, but the database revealed squib. On a whim, she looked up the Tenby art gallery she had visited as a child. It still held some Augustus John works, but the drawing of the girl was not amongst them.

Alice tried the word 'beach'. That brought up articles on blue flag beaches, beach parties and beach towels. But nothing on the *Beach* painting.

Music drifted in from The Bull's courtyard and Alice pictured herself sitting under an umbrella, a cool beer in her hand. An appealing idea at that moment. She thought of the first time she had been to The Bull. Joe took her to celebrate landing the assistant curator job at Gregory's House and they ate dinner in the main restaurant. The walls were packed with pieces by Brazilian artists as part of the town's cultural festival. Joe hated the paintings – too bright, too garish – but Alice loved them, their vim and splash reflecting the optimism she felt for her new job, new home and the new phase of her fledgling relationship with Joe.

They spent the rest of the balmy evening under the stars, planning summer days on the river, bankside picnics and evening drinks on *Daisy*'s deck. She was relieved to have moved away from London and the job that had gone so horribly wrong. Thankful that she had ended up in this delightful town, with a man she liked and a clean slate for another attempt to climb up the greasy corporate pole. For the first time in ages, she felt safe.

As she did not have much to show for her efforts so far, she typed in more search terms. 'Town hall', 'paintings' and the name of the grey-suited man she met at Vivien's: 'Councillor Julian de Havilland'.

SCANDAL. The word pulsed out of the screen. She enlarged the headline and then the full article, a small piece, the sort of filler story that ran down the edge of the *Courier*'s pages. COUNCILLOR DE HAVILLAND IN ELECTION DONATION SCANDAL blared the headline. Alice read on:

A £1,000 donation to Cllr Julian de Havilland's election campaign has been declared illegal by the Electoral Commission. The money was donated by disgraced local businessman, George Shaker, who had been struck off as a company director of Shaker & Sons Furniture, before he made the donation to Cllr de Havilland. Neither Cllr de Havilland or Mr Shaker were available for comment.

Alice searched Julian de Havilland's name, along with the word 'donation'. Only one story appeared, another article of similar size, which read:

Cllr Julian de Havilland confirmed that he had repaid an election donation of £1,000 from George Shaker, once he discovered it breached election rules. He says he has taken steps to ensure that his office has more robust procedures in place to prevent it happening again.

George Shaker was not a name Alice recognised, so she searched for him and could barely contain an audible "No way!" when she found a recent photograph. It was the curmudgeonly man with the broken leg she met in Vivien's drawing room.

Claudia popped her head around the door.

"I'm going to have to throw you out, I'm afraid. We're doing an urgent feature and it needs researching."

Alice clenched her teeth and sent the folder of cuttings to her own inbox.

"I hope you found what you wanted. There's a lot of cool stuff there."

"There is, though I didn't get as much done as I hoped. Can I come back another time?"

"By all means." Claudia nodded to the screen. "I see you're reading about George Shaker and the donation story."

Alice waved the story away. "Oh, that just came up while I was looking for material on councillors."

"That's not surprising – Shaker had a cosy relationship with the council at one point."

"How cosy, exactly?"

"Shaker and Julian de Havilland spent a lot of time together, not that that was unusual given their jobs. But when Shaker started getting more than his fair share of contracts from the council, there was speculation about the real nature of their relationship."

So Livvie was right about the council's contracts all going to the same companies.

"And what *was* the real nature of their relationship?"

"I don't suppose any more than you would expect, for two prominent business people in a small town. George Shaker was an ambitious man who grabbed every opportunity to expand his company and influence. Julian de Havilland was in charge of business and regeneration, so their paths often crossed."

"And that's it? So, what's behind the speculation?"

"What's behind any rumour? Sometimes people choose to see what they want to see, regardless of what's actually there. I don't want to get involved with spreading unsubstantiated rumours."

"Isn't that something of a handicap for a journalist?"

Claudia pulled a look of faux shock.

Alice persisted. "So, there's nothing more to the Shaker and de Havilland story?"

"George Shaker was struck off as a director a few years ago, but he's done his time. And that's it."

"But the dodgy donation? That must have been something, you wrote a piece about it for the paper." Alice poked a finger at the computer screen.

"We did, but in the end, it didn't prove to be anything." Claudia shrugged.

"That's not what the Electoral Commission thought."

"The Commission was right, technically the donation broke the rules. A review of de Havilland's expenses exposed the mistake and the donation was declared illegal. De Havilland's local party association was fined. Really, it wasn't a big deal." Claudia looked behind her. "The real question is: Why did the Electoral Commission decide to examine the expenses in the first place?"

"What do you mean?"

"Someone tipped them off and we know because the regulators told one of Julian's staff. But nobody knows who the whistleblower was."

Alice was finding it hard to believe that the two respectable looking people she had met that morning, were involved in the scandal.

"Who are the likely suspects?"

"The other political parties are the obvious candidates, though they all denied it. But they would, wouldn't they?" Claudia giggled. "Politics is riddled with plotting and intrigue, just like the art world."

A young, bearded man stuck his head round the door, and seeing them still there, started to back out.

"Apologies ladies, I thought the computer was free."

"It is." Alice gathered her bag. "I'm just leaving. Thank you again, Claudia. Perhaps we can catch up on that story another time."

"Absolutely."

Alice was on her way out the front door when she stopped.

"I meant to ask you about the painting the *Courier* is lending my exhibition. Could I take it with me now?"

"Heck, I forgot. It's the lamb dinner in the boardroom, but there's a meeting in there now so I can't get it. I'll send it round tomorrow."

"Er, lamb dinner?"

Claudia clapped her mouth. "I'm so sorry, I shouldn't have said that. It's a dreary painting of sheep grazing on the founder's estate, and the staff nicknamed it 'Lamb Dinner'. Very un-PC, I hope you're not offended."

"I'm more offended by the 'dreary' description. I'm scared of ending up with a gallery full of duds."

Alice meandered into Market Square, where she took a breather by the fountain. She had hoped to find some entertaining anecdotes for her catalogue at the *Courier*, but discovering the election donation scandal was an unexpected bonus.

Julian de Havilland and George Shaker certainly had the appearance of being socially acceptable – a far cry from gangland criminals. Claudia had implied that somebody had snitched on them to the authorities, and she had brushed off George Shaker's behaviour. But the man had form. Being struck off as a director presumably meant he was hardly Mr Innocent.

Perhaps Claudia was protecting him. But from whom? Someone in Great Wheaton who wanted to dump a prominent councillor and a successful businessman into trouble and didn't worry about the consequences.

Chapter 11

ALICE HAD A LOT on her mind; not least, whether she was ever going to see Joe again. He had still not contacted her and when she tried to ring him, his phone went straight to voicemail. After a sleepless night, Alice arrived at the office barely able to string two thoughts together.

She gazed out of the boardroom window, watching someone making tea in the office opposite, while Rosie Knight recounted an incident at a party she'd been to.

Rosie broke off as Duncan stepped into the room and took a seat at the head of the table.

"Okay everyone, let's get going. We're all busy, so we'll keep this week's catch-up brief." He opened a sketch-pad to a clean page and pinched a pencil between his fingers. "So, you all now know about Jenna's accident. She's broken her hip and pelvis, so she'll need surgery, followed by an extended period of recovery. Alice will continue in the role of interim senior curator for the time being. It's a big job, so we all need to pitch in and help her where we can."

Tommy Norton nodded and set off a Mexican wave of nods around the table.

"Rosie, I've just had a difficult conversation with Jasmine Khan, complaining about this week's *Courier* article on her exhibition. She says the criticism is about the curation rather than the artwork."

So, Alice thought, she wasn't the only person who thought the sainted Jenna Farling's work was overrated.

"I'll speak to you about that and the other issues she raised, after this meeting. To mitigate any other complaints from Jasmine, I'll take ownership of taking down her exhibition when it finishes next month. Tommy," Duncan said to the technician, "you and I need to talk about that, book a time in my diary please."

Duncan looked at his pad and tapped dots on the page. "That will free Alice up to concentrate on the centenary exhibition. I'm not going to give another pep talk on how important this show is for us – I hope that's ingrained by now – just a reminder that we need to continue to give this our very best efforts."

At first glance, it looked as if Duncan had randomly sprayed the page with dots, but as he started joining them up, they formed the outline of a dog.

As Alice watched him, Duncan looked up. "How are you getting on with gathering in the paintings?"

"Okay. I've picked up a couple already, they're downstairs along with Vivien's drawing, which arrived earlier. There's a dozen more works coming over the next couple of weeks." She meant to meet Duncan's gaze, but looked at Rosie Knight instead. "I went to a lender's home yesterday and found some beautiful figurines. They're original pieces, absolutely delightful, they would bring a different dimension to the exhibition. So I thought—"

"Wait a minute, Alice. I don't want any changes to Jenna's list. Can we just stick to the script please?"

"Sure, if that's what you want. But these are very special pieces and you did say you wanted our best efforts on this exhibition." Alice looked at the top of Duncan's head, as he finished the house that had joined the dog on his pad. "It won't be any trouble, we could use a plinth left from the Martha Bergman show. I'll bring in some of the figurines, so you can see how special they are."

"I'll think about it."

"Thank you, Duncan, you won't be disappointed." Alice rocked back on her chair and shot Rosie a triumphant look. "It'll make an excellent media story. I took some pictures yesterday, I'll send them over to you."

"I said I would think about it," Duncan said. "That's not a yes. Hold fire, Alice, until I've made a final decision. In any event, the Augustus John will be the main attraction. John is a well-known name and we'll centre our publicity around that image."

"Augustus John is a big name, absolutely, but we had a couple of his paintings here a few years ago, so he's not a new name to the gallery."

Alice's chest tightened. She couldn't let Duncan promote the drawing until she knew for sure it was genuine.

"I'm hoping to get a new work from another well-known artist and someone we haven't featured here before. That could be the star of the exhibition?"

Duncan moved his pencil over the house doodle, then went back to the beginning. The lines grew darker, along with his expression.

"Just. Stick. To. The. List, Alice. Don't make me say it again. Augustus John is the biggest name we have in this show. And even if he isn't, which he is, I want to use Vivien's drawing to sell the exhibition. The council is our biggest funder and I need to keep her happy. Now." He looked around the table. "Is there anything else?"

"There's also the council's painting. They sent the wrong one, so I'm trying to track down the original work, to get it back in time for the opening."

"What's wrong with the painting we have?" said Duncan. "*Peonies,* isn't it? Why can't we use that?"

"There's nothing wrong with it, but it's not the one on Jenna's list."

"Nobody else knows that. The visitors will just see a painting lent by the council." He looked at Rosie for support. "We'll use *Peonies.*"

"I thought you said we should stick to the script," said Alice. "Jenna picked out *Beach* because it's so good. I want to make sure I carry out her instructions and get the painting here for the opening."

Duncan's face and neck flushed. He looked at the ceiling before turning his gaze on Alice.

"You're not spending your time tracking down anything, Alice, you're not a detective. Just concentrate on your own job. Please."

"That's what I'm trying to do." Her voice grew louder. "You said stick to the list. *Peonies* is not on the list and *Beach* is."

Duncan threw down his pen. "We'll use the painting we have and I don't want to hear any more about it."

"But—"

"Just do what I tell you, damn it." Duncan spat out the words, sprung to his feet and sprinted for the door, leaving the staff staring after him.

Rosie gathered her things and shot Alice a pointed glare. "Duncan was only trying to support you. I would have thought you'd be grateful; after all, you haven't done this job before and you need a lot of help." She swept out the door, leaving Alice and Tommy at the table.

"If you keep your mouth shut, you might make it to the end of the day without being fired," Tommy said. "But it would be more fun if you didn't!"

"It's not funny, Tommy. Oh, what was I thinking?" Alice threw out her arms. "I should apologise to Duncan. Should I apologise to Duncan?"

"I'll leave you to decide. In the meantime, we need to talk about layouts for the exhibition and whether you want the wall in the Ann Gregory room taken down. I'll have to book the technicians by Friday."

"I think the wall will have to stay, I even wonder if we'll have to build another one to fit everything in. Let me know what you think."

"I'll book Paul and Keith anyway, how about that." Tommy tucked his notes into a folder and pushed his chair under the table.

"Also, Tommy, would you mind digging out the plinth you made for the Martha Bergman exhibition? I think it'll be big enough for the figurines I want to show."

"Sure. By the way, you are going to get all this signed off by Duncan, aren't you?"

"I'll see him now and get his go-ahead. We'll catch up early next week."

Tommy disappeared, leaving Alice alone. She stretched her legs out in front of her and leaned her head against the back of the chair. She knew she should not have argued with Duncan in front of the others, but she needed him to know how much she wanted to make the exhibition succeed.

With the Augustus John drawing in doubt, she needed other star attractions in the exhibition as back-up. At least Roddy's new painting was genuine, as were Nicholas Waites's figurines. And regardless of what Duncan said, she was going to get *Beach*.

Chapter 12

Augustus John's girl was on Alice's mind as she walked back to *Daisy Dawn.* The girl had been with her ever since she saw her at Vivien's house, following her every move and shadowing her thoughts.

In her cabin, Alice opened the wardrobe and took out an old shoe box. She sat on the edge of her bed and rummaged through birthday cards, photographs and letters until she found her father's postcard. Holding it up, she studied the face she knew intimately. The girl looked back at her.

"Hello my friend, good to see you again. You should know, you've got a doppelgänger out there. She looks very similar to you, but she's not exactly the same. You look serious, but Vivien's girl has a sad, even a troubled face. Did your master draw both of you, or did some clever forger produce Vivien's version?"

Alice needed a definitive opinion and from someone who could not be disputed. And she knew just the man.

She found the number for Stefan Erickson, a noted authority on Augustus John and his era. She called his number and held her breath. Yes, he said, he would be delighted to examine the drawing and if she did not mind making it late, he was free that evening.

There had been no response from Monica Streatham, the officer in charge of the council's art collection, so she dialled the number again. Expecting to reach Monica's voicemail, Alice started her message, but was cut off.

"Alice, stop! It's Helen Yardley here. I'm a real person …"

"Oh, Helen! I'm sorry, I was expecting Monica's voice-mail. Have I dialled the wrong number?"

"No, this is Monica's phone, I've answered it as she's not here. Can I help you?"

Getting Helen instead of Monica might be more useful, as she didn't know much about the collection.

"I wanted to arrange an appointment to see the art collection and also to ask Monica some questions about *Beach*. Is that something you can help me with?"

"Maybe. What do you want to know?"

"I'd like to speak to the benefactor who has *Beach* now and get it back in time for my exhibition opening. Would you give me their name and number please?"

"I thought Councillor Taylor told you the painting wasn't available. She offered you something else, didn't she? Why don't you leave it at that?"

Alice hesitated.

"I should speak to the person who has it first. I'm just looking for a compromise, so that everyone gets a bit of what they want."

Helen sighed. "I'm not sure. That's not what Councillor Taylor agreed."

"Well that's true, but my problem, Helen, is that my boss will be furious if I don't make a good effort to get this special work. The first thing she'll ask me is whether

I spoke to the borrower myself."

She looked out of *Daisy*'s window, as the swan family, mother, father and three cygnets, residents of the reed bed on the opposite bank, fluffed their feathers and set off in single file up the river.

"If you want the borrower's details, you'll have to ask Councillor Taylor. I can't give them out without her authority."

"But Monica said it would be okay when I spoke to her before. She was going to send the details through. I don't know, she must have forgotten."

Alice grimaced. Lies were not her usual stock in trade.

"I don't know. Perhaps you should wait until she's back from holiday, then she can send it to you herself."

"She's gone already, has she?" Alice pushed on. "That's a real pain as she promised she'd do it before she left. I can't wait until she's back, the exhibition is opening soon."

The lies were tripping off Alice's tongue easily now; she was shocked and amused in equal measure.

"I suppose two weeks is a long time. Well, if Monica said you can have the details, I'll send them over. I'm sure she will have told you that the information is confidential, but I'll remind you not to share these personal details with anyone else."

"Don't worry, I'll keep them to myself. Thank you, Helen."

She cut a couple of slices from a sourdough loaf she'd bought at the market earlier and went up the companionway. "Over here!" she called to the swan family, now pecking around Roddy's barge. They turned and glided over the glistening water towards her. She pulled herself far enough under the bottom rail to dangle her legs over the side. Mrs Swan unfurled her elegant neck as Alice dropped a piece of bread into her mouth. She threw a bread shower into the river and the cygnets crowded in, gobbling the food as their mother watched over.

Mr and Mrs Swan had come into her life one cold, bright January morning. She was on *Daisy*'s deck, hugging a mug of hot chocolate, when she noticed the swans fretting around a jumble of wood in the water on the opposite bank. The birds had been using an old section of jetty as a base for their nest and it had rotted away, evicting them from their home. Joe found some odd pieces of wood, and together they rebuilt the platform. The swans constructed a new nest, which became the family home when their brood arrived.

"That's it for today, the rest is my lunch," Alice told Mrs Swan when she tapped on *Daisy*'s side with her beak. "You'll have to try somewhere else."

Alice plopped into a deckchair just as Helen Yardley's email popped up. It had an attachment entitled 'Great Wheaton District Council Art Collection, List of Borrowers'.

The document had three columns. The first gave dates when paintings had been borrowed and subsequently returned, the next column listed titles of paintings alongside their credited artists. Lastly, borrowers' names were recorded along with their contact details.

Alice read through the list. Edward Bawden, Jenny Saville, Gwen John …

Alice skipped to the end and read the last entry: '7 June 2019; *Beach* by Anonymous; Borrower: HSD.' Just last week. Nothing more. No phone number or address.

She ran her finger down the list a second time. The initials 'HSD' appeared many more times, going right back to the beginning of the list in 2002, but there were no contact details. And yet there was Claudia Rowan's name, a recent borrower, along with her phone number and email address. And Councillor Julian de Havilland, his phone number too. Why no details for HSD?

Another set of initials was also preying on her mind – 'JM'. It could not be a coincidence that *Beach* was unavailable the very same day Alice received the mysterious note. But why did Jason want to meet her? And why was he dead before he had the chance to tell her?

Chapter 13

Julia and Alistair Marsh were members of almost every club and society in the town. They knew practically everyone, so surely they would know HSD? Alice pressed Julia during their phone call, but she was adamant. She could not think of anyone with those initials.

Alice was sanguine. She and Roddy were on their way to dinner with Marjorie Cavendish, and as Marjorie had lived in the area "since dinosaurs roamed the earth" according to Roddy, she was bound to have bumped into HSD at some point.

In the meantime, there was still no word from Joe. Uncle Patrick's birthday had been a big family event, with cousins and grandparents that Joe had not seen for years. There would have been music and dancing until the early hours, followed by a hearty lunch.

Caught up with the birthday celebrations, Joe would have left his phone at the bottom of his rucksack and forgotten about it. There was no point sending another message now – he would be on his way to catch the late night ferry. Sanguinity remained intact.

Marjorie Cavendish's dinner was delicious. Alice scraped

her plate, licking the last traces of chocolate from the fork. She took off her sunglasses, setting them on the tablecloth, and breathed in the pungent lemon-scented air of Marjorie's garden. Shadows from a lowering sun spread across the grass; bees hummed as they cruised foxgloves searching for a nightcap.

"That was scrumptious, Marjorie, thank you."

"Have another slice if you want, there's plenty more."

"Well, I would." Alice leaned forward, one elbow on the table. "But three slices of cheesecake would be embarrassingly greedy."

"Dear girl, do not let embarrassment get in the way of your appetite. I'm sure Marjorie and I have seen more ignominious things at the dinner table."

"I know I have." Marjorie laughed. "And it has usually involved you, Roddy. Do you remember Roger's birthday at that Italian restaurant in Charlotte Street, when Roger got the people on the next table to blow out the candles on his cake?"

"And he pushed their faces into it." Roddy howled. "I laughed so much, I split my trousers."

"And yesterday," said Alice. "Roddy proved he was not the world's best guest, when he suggested that Vivien Taylor's prized artwork was a fake."

Marjorie dipped her head and peered at Alice over half-moon spectacles. As if unsure that Alice's words could be true, she turned to Roddy. "Is Vivien's drawing a fake?"

Roddy twiddled a tuft of his beard. "It didn't look like I thought it should do."

"Roddy, you're incorrigible! It looked a perfectly good drawing to me. What's your view, Alice?"

"I must admit I also had doubts. I saw the drawing when I was a child, and I can't quite put my finger on it, but there's something slightly off about it. The girl doesn't speak to me the way she did before."

"Of course she doesn't. It would odd if she did. You were only a child then and children see things differently to adults."

"That's one explanation I suppose. But I know that drawing very well and I'm not convinced it's the same one. In fact, I'm so concerned about it, I've asked a specialist to examine it and give me a professional opinion. Stefan Erickson is an expert on Post-Impressionism and if anyone can authenticate the drawing, it's him."

"Alice," said Marjorie, laying a hand on her shoulder. "That strikes me as an over-reaction. You haven't had time to examine it properly yet. You should go and have another look before you start calling in experts."

"I don't think that will help, I'll have the same doubts however many times I look at it. The point is that it would be irresponsible to hang a drawing on the gallery wall if I'm not sure it's the real thing. I need a second opinion."

"She's doing the right thing." Roddy topped up their glasses. "She *is* the senior curator now and she's taking her responsibilities seriously."

Alice smiled.

"Stefan's a top man, he would be my choice of expert too. And lucky for you that he was available so quickly."

"When I told him I might have a forged Augustus John, he was so excited he said he'd cancel a dinner so he could come tonight."

"What about Duncan Jones?" said Roddy. "How has he taken your news? And will he be satisfied with Stefan's opinion?"

"And Vivien?" said Marjorie. "She is the owner after all. I know I would be furious if someone doubted the authenticity of my artwork. Will she accept Stefan's opinion?"

Alice ran her finger around the rim of her glass. "I haven't told either of them, or anyone else for that matter, other than you two. I don't see any need at the moment, we only suspect that the drawing may not be genuine. Stefan will be here after the gallery closes and nobody will know. I'll see what he says and then decide what to tell Duncan and Vivien."

"Dear girl, please tread lightly," said Roddy. "Reputations are at stake here – for everyone."

Marjorie twisted around, facing Roddy straight on. "You're a fine one to talk, Roddy. If you hadn't opened your big mouth, Alice might not have been encouraged in this silly course of action. I can't believe that Vivien would have bought a fake, she's far too experienced a collector. We can only hope that this expert of yours, Alice, confirms the drawing is genuine and you can stop creeping around galleries in the middle of the night."

Roddy spread his hands. "I hope so too. If it were my work, I'd be mortified if people doubted I'd painted it and brought in some young pup to verify it. So please be discreet."

"But Vivien's not the artist," said Alice. "She's the owner."

"It is the owners, dear girl, who have the biggest egos of all!"

Alice stroked Delilah's back. Marjorie's black Labrador had sat at Alice's side throughout dinner and was now resting her head on Alice's knee. Alice had not given any thought to how Vivien would react. Roddy was probably right, she would be furious if she knew that Alice doubted her drawing. Alice could not afford to upset the gallery's main funder, but she could also not afford to display a fake drawing. She was treading a precarious path.

"Talking of paintings, Roddy," said Alice, "how's the new work coming along?"

"You're painting again, Roddy? That's marvellous. What's the subject?"

"You will see when it's finished." He shook a Gauloise from its paper packet and lit it with a plastic lighter.

"Your abstracts were splendid. Roger loved them, as did I. Especially the fried eggs!"

Roddy scowled. "Heathen! You are the only person I know who can see food in my paintings."

"I eat all day, then I dream of food. Which explains my waistline!"

"Anyway, my work sold well I'm glad to say."

"Some of your paintings must be worth a fortune by now," Marjorie said. "And I bet Walker Hampton's got the most valuable one."

"Walker Hampton!" Alice moved her plate aside and put both hands on the table. "When did he buy one of your paintings?"

"Forever ago. Back in the day he had an interest in a hotel or casino or something in Palma, so he'd go over to Mallorca every now and again to keep an eye on it." Roddy flicked ash into a crystal ashtray. "As he liked art, he would do a round of artists' studios and buy whatever took his fancy. He bought two or three of my pieces."

"I didn't realise you even knew Walker, you've not mentioned him before."

"I only met him a few times and it was a very long time ago. I haven't seen him since." Roddy blew smoke towards Marjorie's darkening garden.

"But the party, Vivien's unveiling– you would have met him then," said Alice.

"Was Walker there?" Marjorie wiped her brow with a napkin. "I didn't see him."

"I only saw him by accident." Alice poured water from a ceramic jug. "I'd been told the best paintings in the house were in the bedrooms, so I snuck upstairs. I was in Walker's bedroom minding my own business, just about to soak up a joyful Frida Kahlo, when I got caught by Walker himself."

"Dear girl," said Roddy. "When I advised you not to do anything impulsive, I meant things like – don't go wandering into your funder's husband's bedroom!"

"I was only interested in the paintings!"

"I didn't think anything else."

Marjorie collected up the dirty plates and stacked them on a nearby trolley. "Walker is a strange fish. He keeps himself to himself most of the time, in fact he's almost invisible. Makes you wonder what he's up to."

"Well I met him and he was definitely there."

"He may have been there in the flesh, but is he really what he appears to be?" said Roddy.

"So, first you think Vivien's drawing is a fake and now you're saying her husband is an imposter?" laughed Alice.

"Oh no, Walker really is her husband." Marjorie pulled a cushion from one of the chairs and put it behind her back. "That is, he's her legal husband, but whether there is any sort of real marriage there is anyone's guess. Still I suppose it suits them both well enough."

"Talking of mysteries, I've found out who has the council's *Beach* painting that I need for my exhibition. Someone with the initials HSD."

Alice searched Marjorie's face, but not a flicker of recognition crossed her round cheeks.

"Vivien told me that he or she was a local benefactor. Do you know who it could be?"

Marjorie shook her head. "How did you find out who had the painting?"

"The council gave me the list of people who've borrowed work from its collection. It had contact details of all the other borrowers, but not this HSD person. No ideas?"

"No, sorry I can't help," said Marjorie.

Alice twirled her glass stem between her fingers. "But until I find out who HSD is, I can't even begin to get *Beach* back. It's such a pain, I'm desperate to have the star of the show safely stored at the gallery."

"Goodnight." A high-pitched voice came from across the lawn. Delilah pricked up her ears, before bounding across the lawn towards a man in a wide-brimmed hat, disappearing behind a lemon tree.

"That's my handyman, he's been fixing a leaky hose pipe," said Marjorie.

"Delilah's a sweet dog, she must be good company for you."

"She is." Marjorie glanced after the dog, a fond smile on her face. "Though she's not been herself since her twin left earlier this year. I couldn't cope with both of them, so I gave her brother to my handyman."

Alice checked her watch. "I should get going soon, I've got to meet Stefan. It's been a lovely evening, thank you for dinner, Marjorie."

"You're very welcome, I greatly enjoyed your company. I'll take you through the house, so you can see some of my paintings on the way out."

They ambled through the large Victorian manor house, taking in Marjorie's eclectic collection of paintings and sculptures. They ended the tour in the kitchen.

On the wall was a photo of a younger Marjorie, underneath layers of pink tulle, being whirled around the dance floor by a tall, handsome man.

"Hey, fabulous outfit," said Alice. "You look amazing."

"I was an amazing dancer too, if I say so myself. That's Roger and me, doing the foxtrot. We won a gold medal." Marjorie held up an imaginary medal, a sunny beam on her face. "I spend most of my evenings in here now that I'm on my own, so I've brought in some of my special things."

"I'm sure Alice would like to see your John Nash, Marjorie, if you've still got it."

"I wouldn't part with my Nash for all the tea in China. It's in the pantry behind you, Alice."

Alice's mouth hit the floor. "Seriously? You've got paintings hanging in the pantry?"

"Not hanging, I just store them in there. I want to hang the Nash over there by the clock, but I haven't got around to putting it up yet. It's in the pantry for safe keeping."

"I'll come over another time and fix it up for you," said Roddy. "Get it out for me would you, Alice, so I can check the fitting."

Alice opened a louvre door and stepped into a walk-in pantry, with tiled shelves up to the ceiling on both sides. The right-hand shelves were filled with tins and packets, along with a chocolate cake missing two slices.

Alice found the Nash on the floor, propped up against a box of wine and loosely covered with a piece of cardboard. Several other paintings were stacked up behind it.

"Now that's a landscape I do like," said Alice. "In Nash's hands those empty fields look inviting and the trees are wonderful. I don't suppose I could borrow it for the centenary exhibition, could I?"

Marjorie hesitated. She reached out and lightly caressed the frame. "Well, why not? I know it will be in safe hands at the gallery."

Marjorie and Roddy walked Alice to the front door. "Thank you for your charming company, my dear. Come again soon, I get lonely rattling around in this big house on my own."

Marjorie wrapped her arms around Alice and gave her a squeeze. The embrace was generous and maternal. Alice could not remember the last time she received such a warm gesture from her own mother. She leant against the older woman's padded body and soaked up the hug.

As she pulled away, Alice spotted one of Jason Marley's protest leaflets, lying on the floor beside a pair of wellington boots.

"I see you've got one of those too. I was talking to someone about the proposed new shopping centre this morning. I don't think the protestors are going to stop, despite that poor man's death."

"It's all guff." Marjorie threw her arms in the air emphasising the guffness. "Once the centre is built, people will flock into it and they'll think it's wonderful. It'll create lots of jobs and there'll be more shops and restaurants, it's good news for the town. People are complaining because they've got nothing better to do."

"It's terrible," said Roddy. "I knew Jason Marley. He used to fish up near Narebridge and he'd drop by on his way back. Only last week, he told me he was making some headway with the Dunn Road opposition. And now he's dead. It does not pay to make waves in this town, clearly."

"Roddy, what *are* you suggesting?" said Alice. "Can I add murder, along with fake drawings and fraudulent husbands, to your list of imaginary criminal activity in Great Wheaton?"

Chapter 14

HIGH ABOVE GREGORY HOUSE's entrance lobby, moonbeams broke through the domed skylight, mottling the black and white tiled floor. A magnificent dark wood staircase, buttressed with a white wrought-iron banister, followed the sweep of a circular wall to the floor above.

"This is an impressive entrance," said Stefan Erickson, his blue eyes sweeping the room.

"Isn't it just? I think it's the most remarkable feature of this beautiful house. Back in the day, it must have wowed the Gregory family's guests."

"It is amazing still, especially for new visitors like me who do not expect something so spectacular."

"Wait here a minute, Stefan. I need to turn the alarm off." Alice opened a door behind the information desk and silenced a determined beep. She typed a number on the alarm keypad, there was a double beep, then the system fell quiet.

Alice strode across the lobby, unlocked another door and beckoned Stefan over.

"The store room is in here. Careful as you go down the stairs, they're a bit uneven."

At the bottom of the staircase they stepped into a disorderly large basement room. Bits of plywood, part-opened boxes of catalogues, fought with broken chairs and a forlorn rabbit sculpture, missing one ear.

As they made their way through the basement, muddle gave way to order. Across the back wall were two rows of compartments, one on top of the other. Each compartment was divided into numbered sections, some housing a painting, some empty. Alice placed Marjorie's John Nash into an empty section and marked its number on a clipboard hanging from a nail on the wall.

"These paintings down here," said Alice, indicating the bottom row. "Are the artworks for the centenary exhibition, and this one here is the Augustus John."

She pulled out a rectangular package wrapped in brown paper and laid it on a table by the side wall. She unwrapped the package, exposing the drawing, and switched on the strip light above.

"Well, here it is. What do you think?"

Stefan rubbed his fingers, picked up the drawing with both hands and eased it close to his face. He moved his head from left to right, up and down, diagonally. He held the work at arm's length, then tipped it backwards, the light from the strip flooding the girl's face. Placing it back on the table, he gathered his long blond hair in one hand and bent deep over the image.

"Where did the owner get it from, I wonder?"

"Vivien Taylor, the owner, told me she bought it from a friend, who'd inherited it from an aunt some years before. But that's all I know."

"So, the drawing has no provenance. That is unhelpful."

"I know, but despite that, do you think it's a genuine Augustus John?"

Alice still shuddered at the memory of an incident at her previous gallery, when she had attributed a painting to the wrong artist. She had to produce labels for the paintings in an exhibition, with the name of the artist and the title of the work. She had left the job till the last minute and in her haste, she muddled up two of the labels, placing them underneath the wrong paintings. Her mistake had been picked up by a journalist at the exhibition opening, who wrote a derogatory story about the gallery's incompetence for an influential arts magazine.

It was an embarrassment for the gallery and Alice was considering her position when Joe spotted an ad for assistant curator at Gregory's House Art Gallery. She applied for the job and it had been a relief for everyone when she was offered the post.

It did not take long for the story to travel around the intimate world of art and artists and Alice spent her first months at Gregory's House trying to repair her damaged reputation. She had made a mistake and if she made another on that scale, she would never get another curating job.

"I am contemplating ..." Stefan dusted the drawing's glass with a blue handkerchief. "It is not straightforward. Tell me, the owner, this Vivien Taylor, does she have any other significant artworks in her collection?"

"I don't know about her, but her husband's bedroom is full of gems. He has a Degas and a lovely Frida Kahlo. Lots more, too."

"So, the husband must be the collector, yes?"

"I was led to believe that Vivien was the main collector, but Walker has bought paintings in the past and he has great taste. From what I saw, he's the real collector."

"Walker! Do you mean Walker Hampton?"

"Yes, do you know him?" Alice rubbed goose bumps on her arms.

"I have met him two or three times, but I know him mostly from his reputation for aggressive bartering. I am told he can beat down the most resilient of dealers with much charm. As you say, he knows his stuff."

"A charming crocodile." She smiled. "I can believe it."

"So, to the Augustus John." Stefan picked up the drawing again. "There is disagreement about the authenticity. You do not believe it is genuine; why is that?"

"I first saw the drawing when I was a child and I've seen the image hundreds of times since. I know that girl. But this one … Whilst the two images are very similar, I'm not convinced they are exactly the same. On the other hand, this looks so much like Augustus John's work that it's almost too good to be a fake. Really, I just don't know."

They both looked at the drawing. A groan from one of the floorboards above interrupted them and Stefan looked up.

"Don't worry. This is an old house and it makes strange noises, it sounds worse now the building's empty. Although, Tommy Norton is convinced we have a resident ghost."

Stefan smiled. He turned the drawing over and studied the back. "Sometimes the back gives us helpful information, but this one is blank." He put it back on the table. "Have you found any other interesting pieces for your exhibition?"

"I've just picked up a lovely John Nash and I've got my eye on a couple of other works, though they're not confirmed yet. I'm hoping that other good paintings will turn up."

"But these good paintings may not appear," said Stefan. "What will you do if you are left with an exhibition of duds? You are taking a risk, it seems to me."

Now she reflected on it, why had she pinned her hopes on so many speculative pieces? Roddy may not finish his painting. Duncan Jones had said no to Nicholas Waites' figurines and Alice had failed to find *Beach*. To top it all, the Augustus John might be a fake.

"I agree. As things stand it's not a show I would want to shout about." She laid her hand on the table next to the drawing. "This should be a central part of it, but I can't include it if I'm not one hundred percent sure."

"You are right to be cautious, even I am not sure." Stefan leant forward and lowered his voice. "However, in my opinion, this drawing *is* an authentic Augustus John work."

"Really?" Her voice spiked an octave. "What makes you so sure?"

"It has John's fluid lines and his superb draughtsmanship. It also has an authentic signature, though the work would speak for its creator even if it were unsigned. But, I agree that it is not the same as the famous drawing of the girl. I believe that what we have here is a different work altogether."

"You mean, we've discovered a new Augustus John drawing?"

"It is possible. But without a provenance I cannot be certain. An investigation is required to establish the drawing's journey from artist, all the way through to current owner."

"If it does turn out to be by John, why would he have produced two drawings so similar?"

Stefan leant against the table, the strip light bathing him in cold light. "Augustus John taught art early in his career. He could have created a drawing as a practical example during class and given it to one of his students to study. My own theory is that he gave away lots of drawings in this way, including incomplete ones. Some of these could have been kept in private ownership and we have no idea they even exist." He flicked his hair over his shoulder. "Another explanation, is that this drawing could be a study for the more famous one. Perhaps he didn't like it so much and abandoned it. That is why we need that provenance, Alice. I can help with research, but I need you to get an accurate account of Vivien Taylor's purchase and of the friend she bought it from."

"Of course. I'll speak to her and get whatever information I can."

"Good. When you know more, call me and we will talk again. In the meantime, I suggest we keep this between ourselves. If the media or, worse, the art world, finds out, they will descend on you like a flock of snow geese."

"I've got an un-dis-cov-ered John, dah, in my baaaa-sement," Alice sang as she locked *Daisy*'s hatch door behind her and skipped down the companionway into the saloon. "I've got the biggest star in the biggest exhibition the gallery has ever had!"

She had romped home after leaving Stefan at the train station, scarcely able to believe her luck. A newly discovered Augustus John would set the art world alight and send her career into the stratosphere. She was bursting to tell somebody the exciting news, but she could tell precisely no one. Not yet anyway.

She flitted around *Daisy*, cleaning up the kitchen, dusting the living space and even cleaning the windows. But it was impossible to keep her mind from racing. She thought of the spectacular opening she would put together. Lots of lights, a cocktail bar, the nation's media. She wondered whether Duncan should hire a PR agency.

After planning and re-planning her imaginary event, Alice switched on the air conditioner. Discarding her clothes, she flung them onto a chair and lay on the bed in her underwear. She turned on her side and watched the stars through a gap in the curtains – fairy lights in a charcoal sky.

Showing the Augustus John drawing could be a career-defining moment for Alice. But first, she had to prise that provenance out of Vivien Taylor.

Chapter 15

THE NEXT MORNING, ALICE emerged through the hatch door to find Joe leaning over *Daisy*'s side, arms resting on top of the railing. He straightened up when he heard her.

"Hey. You get a good sleep?"

Alice hid her face with her hands. She hadn't seen *this* coming. Assuming that Joe would be exhausted from his trip, she had expected him to be at home in bed at this time of the morning.

"Yes, thanks," she said as she sidled over the deck, stopping just beyond his reach. "How about you?"

"The body was creaking after the long ride from the ferry and I couldn't sleep, so I thought I'd wander over and see how you were."

Alice clutched her elbows and hugged herself as though for reassurance. Emboldened, she inched a little closer.

"Joe, I'm so sorry I didn't come with you. I tried to call you …"

Joe held up his hand. "I need some breakfast before you launch into a full-scale apology." He limped across the deck. "I'll make it, sit yourself down."

"That's sweet of you, Joe, but from what? There's no food here."

"I assumed that'd be the case, so I stopped at the market on the way over."

Alice smiled. "Actually, I'm hungry too. What have you got?"

"Eggs. Also cheese, tomatoes and spinach. I'll do an omelette. What would you like in yours?"

"Everything?"

Joe headed into the saloon, emerging in less than ten minutes with a tray of toast, coffee and two omelettes, which he set on a square wooden table. The tang of cheese wafted up as Alice dug her fork into puffy eggs. She swallowed and sighed.

Breakfast over, Joe got up and eased across the deck, stretching his legs with long strides. Alice followed him.

"Joe. Joe. I'm really sorry about Uncle Patrick's party. I …" She ran out of words, despite spending a silent breakfast planning what to say. She waited for Joe to fill the void, but this time he said nothing.

Alice swung her arms back and forth, then let them hang beside her. Over Joe's shoulder, a little family tableau caught her eye – father, sons and fishing gear motoring along the river, their dog barking at the swan family bobbing in the wake of the boat.

"I had to stay, yesterday, um … That is, I felt that I had to stay, that I couldn't run off on my first morning as senior curator." She machine-gunned the words, as if more of them would amount to a rational explanation. "I thought Duncan would think I wasn't serious about the job and perhaps he might even take back the promotion. I'm sorry if I came over a bit hasty. And maybe a bit rude … and thoughtless."

Joe showed no reaction. Then he moved off the railing. He towered above her, his sapphire eyes narrowing.

"You thought that, maybe, you were a bit thoughtless."

She swallowed hard, and her voice faltered. "I definitely was. I could have put it much better, if I'd thought about it first."

"So, if you'd taken a minute to think about it, you would still not have come with me? Is that what you're saying?"

Alice rested her jaw in both hands and contemplated the deck, before she thought it safe to reply,

"I have to be honest with you, Joe, I was afraid I'd get fired if I went away the day I'd been promoted. So I stayed. And I'm sorry I missed Uncle Patrick's party. But I'm even more sorry that I upset you."

As the words spilled out she grew calmer and she gave Joe the trace of a smile.

"Okay, I get it." A little pulse appeared on his temple. "You didn't want to ruin the first day in your new job, so you ditched me." Joe's forehead furrowed. "Well, I'm not going to be dumped out of your life when you feel like it and picked up again when it's convenient for you. And I'm certainly not going to let you trash my family's celebrations at the last minute, with no explanation or apology."

Joe leaned forward until his face was inches from Alice's.

Alice's head thumped and she braced herself for more words to blast through the space between them.

"I don't know what else to say, Joe, except that I was thoughtless and inconsiderate and I'm really sorry. And I promise I won't do anything like that again."

Joe glared, then stepped back and gave a hazy smile. Finally he said, "Okay. I accept your apology."

"I'll call Uncle Patrick and apologise."

"You'll do that. But in the meantime, there's a forfeit to be paid."

Alice's mouth dropped. "A forfeit? What sort of forfeit?"

Joe lunged forward, picked Alice up in his arms and turned towards the river.

"You breakfast with the swans."

And he threw her over the railing, into the water below.

Chapter 16

The Bull Hotel had been serving drinks to Great Wheaton's residents and visitors for over five hundred years. The hotel's original timber structure, exposed beams and enormous stone carved fireplace, were visitor attractions in their own right. A young woman, positioning herself for a selfie, slid backwards along the bar, parting customers from their drinks.

Alice placed her order with Flora and glanced at photos of some of the bar's most famous customers. Politicians, artists, writers and a border collie named Bailey, who in the 1890s had accompanied his master to The Bull every day.

Alice and Joe took their beers into the courtyard, which was as packed as expected on this sunny Thursday lunch time. In the midst of the throng, Alice spotted Claudia Rowan waving, so she weaved through the customers to join her. Finn Kinnaman was there too.

"Sorry, we didn't see you, we only got two drinks."

Alice introduced Joe to Claudia.

"Good to meet you, Joe. Don't worry about drinks for us, we're already sorted."

"Okeydoke," said Joe. "Hi Finn. What's brought you out this way?"

"You two know each other?"

"We met when we were covering Lenny Livingstone's trial in London a couple of years ago," said Finn.

"Well you won't get that sort of job here," said Alice. "There are no organised crime bosses in Great Wheaton." They all laughed.

"Actually, we were just talking about you, Alice," said Claudia. "Finn was showing me the pictures he took at Vivien's party. There's some good ones of the Augustus John drawing and now that you're here, you can help me choose which one to use in next week's feature."

"Wouldn't it be better to run the story a bit closer to the opening date?"

"I thought you were keen for some advance publicity. Tell people about it now and build up the anticipation, that's what you wanted, right?"

"Well yes." Alice worked the label of her beer bottle with a fingernail. "But it's still six weeks away. People might forget about it if we tell them now."

"They won't forget if we keep reminding them in the weeks leading up to the event, which is what we planned to do. And it's only just over five weeks away, which isn't that long."

"Surely a couple of weeks won't make any difference?"

"Vivien Taylor would kill me. She specifically asked me to big up this event. It's for your benefit too. You seemed keen enough the other day, so I'm surprised you're stalling now."

Alice looked at Joe, willing him to jump in and change the subject. But he missed her entreaty.

"I'm a bit concerned about you publishing pictures of the drawing. Just in case we decide not to put it in the show."

"Nice try, Alice. You know better than I do that that drawing will be centre stage in the show. Or else Vivien will pull every penny of council funding from Gregory's House."

"Can I at least see the article and pictures before they go to print? Just to double-check the details?"

Claudia pursed her lips and glanced around the courtyard. When she faced Alice again, her lips had softened but her eyes were cold.

"I don't usually let the subject of my stories approve my work and I'm not sure I can make an exception for you."

Claudia sipped her wine and fixed Alice with a stiff stare. "I'll think about it, but don't hold your breath."

"I heard about the drowning incident outside the gallery the other night," said Joe. "Are you involved in reporting that story, Claudia?"

"No, that's being handled by our crime reporter. It's a terrible thing, I knew Jason Marley well, nice man. Just when he was making some headway with his protest against the shopping centre too."

"Really?" Alice perked up. "You think he was actually getting somewhere with it? What had he achieved?"

"I don't know for sure, but I do know the council officers were in a flap about him. Apparently, Jason found out something that scared them. A lot."

"So, his death has come at a convenient time for them?" said Alice.

"It would appear so." Claudia lifted a hand as though to stop a thought in its tracks. "But I don't think for one minute it was anything other than a tragic accident."

"I'm not so sure," said Finn. "My police source hinted that it might not have been a straightforward drowning. Not that he would expand any further."

"You must have a special source, Finn, as the official police line is that it's being treated as an accident." Claudia brushed a fly from her glass. "While I think of it Alice, you know the George Shaker story we talked about the other day? His donation to Julian de Havilland's election campaign?" Alice nodded. "We had an intern working with us at the time, who did the research for that piece. Finn reminded me when I mentioned it to him earlier; actually, Finn knows him."

"Yeah, we worked together on a couple of stories while he was at the *Courier* and we kept in touch after he left. If you want to speak to him I can give you his number."

"That would be great, thanks," said Alice. "I would like to know more about George Shaker, actually Julian de Havilland really. What's the intern's name?"

"Freddie Garfield. He's a staff reporter on the *London Standard* now."

"I know a bit about George Shaker," said Joe. "In fact, I've met him a couple of times. His reputation for dodgy dealing doesn't stop people inviting him to their parties."

"He was at Vivien's unveiling the other day and he seemed quite at home."

"He's Great Wheaton's most glamorous criminal, so he adds a certain cachet to drinks receptions," said Claudia.

"So, what else did he do to get such a bad reputation?" said Alice. "Surely there was more than just that dodgy donation?"

"He was barred from being a company director, something to do with the finances at his own company. Freddie will know the details. It happened before the donation scandal, so it gave the impression he was a serial fraudster."

"Here's his number," said Finn.

Alice punched Freddie Garfield's details into her contacts list.

"What other stories did he work on?"

"A whole host of things," said Claudia. "He was such a good researcher that everyone wanted him. A classic terrier – once he'd been given a brief, he just had to get to the bottom of it."

Alice contemplated questions she wanted to ask Freddie Garfield, but stopped when she caught Joe's anxious glance.

"But this afternoon, we'll enjoy hot rays and cold beer."

Alice reflected on Claudia's comments about Jason Marley. He knew something that had the council worried. Whatever it was, there was something he thought Alice should know. She had to find out what it was.

Chapter 17

Later, Alice sat on *Daisy*'s deck, working up an article for the centenary exhibition catalogue. Her fingers flew over the keyboard, hammering out a description of Ann Gregory's paintings.

Freddie Garfield had been delighted that someone was interested in his research and had invited her to meet him in London. Joe was going with her and they would spend the day together – giving her a chance to make up for missing Uncle Patrick's birthday.

Guests from a neighbour's party spilled across Sam's Lane, seeking shade under a leafy plane tree near *Daisy*'s bow. Their chatter masked the trilling at first, so it was only when the noise persisted that Alice realised her phone was ringing down in the saloon.

She let it ring, not wishing to break the flow. The caller had other ideas, however, and tried again. And again. Finally, Alice groaned and got up to answer it.

"Get over to the gallery as fast as you can," said Duncan Jones. "We've had a break-in."

By the time Alice arrived at Gregory's House, the police had blocked off both ends of Albany Street, along with access to the gallery. She had to fight her way through a knot of onlookers and the uniform on the front door. Once inside, she found an agitated Duncan talking to an unexpectedly familiar man.

"What happened?" she said as she ran across the lobby.

"Somebody broke in," Duncan said in a quiet, pinched voice. "And stole the Augustus John drawing. From the store room. In the basement."

Alice's limbs weakened; she felt as if she was going to faint.

"What? No. It can't be gone. It just can't."

"Hello, Miss Haydon," said the tall, handsome man beside Duncan. "I'm Detective Inspector Nathan Salisbury and I'm leading this investigation."

The words, spoken with studied formality, did not register, but the face did. Nathan Salisbury had been her first serious boyfriend, when she was at college and he was a police recruit. She had not seen him for many years, but here he was again, right on her doorstep.

Nathan turned to Duncan and gave a little smile. "Actually, we know each other." To Alice he said, "I realise this is a shock, but we want to ask you a few questions. Is that okay, Alice? We need to establish a timeline, so we can begin our enquiries. And I have to give the owner a preliminary account of what's happened."

Alice saw whatever colour was left in Duncan's face drain away at the thought of explaining to Vivien Taylor that her prized Augustus John drawing had been stolen from his gallery.

"My officers are in the store room, so if you would go and give them as much information as you can please, that would be helpful. Ask for DS Riley."

"Of course."

Alice's heart galloped as she made her way to the door to the basement. She was disorientated, clinging onto the banister as she crept down the stairs. The last time she was on these steps, she had felt giddy too, but with excitement. Stefan had just told her that she might have something special on her hands, and she had already been planning the rest of her career around it. How could it have all disappeared so quickly?

She found a pale and strained Tommy Norton in the basement, with a uniformed police officer. Another man was poking around, making notes in a black book.

Debris littered the basement. Dollops of red paint splayed across the floor and halfway up the side wall beside some overturned shelves. The thief must have rustled around the shelves, knocking off tools, brushes and tins of paint in the process.

In the storage units, paintings sprouted torn bubble wrap, with some hanging out of their compartments. Others lay on the floor, wrappings ripped open, exposing the images inside. They looked disheartened in the dull light, ashamed at not being good enough to steal.

Tommy hurried over, running a hand through his hair.

"Hell, Alice! The drawing's been stolen. I can't believe it."

"So I hear. The Augustus John. Was anything else taken?"

"Yes, we think two others, at least."

The officer who had been taking notes introduced himself as DS Nick Riley, and he handed Alice a clipboard.

"I understand from Mr Norton that you're the senior curator." Alice nodded. "I've been told this is a list of paintings for an upcoming exhibition. Can you confirm that please?"

Alice looked at the clipboard. Squiggles danced on the page, but she assumed it was the right list, so she nodded.

"The titles with a red tick are paintings that you checked and deposited down here? Is that correct?" Alice nodded on cue. "From our preliminary investigation, we know that three of these paintings are missing. The ones highlighted in green."

Nicholas Waites' painting was marked, as was a fine nineteenth-century watercolour of Great Wheaton's High Street, which usually hung in the bar at The Bull Hotel. But it was '*Untitled* by Augustus John; lender Vivien Taylor' that screeched at Alice. Her precious Augustus John had been stolen.

There had never been a break-in at Gregory's House before. Why now? She felt sick, wishing the ground would open up and leave someone else to deal with … everything.

"Are you sure?" she said. "I mean are you sure those works have actually been stolen? They're not still here somewhere?"

DS Riley smiled. "We've searched thoroughly, but the paintings are not in the building and we've found clear evidence of a break-in. We'll search the area outside of course, but in the meantime, we are assuming the paintings have been stolen."

DS Riley pointed to the clipboard. "I need a copy of that list please. We have more questions, too, so I'd appreciate it if you stayed around a bit longer." He moved away, leaving Tommy and Alice alone.

"When do you think it happened, Tommy?" Alice whispered, peeking at the police officers, though their backs were turned.

"I don't know. I didn't notice anything unusual when I arrived this morning. But I discovered the store room door was unlocked when I went to get some tools. I came down and found this mess. So, I guess it must have happened sometime during the night. Though I don't know how they got in the building without setting the alarm off."

Alice's stomach lurched and she leaned against the wall, afraid she really would fall over. She went over her movements with Stefan. They had wrapped up the drawing and put it back in its storage unit. She was sure about that. Then they had locked up and left. But had she remembered to put the alarm back on?

She was not even supposed to have been in the gallery at all. She felt hot and clammy and her heart hammered in her ears. She had to get away, so she ran for the stairs.

"Hey, where are you going?" Tommy shouted.

She turned and held up the exhibition list.

"I'm going to get a copy of this for the police," she said, and ran up the stairs to the office.

At her touch, the photocopier clicked and whirred into life, flashing blue lights before it settled into action mode. There was no settling for Alice though, as she paced around the office searching her memory of the night before, going through the sequence again and again.

What would she tell the police when they asked her when she had last seen the drawing? She did not like the idea of premeditated lying, but what would be the harm, if she just said she had been at home? Quietly by herself. With no witnesses. She had not stolen the drawing herself, surely everyone would know that.

The CCTV cameras were dummies, so there would not be any footage of her entering the building. But the alarm.

It would register that it had been disarmed, and the time that it had been turned off. She could say she'd come into the office to pick something up. But what? She'd have to find a good reason – and fast.

What about Duncan? What would she say to him? She couldn't tell him she had brought Stefan to the gallery. Not now.

Stefan! She had to tell him. She dialled his number but got his voicemail. She left a message asking him to call her urgently and on no account to speak to anyone else first.

Her hands were shaking as she put the exhibition list on the glass and pressed Copy.

Her eyes swept the room and lit on the cupboard in Duncan's office. He usually kept a bottle of whisky inside, so she tiptoed into the office and opened the cupboard door. Sure enough there was a half-full bottle of Jameson, partially hidden behind a stack of plastic cups. She picked up the bottle and poured a measure, her hand shaking, into one of the cups. She took a large gulp and closed her eyes, relishing the hit to her head and the burn at the back of her throat.

"What do you think you're doing?" Duncan's voice came from behind her with unusual authority.

A layer of embarrassment on top of her anxiety rendered her speechless. All she could do was hold up the cup to show a smidge of amber liquor at the bottom.

Duncan gave her a look of uncharacteristic sternness that filled her with dread. He hesitated, then his face softened.

"Here, pass it over."

Duncan perched on the edge of his desk and took a swig from the bottle.

"What am I going to do, Alice?" He put a hand on the top of his head. Alice had no answer.

"DI Salisbury said he would speak to Vivien Taylor. It's for the best I think."

"Yes. Better it comes from him."

"And he's going to ask the media for a black-out over the next couple of days. He doesn't want details in the press yet."

"Thank God for that."

"It's the end of the gallery. And the end of me. You don't survive things like this, not in a small town. Perhaps I should resign immediately. What do you think?"

Alice tried to consider his question; but her thoughts were on her own future. Now might be a good time to tell him about Stefan's visit to the gallery. He would surely understand that she was only being diligent, authenticating a work that was in doubt. Duncan admired Stefan and would trust to his professionalism in ensuring the drawing was stored correctly.

But when she opened her mouth to speak, something entirely different came out.

"Somebody has stolen a masterpiece. It's the second piece from the centenary exhibition that's gone missing. I'm going to hunt down both those artworks and I won't stop until I've got them back."

Chapter 18

Nathan Salisbury's face smiled from Alice's open book. She smiled back. He blew a kiss; Alice giggled.

"Huh?" Joe looked up from his phone.

"Oh … just something funny in my book."

She held up the offending object, hoping it would hide her heated cheeks. Joe went back to his work and Alice watched the countryside trundle by, until the train reached London.

They ambled along Kensington High Street. A man was selling cut-out masks of the royal family, and tourists with faces locked on mobile screens occasionally surfaced to check where they were. Joe walked ahead of her, heading for Kensington Palace Gardens. Alice had not been to London since moving out over a year ago and had forgotten how … London it was.

On the journey down, she decided that she would forget about Jason Marley and the Augustus John theft. She wanted to focus on Joe. They planned a stroll around the park, followed by a leisurely lunch, just enjoying each other's company.

But first, she had an appointment with Freddie Garfield and she mulled over the points she wanted to cover with him.

They entered a gloomy, dingy pub that smelt of yesterday's chips and today's sweat. Alice recognised Freddie from Finn's description. He was sitting up at the bar, sweeping through his phone, occasionally glancing at golf highlights on a large-screen TV on the wall.

"Thank you so much for meeting me, Freddie. I appreciate you taking the time."

"It's no problem, I had a free slot before my next meeting. I should thank *you* for coming all the way down here, I'm delighted someone has finally taken an interest in my research at the *Courier*."

Joe ordered drinks and sat on a bar stool. He nodded at the TV screen. "I'll catch up with the Open while you two chat."

Alice noticed a table of smartly attired older customers and pulled at the bottom of her shorts.

"Actually, I was intrigued by your call," said Freddie. "It's been a while since I worked on the de Havilland story."

"I only found it by chance, but I'm glad I did." Alice pulled out a high stool and plonked her bag on the counter.

"It was a shame the paper didn't make more of it. But Julian de Havilland kept his seat at the by-election, as well as the business portfolio. He was an influential councillor, so the editor buried the story. I moved on and I guess it got forgotten."

"Is Julian de Havilland really that powerful? I don't mean to sound naïve, but he's only in charge of one part of the council's business. How far can one councillor's influence extend?"

"As his role is effectively head of the local business community, potentially everywhere. He helps local companies grow and attracts businesses from outside the area. He's a good networker, too. He's been a trustee on charity boards, a school governor and patron of a whole load of other organisations." Freddie tipped the last peanuts from a bag into his open palm. "Personally, I think that's a problem and that was the bit of my story the editor didn't like." He threw the peanuts in his mouth.

"What bit of the story? There's more than just the donation?"

"Sorry, I thought that's why you wanted to meet me, to talk about the other stuff."

"Please, do enlighten me."

"Shall we sit at one of the tables? They're more comfortable."

Freddie squeezed himself between a round table and a studded burgundy leather couch. Alice slipped in beside him.

"I got interested in Shaker and de Havilland after the donation story. Shaker had already been barred from holding any directorships and he sounded like a shady character to me, so I did some digging around. I discovered that he was one of three directors of a family business, which did very well. But when he got involved with some new companies, he left the day-to-day running of the family business to the other two directors."

Freddie's phone lit up and he turned it over.

"But behind his back, the other two were syphoning money off from the company into their own bank accounts and eventually they ran the business into the ground. The company ended up in the hands of receivers, who discovered some kind of internal irregularity in a sale of shares from Shaker back to the company. He had to give all the money back and he was barred as a result."

"It sounds like it wasn't really his fault?"

"Well, not directly. But when you're a company director, you're responsible for everything whether you know about it or not."

"It must have given him a bad reputation, especially after the donation scandal. It's odd that Shaker got caught out twice by deals that someone else hadn't done properly. Apparently one of his advisers organised the donation to Julian de Havilland. It seems he's been unlucky."

"Or perhaps he was just careless." Freddie smiled. "And the moral of the story is …?"

"Something about advisers!" Alice laughed.

A loud "Cheers!" erupted from the older men on the next table. They clinked their glasses together and gulped down whisky.

"So, what else did you find out?"

"I was researching the new shopping centre at Dunn Road and I looked through some of the council's tendering procedures. One of George Shaker's companies had submitted an application to provide all the fittings for the development. Other companies also tendered, but Shaker got the business. Signed off by … "

"Julian de Havilland," said Alice. "When was that?"

"A few months before the election donation business."

"So, it looks like a contract from de Havilland in exchange for a campaign donation from Shaker. That's a nice little deal!"

"It is, and I'm not convinced it was the only one between them either. Anyway, at that point I was told to drop the story."

"My friend Livvie complains that she never gets a contract with the council, that all the business goes to the same few companies."

"That was my feeling too, though I'd not done enough research to confirm it."

"And nobody at the *Courier* picked up any of this when you left, I take it?"

"I don't think so. But I'd got so interested in it I couldn't let it go. I carried on poking around and gathered together a pile of material. But then I got this job and dropped it. I kept everything though. If you're interested, I can dig it out for you."

"Please do, I'd love to see it. So, what do you think of Julian de Havilland? Is he a real baddie, or a goodie disguised as a baddie?"

"I like to keep an open mind on people and it could be that George Shaker's companies won the council's business because they were the best. And that he happened to donate to Julian's campaign because he wanted to. But I don't think so. I can't explain it – it just didn't feel right."

Alice finished her lemonade and put the empty glass on the sticky table top.

"There was something else I wanted to ask you. I'm trying to find out the identity of someone with the initials 'HSD'. Does that mean anything to you?"

Freddie glanced up and moved his head from side to side as if he was reading the answer on the ceiling.

"No, I can't say that it does. Is it someone from Great Wheaton?"

"Yes. Whoever it was borrowed a painting from the council's art collection which was already promised to my gallery."

"I didn't know the council had an art collection, or that people could borrow from it."

"It's not a well-known fact. Perhaps there's something in your box of tricks that will help me identify HSD. I'm impressed that you've still got all your research material – I don't keep any of my notes when I move companies."

"I try to keep all my research, you never know when you'll need it." He waved his phone. "Actually, I think I've got something here for you."

Freddie scrolled through his folders and Alice pondered the turn the Julian de Havilland story had taken. Dodgy contracts could now be added to a dodgy donation.

"Freddie, did you ever come across Jason Marley?"

"Talk of the devil. That's what I'm looking for – it's about Jason Marley."

Alice told him about the letter she received from 'JM' and Jason's subsequent death.

"Jeez, poor guy." Freddie put the phone down, held the table and pushed his shoulders back into the couch. "Matter of fact he contacted me about eighteen months ago, asking for a meeting."

Chatter rose at the next table, so Alice moved closer to Freddie. "Really? What did he say?"

"He was more interested in what I had to say. He pumped me on what I knew about the Dunn Road development, which as it turned out was less than he knew."

"Here we go," said Freddie. He picked up his phone and turned it towards Alice. "It's a note I made during our meeting, me and Marley. He kept going on about who owned the Dunn Road site and that I should look into it. I was going to get someone to check the Land Registry, but I never did. Not after that letter."

"Letter?"

"Yeah, it was delivered to my office. A sheet of lined paper, like something you would tear out of an exercise book, with letters cut out from newspapers. 'Drop Dunn' it said, or something similar." Freddie laughed, wiggled his fingers in front of his face. "Ooooh! Real Scooby Doo stuff."

"A threat? Oh my God, you must have been terrified." Alice gripped Freddie's arm.

"Not really. I've had a few warnings in my time, even a punch or two, but this was kindergarten stuff." He smiled and winked at Alice. "I wouldn't worry about Jason Marley if I were you. He probably didn't know any more about *Beach* than you do."

A light breeze played on the back of her neck, as if someone was blowing on it. She swirled around, but there was nobody there.

Freddie put a hand in his trouser pocket and pulled out a memory stick.

"Here, take this, it might come in handy one day. You plug it into a laptop and follow the instructions, enter the keywords you want it to pick up. It downloads all documents containing those words. Real James Bond stuff."

Alice took the stick. "So this is how you get your material is it?"

"Oh, I don't use it for my stories, that's just to spy on my girlfriend!" He laughed. "I've probably made it sound as if councillors are all a bunch of crooks, which they're not. Most of them are decent people doing a difficult job the best they can. But sometimes they make mistakes."

"But how can the rest of us be sure of that, when the local paper won't print stories when councillors do something they shouldn't?"

"That's a good question. There is nowhere near enough scrutiny of local government in my opinion. Very little of what it does gets reported in the media. I suppose people aren't interested. Now ..." He stood up. "I must go or I'll be late for my meeting."

"Well, thank you so much, it's been fascinating."

Alice watched Freddie saunter out of the pub, then she tapped Joe on his arm.

"Ready?"

"Would you wait a while now. Rory McIlroy's only on the sixteenth."

Chapter 19

ALICE GOT OUT OF bed, stumbled into the living area and checked the news. The *Courier* had a small story on the break-in at the gallery, saying only that it was investigating further. The police had contained the news, for the time being at least.

Whilst she was at the laptop, she ordered a copy of the title register for Dunn Road from the Land Registry, as Freddie Garfield had suggested.

After the meeting with Freddie, Joe had treated her to lunch and they had visited the summer exhibition at the Royal Academy. Joe's mood was easy, Alice was relaxed and neither of them mentioned Uncle Patrick's party. Or her moving in with him.

Alice heated a couple of flatbreads and filled them with the remains of the previous evening's chicken chow mein. She stepped onto *Daisy*'s deck, stretched out both arms, lifted her face to the sun and turned a slow circle on the spot. She gulped in a big breath and exhaled. A seagull watched her from *Daisy*'s roof until Alice shooed it away.

She walked along Sam's Lane to Roddy's barge and stepped onto the gangway. He was on the deck, lying back in a deckchair. He pushed hands and feet away from his body and luxuriated in a long stretch.

Alice wanted to tell him about the Augustus John theft. She craved his coolness after Duncan Jones's panic and indecision, but now that she saw him she was not sure if she could face him. It would mean relating the whole naked story, with no made-up bits. Lying to him would be impossible.

He hadn't yet noticed her and she stalled, watching as he reached underneath the deckchair feeling for a packet of Gauloise and a lighter. He took a long drag and blew out a train of smoke. He rested his head against the deckchair and let his hands drop to the barge's deck.

"Hey, Roddy!"

He looked up with a start. "I was just having a break. I've been painting."

"So I see." Alice studied the work on the easel. "That's the old mastery beginning to shine through, Roddy. Gosh, it's exciting to see a painting emerge from a blank canvas. It's looking strong – I really like it."

"It's coming, I suppose, if slowly." He hauled himself out of the deckchair and straightened up.

"I mean it, Roddy. What do you think – would you like it to go in the show?"

Roddy tugged his beard and examined the painting. "Well, I *was* starting to think it was okay. If you really do like it, I could consider submitting it."

"Excellent. There's plenty of time before I close off submissions, so take your time."

Roddy took a deep breath. "Okay. I'm in."

"Yippee!"

"Finish the painting. Write a catalogue of amusing stories. You are quite the taskmaster, Miss Haydon!"

He grinned. "Now, give me a couple of minutes to get changed and you can come with me to drag a funny story out of Sarah Duxton."

"Seeing as you're on a roll, why don't you carry on painting. I've got plenty of work to do."

Roddy's shoulders dropped a little.

"I'll crack on then," he said. "If you insist …"

Alice walked away, then stopped. She *would* tell him now after all. She started back, but when she got to the gangway, Roddy was lying back in the deckchair, his battered hat covering his face.

Livvie Manners leant over The Coffee Pot's counter, one hand tucked under her chin, reading from a sheaf of papers.

"Slow morning?"

Livvie slid the papers into a clear plastic wallet and clipped it closed. "It's Jason Marley's. He's put together a history of the Dunn Road opposition group's activities. I thought it would be helpful background, as I've joined the group."

"Does that mean you'll be making protest banners?"

"You bet! I'm so pumped about this – it's my chance to stick it to the council big time."

Alice dropped her bag on the floor and was about to climb onto one of the high stools.

"Hey," she said. "Let's sit on the sofa, I've got some free time and we can have a proper chat."

Alice kicked off her burgundy Vans and curled her legs underneath her as she settled into the massive brown leather sofa. Livvie set down glasses of cold water on a low table and sat beside her friend.

"So, what's up with you, Alice? You don't look your usual perky self. Is something worrying you?"

Alice wanted to spill the whole story – everything. Keeping it to herself was a burden she could do without. However, fond as she was of her friend, she knew that Livvie liked to talk, and with so many customers the news would be around the town in five minutes.

"There's lots of work stuff that's not going how I'd hoped," she said. "The centenary exhibition seemed like such an easy show to put on ..." She rubbed her hand over the sofa's worn arm.

"Well, I'm sure nobody expected an attempted break-in at the gallery. That can't have happened many times before."

"No, I don't suppose it has." Alice's voice sounded small, even to her.

A customer strode across the café and handed Livvie his bill along with a ten pound note. "Thanks, Livvie, keep the change."

When he'd gone, she turned to Alice. "Hey, it's only work. Now, more important: how's that gorgeous man? Good day in London yesterday?"

"Yeah, it was lovely. We didn't do a lot, but it was fun being together."

"How did his uncle's birthday party go? I bet he loved catching up with his family."

"He adores big family get-togethers, so he had a great time." Alice dropped her chin to her chest. "Furious with me for not going, though."

"You can't be surprised, Alice, you did let him down right at the last minute." Livvie's words were firm, but her eyes were soft. "To be honest, I don't know why you don't move in with him. He only lives around the corner and you can still keep *Daisy*, somewhere to go if you need some space. What are you afraid of?"

Alice moved her feet off the sofa and slipped back into her shoes.

"I'm not afraid, I just don't feel it's the right time."

"You know you can't spend your life running away from men and relationships." Livvie squeezed her arm. "Is this about your father?"

Alice flinched.

"The thing is Livvie, there was no warning. One day my father was there and the next he wasn't. He walked out one morning and I never heard from him again. I searched for him everywhere I went; bus stops, parks, shops ... But I never found him. And now I feel as if I never existed for him, as if I was never really there. I just couldn't cope with another man walking out on me, and as long as I'm not actually living with Joe, well, there's a distance. Do you see?"

Livvie pulled Alice's head onto her shoulder. "Your father abandoned you and hurt you badly. He should have kept in touch, that's what fathers are supposed to do. But what he did was not your fault. You mustn't blame yourself."

Alice searched Livvie face. "How can you know that?"

"You were only a child when he left; he was a responsible adult. Or should have been." She brushed a stray hair out of Alice's eye. "But not every man behaves like that. Joe wouldn't. He's sweet and considerate. He'd sooner throw himself in front of a train than leave you without saying a word. Okay, he was angry with you for not going to Galway with him, but he came back didn't he? He's here Alice. Your father's not."

"I suppose."

"And that means a lot. Honey, what I'm trying to say is that while your father will always be a part of you, you have to move on. He left you, but you can leave him behind and you should. Instead, open up to Joe. He's far more reliable!"

Alice pushed herself up and held both Livvie's hands in hers. She felt a lightness she hadn't felt for days.

"Thank you, Livvie, I'll have a think about it, a proper think. I know that Joe's a good man and I don't want to lose him. I'll just have to pluck up the courage to tell him I like him."

"Atta girl. Now off you go and find the Augustus John that was stolen from the gallery."

Alice's mouth dropped open. Everyone must know that the drawing was missing, despite the best efforts of the police to suppress the news.

The centenary exhibition was turning into a car crash, and she was beginning to wonder whether being a senior curator was worth the aggravation.

"I don't know why you're so surprised. It's a small town, Alice."

Back home, Alice slammed *Daisy*'s hatch door shut and leant her head against it.

"Holy frick," she said. "What am I going to do?"

She stumbled into the bathroom, threw off her clothes and stepped into the shower, turning it up to the maximum. Shafts of cooling water pummelled her skin, stinging yet revitalising. Feeling refreshed, Alice pulled on a pair of navy shorts and a white vest top and plaited her wet hair.

She picked up her laptop and sat on the sofa. *Great Wheaton Courier*'s Breaking News page flashed across her screen:

Valuable artworks stolen from Gregory's House Art Gallery.

Rats! Still, they didn't mention any names, or show pictures of the missing works. And nothing more on Jason Marley.

She slammed the laptop lid down and paced around the saloon. A call to Stefan Erickson elicited no response. Waiting for something to happen was killing.

Round the saloon again. At the bookshelf, she ran her finger along the collection of paperbacks she had bought from charity shops but had yet to open. She passed the elephant painting she had brought back from India. Alice loved this piece – the majestic animal, the intricately patterned cloth over its back, the young girl in a crimson sari leading it. Painted on brown silk, the delicate work always brought a smile to her face.

She pulled out her special CD and danced her way through Taylor Swift's "Shake it Off". Then she clicked back to the beginning and turned up the volume. After four takes, she sat on the sofa, picked up her laptop and braved her inbox.

An email from Freddie Garfield, with documents attached that he thought she would find interesting. She printed them out on her old printer, picked out a couple of red liquorice shoelaces from the sweet jar and lay back on the sofa to read them.

First was a blank tender application for a council catering contract. She flicked through it, skipping over the boring parts – essentially all of it. She thought of Livvie, and the hours she must put into these things.

She allowed the form to slip off her knee and glide to the carpet. She bit off the top of a shoelace and wrapped the rest around her finger.

The rest of Freddie's package was a mix of reports, newspaper cuttings and party policy papers. But there was one thread holding everything together – the name Julian de Havilland appeared in every one.

She read Freddie's handwritten notes of a conversation he had had with the Electoral Commission about the dodgy election donation. The Commission had received an anonymous tip-off. "*Who*?" Freddie had written in the margin, but if he had attempted to answer his own question there was no evidence of it.

There were photos of Julian de Havilland shaking hands with all kinds of people. He always struck the same pose for the camera, standing with the other party to his left, his right arm across his body, clasping their hand with studied machismo. He even wore the same grey suit. In one picture, he was standing in a building site wearing a hi-viz yellow jacket over his suit, a hard hat almost covering his eyes. Alice did not recognise either of the men flanking him, and squinted at the caption underneath.

Bang!

"What the—?" Alice turned to find Roddy knocking on the window.

"Alice Haydon, open up!"

She returned his wave, though her eyes were pulled back to the picture.

Roddy opened the hatch door and stepped in. "Dear girl, what have you been up to? I rapped on the door loud enough to wake the dead, but you didn't answer. Are you alright?"

"Yes, I'm fine, I just didn't hear you." She sat up. "Did you want something?"

"Only to ask you over for a drink, I've finished painting for the day. I thought you might like a break too." He pointed at the papers littering the floor. "Good grief, what is this mess?"

"I've discovered the identity of HSD, the person who has *Beach.*" Alice waved a newspaper cutting in the air. "It's here, in this picture. Julian de Havilland is standing next to Edward Hacker, managing partner of Hacker, Stanley and Dole. HSD."

Chapter 20

"THEY'RE THE LAWYERS ON the high street aren't they?" said Roddy. "But are you sure about the connection? I thought HSD was a person."

"Vivien Taylor told me that HSD was a benefactor and I just assumed it was a person. This picture from the *Courier* shows Edward Hacker as sponsor of the 2014 Great Wheaton Arts Society annual exhibition. That proves he has an interest in art." She put the cutting on the table. "It also proves that the most senior person at HSD knows Julian de Havilland. And both HSD and Julian borrowed paintings from the council. Surely, it must be the same HSD?"

"It does seem likely." Roddy perched on a corner of the coffee table. "What are you going to do now?"

"Vivien said *Beach* was in this benefactor's office, so I'm going to ask him to give it back."

Roddy raised his eyebrows. "But—"

"I don't see why he wouldn't. It's not his painting after all."

"Now that you've got the Augustus John drawing, does it matter that you don't have *Beach*?"

Alice felt a little wave of nausea. She should tell Roddy about the drawing. He would find out sooner or later – better he heard it from her first. She fiddled with the plait lying over her shoulder.

"Dear girl, whatever's worrying you, spit it out, and quick. I can't abide girls who play with their hair."

So, she told him. He listened without interruption and then said:

"Losing Vivien Taylor's prized drawing, then bullying her generous benefactors into giving you their favourite painting, and all in the same twenty-four hours. Some chutzpah!"

"What do I do now, Roddy?" Alice stretched her arms wide.

"The last time I asked myself that question, I woke up ten years later with a monumental hangover. However, seeing as you've asked me so nicely, I'll try think of another solution."

Alice's mobile beeped and she snatched it up. "It's Stefan Erickson."

"Good, ask him for his advice."

Alice related the story again and as the Swede responded, his monotone voice cooled her aching head and calmed her breathing. She closed her eyes and listened.

"Thank you," she said finally. "I know that's good advice."

She put the phone down.

"Well, what did he say?"

"He said to stay calm."

"That's Scandinavian pragmatism for you." Roddy gave a little snort. "Did he have any practical suggestions?"

"He said we have to stop the *Courier* printing pictures of the drawing. Claudia has already agreed to put off the piece on Vivien's unveiling party until next week. But I don't know how to stop her publishing pictures of the drawing, especially now she knows about the break-in."

"Hmmm. There's a question. And one that requires an urgent and serious answer …" – Roddy shifted to the sofa – "which I can't supply, regrettably."

"We need to get the drawing back." Alice jumped off the sofa and knelt down beside the coffee table. "If we can track it down quickly, we'll avoid having to deal with Vivien and my reputation *may* remain intact."

"This tracking down of paintings is becoming exhausting. Besides, we are not detectives."

"Let's pretend that we are. If we think like detectives, we can follow the trail straight to the drawing." She tapped her palm on the table top. "So, the first thing we need is a list of suspects." She turned over a pizza delivery leaflet and picked up a pen. "Who are the prime suspects?"

"Every art dealer, collector and crime lord in the world. Oh, and your average thief!"

"Very funny. Though I suppose you're right, a rare Augustus John would attract that sort of attention. Okay, we'll narrow it down and concentrate on the people in this area. Let's have some names."

"I'll consult my little black book and pick out the ones with 'arch criminal' beside their name."

"Roddy, please help! Now, a whole party full of people saw the drawing at Vivien's, so its existence was common knowledge. However, it was taken from the gallery and because of Vivien's fear of the work being stolen – God, to think of it! – only a few people knew when it would be delivered."

"Good, start with those. Who are we talking about?"

"Well there's Duncan and Tommy, actually everyone at Gregory's House as I told them at the team meeting that the drawing had arrived. Vivien herself, of course. Other than that, I don't know."

Roddy twirled strands of beard between his fingers. "I think we can discount all of those."

"There has to be someone else who knew when the drawing would be at the gallery. And it must have come from Vivien. Though other than asking her who she told, I don't know how we'd find out."

"Ask her then. When you're apologising for losing her drawing."

Alice felt the colour drain from her face.

"Someone from the gallery should speak to her and I'm sure it won't be Duncan. I suppose as senior curator, it will have to be me. Though the thought of facing Vivien Taylor makes me want to heave."

"It's tough at the top!"

Chapter 21

ALICE PARKED THE DEFENDER in Vivien Taylor's driveway, while Walker Hampton watched from the doorstep. During her vomit-inducing journey to Larchmore she had run through what she would say to Vivien. But she had not factored in seeing Walker first. Whether he was a better or a worse prospect was a moot point, but she was thrown by his presence.

She got out the car, shaky legs unsteady on the gravel, and walked around to the passenger side, retrieving an arrangement of flowers.

"Thanks." Walker raised an eyebrow. "But I would have preferred wine."

"They're for Vivien," said Alice. "To apologise for the disappearance of her drawing." She was going to say "theft" but it sounded too final.

"You won't calm Vivien down with flowers. Still, at least you've made more effort than your boss. We haven't heard a thing from him."

"I'm sure he'll be in touch soon," she said, without conviction.

"Whatever. Vivien's not here by the way, so you can leave those on the doorstep. I'm just off out too."

"Oh, that's a shame. I wanted to ask her something – something that might help in tracking the drawing down." Walker raised both eyebrows this time. "And to apologise, of course."

"What do you want to know? The police have already been here asking lots of questions. I'm sure they have it in hand."

"I know they do, but the disappearance happened at our gallery and I feel responsible. And I can help. With our contacts in the art world, we have a reach the police don't."

"In that case, you can ask me. I'm just off for a whirl with Greta. Come over and say hello."

Walker strode across the driveway; Alice followed. He stopped at a timber-framed carport and with an imbecilic grin said, "Just arrived. My new car. What do you think of her?"

A sports car, glistening like a newborn, stood alone on the gravel.

"Please excuse my car ignorance, but what sort is it?"

"Porsche Cayman GTS convertible. Bit of a hybrid between the 911 and the Boxter. Newish car, no real history, but I thought I'd give it a go. I had it sprayed Atlantic Blue – a bit smarter than the original grey. So, do you like her?"

"She's the nicest Cayman I've seen."

"How kind of you to say so. Though don't tell the missus, she'll get jealous!" He patted the car's bonnet. "I was going to take her out for a drive. Jump in and you can see how she moves."

Walker opened the passenger door and gestured Alice to get in. He was wearing the same faded jeans he had worn at Vivien's party, but with a casual caramel shirt and a ridiculously broad smile.

It was the perfect afternoon for driving around pretty country lanes in a flashy sports car, but Alice couldn't help wondering whether a spin with Vivien's husband was appropriate in the circumstances. Or in any circumstances.

"Thanks, but I really should get back to work."

"You've just arrived. I'll put the roof down and we'll go around the block, won't take long. Hop in."

At least she could ask him whether anyone else knew when the drawing was to be delivered to the gallery. Alice had never been in a sports car before, though she had once ridden on the back of Joe's motorbike. They had just met and she was intrigued enough to want to spend some time with him, otherwise she would never have agreed. She had regretted it the minute they set off. She had struggled to hold on to Joe against a side wind that threatened to turf her off at every bend – added to which it was freezing cold.

But Walker's car was another matter. The roof folded in on itself and disappeared behind the back seat, and Walker guided the car around the gravel turning circle and down the driveway. The sun warmed Alice's face. On the road, Walker pressed the accelerator and the car sped away, leaving Alice's breath behind.

It was too noisy for conversation, so Alice relaxed and enjoyed the ride. Little Cornbury zoomed by and soon they were speeding along the river road towards Narebridge.

Before they reached the town, Walker turned off the road and pulled into the car park of The Shepherdess pub.

"Let's have a quick drink. It's a pity not to on such a nice day."

Walker leapt out and opened Alice's door. He headed inside the pub, directing Alice to the garden on the river bank, where she sat at a wooden table with a canvas umbrella. On the next table, office-dressed people dipped French fries into pots of ketchup over lunchtime chatter.

Walker appeared with two glasses of white wine. "Here's to sunny afternoons and good wine."

"And to Cayman convertibles!"

"You remembered the name." Walker took off his sunglasses, revealing bright, playful eyes. "I'm impressed."

Alice returned his easy smile.

"Now, if you want to carry on apologising for losing Vivien's drawing, I'm ready and waiting!"

"I don't know what I can say, other than I'm really sorry. The gallery was locked and alarmed, it's a mystery to us how the drawing could have disappeared."

"Perhaps it was an inside job, that's usually the story behind these thefts. Not that I suspect you of course, and Jones wouldn't have the guts to do it."

A pang shot through her chest. Her palms and forehead began to sweat.

"You look hot." Walker took off his watch and rubbed pale skin underneath. "Do you want to sit inside? It's cooler in there."

"No, I'm fine. Actually" – she paused, gathering the words – "I wanted to ask you about the drawing, whether *you* have any idea who might have stolen it. It's odd that it was taken from the gallery and not from your house." She rubbed the pad of her finger with her thumb. "Vivien insisted that details about its delivery to the gallery were kept confidential, but somebody must have known when it was going to be there, as it disappeared shortly afterwards. Perhaps Vivien inadvertently told someone else the delivery time. Is that possible, and if so do you have any idea who?"

"No, I don't. Though Julian knew of course."

"Julian de Havilland?"

"Yes, he had dinner with us the night before the party and Vivien mentioned the delivery then. I remember them discussing when would be the best time."

Julian de Havilland again. The man was everywhere.

"Well, that's one man who's not making himself popular, what with his plan for the shopping centre. I've yet to meet anyone who supports it."

"You can count me with them too, it's going to look hideous. I've seen an artist's impression and it looks like an old Soviet prison block. I don't know what he was thinking of."

"Perhaps you should sign the petition against it."

"I already have. You should too, seeing as there'll be a commercial gallery on the site."

"I didn't know that. Still, that's not really a competitor as we don't sell art. I don't suppose Vivien is pleased about your opposition, seeing as it's her own council's proposal."

"The project will go ahead whatever I think. Besides, Jason Marley was a friend of mine and Vivien always knew I would support him." Walker looked over the river. "Not sure what will happen to the group now that he's gone. He'd put so much into it."

Alice stopped her glass mid-air.

"How well did you know Jason?"

"We grew up together. His family were tenants on my father's land. Jason and I were the same age and we both hated school." Walker's face lit up and he moved his glass to one side, allowing room for his constant hand gestures. "When we met, I'd just been expelled from my second school and Jason had bunked out of his. We spent the afternoon fishing in this river, up near Narebridge, and the next day we went hunting for rabbits in the woods. Those were the days."

Alice gazed into her wine.

"I think that Jason sent me a letter just before he died. It was signed 'JM'. As you knew him so well, do you think you could tell if it's his handwriting?"

"Probably. He was fond of writing letters. I've still got a few at home, but those are signed 'Socks'." Walker winked. "Don't ask!"

Alice took the letter out of her bag and handed it to Walker. "Did he write that?"

Walker's face clouded. "Yes, that's definitely his writing. But why did he want to speak to you about a beach?"

"It's complicated!" Alice smiled. "I didn't know you were from around here. Where did you live?"

"The Hamptons used to own everything you can see around us and our house was that one over there. But it was sold years ago, along with most of the estate."

"Is Larchmore part of the estate?"

"No, that belongs to Vivien. My family fell on hard times, which is to say, my uncle gambled the family fortune away. When my father died there was hardly anything left and I've had to live on my wits ever since."

To Alice, the poor-boy-made-good backstory sounded suspiciously like the preamble to a pick-up line.

"I was surprised to see you with that old lush Rafferty the other day. Doesn't seem your type."

Et, voilà!

"He's helping me with the exhibition. But he's also doing a piece specially to submit."

She immediately regretted saying that out loud. Roddy would be furious.

"A new work by Roddy Rafferty, now that is a coup. I'd love to see it. Would it be possible to get a sneak preview?"

"I'm not sure." Alice avoided his eyes. "We're not telling anyone about it yet – it's a surprise. You'd need to keep it to yourself."

"You bet. I wouldn't want anyone else getting their hands on that painting first."

"You've bought Roddy's work before, I believe."

"I have indeed, good stuff they were too, back in the day. I wish I'd hung on to them, they'd be worth a lot more now. Still, who would have known that terrible accident was coming. Threw his career off course for years."

Walker drained his drink and forced a smile.

"Time to head back."

Chapter 22

WALKER PULLED UP IN front of the carport and killed the engine. There was no other car around – Vivien wasn't back.

Alice let herself out before Walker got to the door.

"That's a big garage for only two cars," she said.

"We've got other cars. The BMW's having a prang repaired. I've also got a Defender like yours, which I've lent to one of our neighbours."

Alice shuffled on the driveway, moving the gravel beneath her blue Vans.

"If you've got time, I'll show you some of my own paintings." Walker flicked a speck of dust from the car's bonnet.

Alice hesitated. She should head on really, but the opportunity to see Walker's studio was irresistible. She nodded, following him along a path that took them past the carport and through a spinney.

The path tracked up through the trees and opened into a clearing at the top of a hillock, where a lonely whitewashed summerhouse stood, encircled with a covered veranda.

Walker unlocked the door, revealing a deceptively large, open studio, flooded with light from tall windows on every side. A couple of easels held paintings at different stages of progress. A selection of palettes, an electric kettle and a collection of dirty rags made up the usual artist's paraphernalia. Not many studios, however, had a smart shower room and kitchen like the ones she found through a door at the end. Or a gun cupboard!

"Those are my father's rifles. Vivien won't have guns in the house. That Remington there?" Walker pointed to one of the four rifles in the glass-fronted cupboard. "That's the one that Marley and I used to hunt rabbits."

"Did the rabbit population tremble with fear when they saw you and your Remington coming?"

"You better believe it. I'm a crack shot."

On the other side of the studio, a deep wooden shelf cut the wall into two halves. A line of racks along the bottom, similar to the storage units in Gregory's House, held a few framed canvases, though from the edges of the paintings Alice could see that most of the pieces were unfinished.

Walker thrust out both arms. "Welcome to my hideaway. It's quiet and relaxing and the views are great for painting. But best of all, as you can't see the studio from the house, nobody knows I'm here."

Alice looked through the windows at the panoramic views of the surrounding countryside. There was no getting away from it – this was a magical spot.

Walker rummaged through the racks and pulled out a few canvases.

"Most of my work features the immediate surroundings." He pointed east, across the river. "I did this series of paintings last year, the same scene through each of the seasons."

He lay four canvases in a neat row across the table. The series began with a snow-covered landscape, which burst into greening spring in the second canvas. A languid, hazy summer scene followed and finally autumn, with lush burgundy leaves and bushes heavy with berries. Alice examined the canvases, taking in the small details. There was a single bird, appropriate to the season, in a corner of each picture.

She tried to keep the surprise out of her voice.

"These compositions are thoughtful and interesting, Walker. They're good. I really like them."

"That's sweet of you, though I'd give anything to be able to paint really well." Walker sighed and Alice gave what she hoped was an encouraging smile. As she did so, Walker's face moved closer and his eyes anchored on hers. Alice felt his breath on her cheek.

She flinched, turning her head away and instinctively raising her hand so that it occupied the space between them. Not only was he old enough to be her father, but—

"Yeow!" A high-pitched squeal made them both jump.

Saved by the bell …

"What on earth was that?" Alice looked around her.

"It sounded like an animal in pain. I think it's coming from down there." Walker went to one end of the storage unit and began rifled through canvases.

"You start at the other end, I'm sure it's somewhere here."

Alice began moving canvases. They had been placed at the front, leaving an empty space behind – ample room for a small animal to hunker down, hidden from view.

"Meow." The sound was softer this time, but it was close by, so Alice pulled out all the paintings in the next rack, and at the back of the unit she found a marmalade kitten, its green eyes staring out at her.

Alice pulled the kitten out and held it into her chest.

"Here's the culprit. Must have been there all night. It's so tiny!" She stroked the top of its head. "I wonder where it came from."

"There are loads of cats around here. They sleep outside on the veranda. I feed them sometimes, so they've probably told all their friends there's free food here."

The kitten looked at Alice with big, soulful eyes.

"It's gorgeous."

"Well I hope the little blighter hasn't damaged any of my work."

Walker examined his canvases, while Alice played with the kitten. He took out a framed painting, propping it up against a table leg.

"Damaged?"

"No, it's fine. It shouldn't be here, it belongs in the house." Walker picked up the painting, tucking it under his arm. "We should go."

Outside, Walker led Alice around the veranda to the back of the studio.

"You can put the kitten down here, this is where the adults tend to hang out."

Alice crouched down and the kitten jumped out of her arms. It steadied itself on the wooden decking and, finding its feet, leapt off the side, scampering towards the woods. They watched it until it disappeared under the foliage.

"The views up here are spectacular. No wonder you like it so much."

"There's always something interesting going on; I never get bored of looking at the river."

Alice followed the decking around the studio. They were just a few minutes out of Great Wheaton, but concrete gave way to plants and trees that looked as if they went on forever. The Narebridge road they had driven along earlier was just below. Alice followed the line of tarmac as it swept around the bend, disappearing underneath an elderly chestnut tree, its branches stretching across the road.

"Thank you for bringing me here, Walker, and showing me your paintings. They're very impressive."

"You're being kind, but I'll take the compliment."

"Have you thought about putting a piece in the centenary exhibition? I'd love to have more original work from local artists."

"Thank you, but no. I'm not going to subject an unsuspecting public to my doodles."

"Well, if that's how you feel. I won't twist your arm – but please think about it, there's still time before the opening."

"Don't hold your breath."

They were heading along the path and back towards the house, when Walker stopped suddenly.

"I've just thought of something. There *was* someone else who knew when the drawing would be delivered to the gallery. He popped in for a drink the evening before Vivien's party, and I'm pretty sure it was discussed. He didn't hang around and I'd forgotten all about him. The solicitor, Hacker. Edward Hacker."

Chapter 23

As Alice drove back to Great Wheaton, one question kept popping into her head: *What just happened*?

Did her funder's husband just hit on her?

She only went over to pump his wife for information and the next thing she knew, he was plying her with alcohol … Without the kitten, who knows what might have happened. It wasn't as if she gave him any encouragement. And it was hardly the behaviour of the distressed owner of a stolen – missing – artwork. Was he so rich he didn't care about the drawing, about art? It seemed to Alice he did care – he cared very much.

On the high street, she spied a rare free space and parked the Defender. As she was getting out, she received a phone call from Claudia Rowan. The *Courier* would run the Augustus John theft story in the next edition and it would be accompanied by photos. The theft was a genuine news story and she could not hold it back any longer.

Just when she thought it couldn't get any worse …

Alice messaged Stefan Erickson, warning him that they about to be deluged with enquiries about the newly discovered Augustus John. Then she made her way to Hacker, Stanley & Dole's office. Edward Hacker had known when the drawing would be delivered to the gallery. The firm was down as having borrowed *Beach* and Vivien Taylor had said the painting was at its office. What was the harm in asking Hacker if she could see it?

According to a gaudy yellow sign stuck to the inside of their window, the solicitors offered clients discreet and discerning representation. Alice pushed open the door and entered a contemporary, if bland, reception area. A young man with a Great Wheaton Rowing Club tie introduced himself as Toby and asked how he could help. By contacting Edward Hacker and telling him that Alice Haydon would like to see him, she said.

"He's busy at the moment, but I can book an appointment for another time?"

"In that case, perhaps someone else can help. It's about a painting he borrowed from the council's art collection. I've been promised the same work for an exhibition I'm organising, so I've come to collect it."

The man huffed and consulted his computer screen. "I don't know anything about that, I'm afraid. I'll have to ask—"

"Thank you, Toby, I'll take this."

Alice turned at the guttural voice and recognised its owner from one of Freddie Garfield's cuttings. The man was tall and balding, with rounded shoulders which made his suit appear a size too big.

He walked across to Alice and offered his hand. "I'm Edward Hacker. And you are?"

"Alice Haydon. I'm the senior curator at Gregory's House. I'm here to enquire about a painting which I believe is hanging in this office. I'd like to have it for our centenary exhibition."

"Come through to the meeting room."

He pulled out a chair at a large oval table, seemingly from habit rather than good manners, then sat down on the opposite side. He placed both hands, palms down, onto the table between them.

"We did borrow a painting from the council – *Beach* I believe it was called – and we were told we could have it as long as we wanted. Which means, sadly, that it is not available for your exhibition."

He pushed his hands more firmly into the table and crossed a little finger with a purple-stoned ring over its neighbour.

"Well, that's inconvenient. My gallery has been promised the work too. It's intended as the centrepiece of the exhibition."

"I don't know anything about that. All I know is that we have it now, and all things being equal we plan to keep it for the foreseeable future."

"Perhaps we can come to an arrangement? Between the two of us?" Alice rocked on the chair, trying to find a more comfortable position. For such impressive-looking chairs they were stone hard. "How about I borrow it from you for the run of the exhibition and give it back afterwards?"

"I'm afraid not." He smoothed a hand across his bald head.

"Just for the opening then. I can let you have it back almost immediately. You'll only be without it for a couple of days."

"It's not possible. I wish I could help, but I can't."

A money spider moved across Edward's jacketed shoulder and stopped at the edge of his shirt collar. For a full minute, spider and man refused to shift. Then, sensing victory, Edward lifted his hands off the table, leaving sweaty prints on the polished surface. He twisted his head a few degrees to glance at the spider, then looked back at Alice with a 'See how I didn't budge an inch?' look.

Not having engaged a solicitor before, Alice wondered whether this was a normal pose or if it was just for her benefit.

"Councillor Taylor was telling me about your generous charitable support. Have you considered holding one of your events at Gregory's House? Our garden is perfect for drinks receptions and parties, especially at this time of year. Warm summer evenings and a lovely view of the river."

Edward leaned forward and broke into a big smile.

"I know, I've been to a couple of events there myself." He flicked the spider away. "I agree it's a lovely spot. I would certainly consider it for our next fundraiser. Actually, the more I think about it, the more I like the idea."

Now that he was onto something he enjoyed, Alice decided to go in for the kill.

"And when are you planning the next event?"

Edward pushed the chair back and crossed his legs. He outlined a celebrity charity auction he was planning for September. "I'm friends with Luke Evans, the actor, and …" – his cheeks reddened as he became more animated, and Alice could not take her eyes off the spreading blush – "and I want to smash last year's total."

The man could bore for England, thought Alice.

"That does sounds interesting. If you send me an email with the details, I'll see how we can help."

"That's kind of you, I appreciate it."

Alice looked over Edward's shoulder to a painting on the wall behind him.

"That's a fine portrait. An ancestor of yours, by any chance?"

"Yes, it is," he said, flashing another smile. "That's William Hacker. He was my great, great grandfather and a founder of the firm along with William Stanley. I've done a lot of research on my family history and according to the records, this portrait is a good likeness. Stanley's portrait is in the other meeting room."

"I'd love to see it. Do you have time to show me?"

She followed Edward along a corridor to the other side of the building. She peered into the offices, which were as silently frantic as the *Courier*'s. In front of William Stanley, she offered some suitable platitudes, then asked if she could use the bathroom.

"Of course. It's upstairs, turn left and first on the right. I'll say goodbye now and Toby will see you out when you're ready."

Alice checked the few paintings that lined the stairs as she climbed to the first floor. She checked the corridor too. And the toilets. But *Beach* was not there. Mission over, but not accomplished, she trudged back downstairs.

The front door was straight ahead, so it was only by luck that she turned her head to the left. He had his back to her, but Alice could hear Edward Hacker's guttural voice. He was talking to a grey-haired, grey-suited man, and Alice recognised him immediately. Julian de Havilland.

Chapter 24

ALICE MOVED THE SOFA from beneath *Daisy*'s riverside windows to the middle of the room, facing the wall that separated the living space from the cabin. She moved the coffee table in front of it. Clearing the clutter from the low bookcase, she deposited the items she had bought on the way home.

First, she unwrapped a cork board and propped it on the bookcase, against the wall. In the centre she pinned a photo of Jason Marley, and in the top left-hand corner, her father's postcard of Augustus John's girl. Below that, she pinned separate pictures of Edward Hacker and Julian de Havilland, linking the two men to the postcard with a line of thin, red gift-wrap ribbon.

On the other side of the board, she placed an index card with the word '*Beach*' written across the middle in green pen. Below that went a picture of Hacker, Stanley & Dole's office, which she joined to the index card with a piece of green ribbon.

"Knock, knock." Roddy's voice drifted through from outside the hatch door.

"Come on in, Roddy, it's open."

He clumped down the companionway, dragging a pair of canvases, roughly one foot square, attached to bamboo sticks with sellotape. He was about to speak when he saw the cork board.

"Heavens, child, whatever are you doing?" He propped the sticks against the sofa and hurried to the board.

"I'm determined to get the Augustus John drawing and *Beach* back, so I've set up an incident board. I've pinned up what I already know and I was going to work out what to do next."

"Dear girl." Roddy removed his straw hat. "You are dealing with missing works, not a homicide."

"It'll be the death of my career if I don't find those artworks. I need to restore my good name; it has been shredded in the few days that I've had this job. Ironic, as I'd hoped promotion to senior curator would improve my shaky curatorial reputation."

"Oh, I shouldn't worry. Dubious reputations can take you a long way. I've been living off mine for years. So, who are your main suspects?"

"For the Augustus John drawing, I've got Edward Hacker and Julian de Havilland. Both of them saw the drawing at Vivien's house the night before her party and crucially, they both knew when it would be delivered to the gallery."

"That sounds reasonable. Anything else?"

"The two of them know each other, pretty well from what I can gather. I've done a bit of research on HSD's activity in the town and the firm does have a longstanding relationship with the council. Oh, and I saw them together, only today, in Hacker's office."

Roddy sat on the sofa, Alice next to him. She passed him the sweet jar. He selected a pear drop and she took a flying saucer. Together they contemplated the board in silence, like a married couple watching their regular television soap opera.

"Can you think of any other suspects, Roddy?"

Roddy tugged at his beard.

"One doesn't like to cast aspersions on one's friends; but there are people I know who would happily pay someone to steal a rare Augustus John – and could afford to do it. Though whether they've taken this particular John drawing is debatable."

"As for *Beach,* I've got Edward Hacker down for taking that too," said Alice. "He admitted that he borrowed the painting and that he still has it. But he was most evasive. He didn't say where it was or what he's doing with it, or when it would be returned. And I didn't see it in his office when I looked, though that's where Vivien Taylor told me it was." She lifted one foot onto the sofa and clutched her knee with both hands.

"So," said Roddy, "we have a double theft on our hands."

"I think so. And I wonder if they might be linked. I don't think we can rule out Hacker and de Havilland acting as a team. Julian is used to doing what he wants and ignoring the rules when it suits him, even his own ones. And then there's his penchant for awarding contracts to friends."

"Talking of which …" Roddy got up and fetched his canvases. "I want your opinion on these placards." He held a stick in each hand, waiting for Alice's reaction.

"They're very good, but what are they for?"

"Livvie's organised a protest march to coincide with Jason Marley's funeral tomorrow, which she thought would be a fitting tribute. I'm going, so I made these placards to take along."

"They're lovely, Roddy." She knelt on the sofa and twirled the sticks around. "It seems that everyone is against the shopping centre, so you should get a good turnout."

"Why don't you come along? There's nothing like causing a commotion on a summer's morning."

"Maybe. I'll think about it."

Alice's phone rang and Stefan Erickson's name lit up the screen.

She listened in silence for a minute, then thanked Stefan and hung up.

"He's going to send me names of people he thinks would be in the market to buy the Augustus John. I'll add them to the list of suspects. I'm glad he's involved with this, he's being so helpful."

"Of course, he is. He's giving you other people's names so you won't think it was him that stole the drawing."

Alice shook her head. "I really wouldn't—"

"Well I really would. I'd put Erickson down as my prime suspect. He knows the drawing's value and the effect it will have on his reputation. Even better, he saw where it was stored in the gallery. He could have nipped back later that evening and taken it."

Alice laced her fingers together, her chin on top.

"It pains me to agree, but I suppose he should be a suspect."

She pinned an index card with Stefan's name on the incident board.

"There we are. Three suspects already. This is going to be a tricky investigation."

"What's that doing there?" Roddy jabbed a finger at the board. "Why Jason Marley?"

"Because he's dead. We know he was found in the river, but we don't know why or how he got there."

"You're not seriously thinking of investigating that too?"

Alice showed Roddy the 'JM' letter.

"I think he knew who had *Beach* and he was going to tell me. Until we know what happened to him, I have to assume he's somehow connected to the painting."

"Dear girl, do be careful. You are making some big assumptions here. And treading dangerous ground."

Alice took the letter and pinned it up on the board, underneath Jason's picture.

"Roddy, I have to know what happened to *Beach.* I think it's possible it will lead us to the Augustus John." She hesitated. "And I will be careful."

Roddy arched an eyebrow, but said nothing. He picked up one of the placards, leaving the other against the sofa.

"You can carry on playing with your board, while I get on with the serious work of protesting."

"Actually, before you go, Roddy, the *Courier*'s editor is adamant that the John theft story runs this week. Other than you, me and Stefan, nobody knows it's a special drawing and publishing pictures will only flag it up to the wrong people. Any ideas?"

"That odious man won't respond to reason, as I found out when he ran a scurrilous story about me a few years ago. I'd have sued him if I'd had any money." He banged the placard on the floor.

"I seem to remember that Marjorie Cavendish has a connection to the *Courier*. Isn't she a trustee or something?"

"Roger was a shareholder, and after his death Marjorie inherited his shares. She knows the owners and the editor well."

"So, we could get her to ask the editor to run the story but pull the pictures?"

"Is that *we* or *you*?"

Alice pulled her most winning smile.

"Would you mind, Roddy? You know Marjorie much better than me."

"You know you're becoming very bossy, young lady."

Alice felt a blush spread over her face and neck as she watched Roddy make for the exit.

"Roddy, I'm sorry. I had no idea I was being so … pushy. I just want to get the drawing back."

Roddy half-turned. "I know how keen you are to do a good job and I'm happy to help you." He smiled and held out a hand. "Now, do you want to come over for a drink later and we can discuss our protest tactics for tomorrow?"

"Thanks, but I'm cooking dinner for Joe tonight."

Roddy laughed. "Shall I order a Chinese? A Plan B?"

"I don't know what you think is wrong with my cooking, I eat it all the time."

"Dear girl, if only you knew," he said. "I'll see you on the stump tomorrow. Don't forget your peaceful protest weapon."

Alice picked up Roddy's placard. The words 'Nature not Profit', in green paint, were surrounded by images of flowers and wildlife. She ran a finger around a rose. The original plan, for a communal garden and play area, had been somewhat more inspired than the concrete shopping monstrosity that Julian de Havilland wanted now.

Opening her inbox, Alice found a response from the Land Registry. Title for Dunn Road appeared to be in the name of a company called Carrie Developments.

The name was unfamiliar, so she searched the internet and found the organisation's website. There were some sketchy details of the construction company's history, along with a broad mission statement that could have been the mantra of almost any company. Two case studies revealed that the company had built a holiday resort in Antigua and a block of luxury apartments in Belize. And that was about it. No Contact page, so no email, phone number or address.

Alice searched the council's website. She found a report on the agreement with Carrie Developments for a joint project to build the proposed shopping centre on the Dunn Road site. She skipped through the report, written in legal speak that went over her head, and went to the signatures at the back, where she found addresses for both organisations. The council's was listed as High Street, Great Wheaton and Carrie Development's was in the British Virgin Islands.

There was a knock on the hatch door.

"Come in, Roddy," she yelled.

The door opened. "It's me," said Joe. "I'm not interrupting, am I?"

"No, absolutely not, come on in." She caught the clock on the wall. "Gosh, is that the time already? I haven't even started dinner."

"Don't worry about it." Joe put a bulging plastic bag on the kitchen counter. "I'm cooking."

"No way. I've planned what I'm going to make, bought all the stuff and even printed out the recipe. I'm determined to cook for you for a change. Here's a cold beer – why don't you sit on the deck until it's ready."

She had not made a pasta sauce from scratch before. But if Nigella could whip up a sauce in five minutes, how hard could it be?

She fluffed up her hair, pouted at the frying pan and set about preparing dinner.

Chapter 25

Duncan Jones' email could not have been clearer.

'*I am not paying for plinths – use the painting you already have.*'

With Nicholas Waites' painting and the Augustus John drawing stolen, Alice was rapidly out of stars for the centenary exhibition.

She could still save face if the exhibition was a critical and popular success. She wanted Roddy's new work in the show, but she could not bank on him finishing it in time. That only left Nicholas' figurines.

She wondered how Nathan Salisbury's police investigation was progressing. And then she wondered how Nathan Salisbury was progressing.

"Morning." Joe emerged from the cabin. "How's it going?"

Alice snapped back into the real world.

"Slowly. I'm spending so much time on my investigation that the day job is taking a hit."

"You could leave the investigating to the police you know, it is their job after all."

"I could. But I want to do it."

Joe rubbed his chin and padded over to the kitchen. Alice fiddled with her phone, avoiding his gaze.

"I was thinking I would join you at the demo this morning," said Joe. "I'd like to take a few action shots. That's if you've decided to go."

"I am going, so by all means come too." A thought occurred to her. "Do you ever regret giving up the war reporting, Joe? Shooting demos is hardly the same as shooting war zones."

"The only real difference between a demo and guerrilla warfare is the choice of weapon. They are both about conflict and both generally pitch the establishment on one side and the resistance on the other."

He sat on the sofa arm and moved a strand of Alice's hair away from her eye. "Do I miss traipsing around the world's trouble spots instead of spending more time with you?" He brushed her forehead with his lips. "No, I don't."

She looked at him, but could not meet his eyes, so she watched her finger as she ran it along his forearm. "There's some leftover pasta from last night's dinner if you want to heat it up."

"Thanks for the offer, but I'll pick up some breakfast on the way."

The traffic lights flicked from amber to green but the cars remained still, blocked by a row of bodies lying across the road.

Protestors, arms aloft, banners and posters raised to the sky, surged down the footpaths on both sides of the street. Many chanted "Play parks not retail parks!" and "Our children's future!", the slogans scrawled on the back of cereal packets and stuck onto wooden poles with duct tape. Protestors weaved around stationary cars, defiantly thrusting their banners at the occupants.

Earlier, Alice had joined Roddy and Livvie at the beginning of the march. Holding one of Roddy's placards, it was not long before she was swept up in the crowd, feeding from its energy.

"No to retail parks!" she shouted with gusto. "Yes to play parks!" Intoxicated by adrenaline, she chanted louder and marched harder. When the rally reached the stationary traffic, Alice ran ahead to get a better view of the lie-in protest.

A car horn blasted loud and insistent, and other horns joined in solidarity. People got out of their vehicles, craning necks for a better look. The protestors' chants were countered by shouts from the occupants, the two factions squaring up like opposing teams at a football match. A police siren sounded from behind, then faded into the cacophony of shouts and blasts.

Alice hovered on the footpath near the traffic lights, right by the lie-in. She scanned the scene behind and in front, soaking it all in. Faces filled with aggression, passion, distaste. Faces looking out of windows high above the street, some passive, some cheering the crowd on, taking sides. She recognised Flora from The Bull, waving her arms as she hung out of a top storey window.

Outside the town hall opposite, security guards and police officers stood by the locked front door. They edged closer together as the stand-off intensified. Two floors up, safe behind a window, a line of onlookers surveyed the scene with varying degrees of amusement and annoyance. Alice did not notice Julian de Havilland at first, but when she did spot him, his eyes were already locked on her. It was too late to duck away, so she stared back. Two sets of eyes boring into each other, one in reproach and one in defiance.

A woman circled around a blue Mercedes chanting "Development out!", swaying her banner in time to her incantation.

"Get that banner off my car," shouted the driver. "You may not have a job to go to, but I do."

"We have a right to protest. And I didn't touch your car."

"Take your protest somewhere else!" yelled another.

"Stop complaining, we're doing this for everyone's benefit."

Recognising her, Alice shouted out, "Julia! Over here!"

Julia Marsh looked up and wended her way through the cars to join Alice. She was holding a Roddy Rafferty special, one with a pair of squirrels in the corner.

"Isn't this exciting?" said Alice.

"It's a good turnout," Julia shouted. "Lovely that people want to support Jason Marley and I'm delighted to see you here too."

"I'm so glad I came. It's just brilliant."

"I hope we'll get a positive outcome."

"I thought it had already been decided that the shopping centre was going ahead."

"It has." Julia moved closer, shouting louder. "But Jason was pushing for a judicial review, which could stop the process. He seemed to think there was a chance it would work, as he knew all about Carrie."

A shrill scream from one of the prostrate figures on the road pierced the air.

"Let go of me, you fat toady!" yelled a bearded man from the tarmac, as someone in checked shorts tried to drag him away by his foot. The protestor flipped onto his stomach, lashed out with his free arm and thumped his attacker's leg.

"Leave him, Darren." An ash-haired woman pulled him away. "It's not worth it."

Darren, apparently trained for obedience, duly desisted and the protestor resumed his prostrate position on the road.

Alice's heart clanged and her stomach danced. "Here, hold this." She shoved her placard at Julia and flew across the road towards a group of spectators.

"What are you all looking at?" the bearded protestor snapped. "Don't stand there gawping, join us!" He grabbed a handful of leaflets from underneath his head and threw them at the onlookers.

A man next to Alice stepped forward, grabbed the leaflets and threw them across the road. "I've had enough of this." He placed his foot on the side of the prostrate protestor's thigh and nudged him a couple of times. "Time to get up, mate."

The protestor grabbed the man's ankle, yanking it towards him, then let go. The attacker lost his balance and fell over. A punch was thrown and one returned. Hair was pulled. Someone yelped. Alice gulped. The two men wrestled. Arms and legs thrashed. A foot kicked Alice's ankle. She shuffled backwards, but was blocked by the crowd behind.

Shouts of encouragement interspersed with jeers came from the swelling mass. The crowd packed together, penning Alice between the brawlers and the mob. She pushed back against the wall of bodies, groping for a gap.

Another fight broke out beside her and she was buffeted one way, then back again. Bodies closed in, blotting out the light. A placard slammed into her face, and she felt the hot sting of blood above her eyebrow. It trickled over her eye and down her cheek. Tears welled, blinding the other eye.

Alice fell and, struggling to get up, crawled through and around a thicket of legs. She fell again. She rolled over and found herself back among the original fighters, still hammering each other on the tarmac. She felt a blow on her shoulder and lashed out. Someone trod on her hair. She yelped and crossed her arms over her head. The crowd seemed to close in, towering over her. Darker. Louder. A kick. A bellow. A whistle.

A strong grip grabbed her arm, hauled her to her feet and pushed her along. She dragged a hand over her eyes, wiping stinging tears and blood, but it blurred her vision further. She had no idea where she was. One foot tripped against the other, but her invisible helper held on, steadying her with a hand on each elbow. Half-blind and now unable to move her arms, she allowed herself to be pushed up a couple of steps and thrust into a seat.

A door slammed. A van door. Silence.

"Crap!" she said aloud. "I've been arrested."

Chapter 26

Alice perched on a sun lounger on *Daisy*'s deck. Joe crouched beside her, his hand in hers.

"It wasn't until I heard the woman say I was in an ambulance," Alice said, "that I realised I hadn't been arrested. It was all so confusing." She fought to contain a sob, but it escaped and she tightened her grip on Joe's hand.

"It was chaos, I know." He stroked her arm. "Good job that para saw you when she did. That's a nasty cut on your forehead."

Alice reached above her eye, tracing the strips of medical tape with her finger. A slow stretch down to pull off her black Vans released blistered toes.

"Gosh, my feet are killing me. Someone stamped on my toes, so they were already hurting when I found Chatsworth Road blocked off and had to walk the long way home."

Tears trickled down her face. She lifted a hand to brush them away, but couldn't find the energy. Joe cupped her elbow, inching her towards him. She crumbled into his arms, nestling her cheek in the soft curve between neck and shoulder. His hand stroked the back of her head and her body slackened.

"I was so scared."

"I know."

Alice broke from the embrace.

"Are you feeling okay, Alice?"

"I'm just tired."

She lay back on the lounger and closed her eyes. Her head throbbed and the bruises on her arms and legs seemed to throb in sympathy. Opening her eyes, she saw Joe leaning against *Daisy*'s side.

"So, how did you get on? Did you take many pictures?"

"Yeah, lots. It was surprisingly heated for a respectable middle-class demo. To tell you the truth, I was only expecting a quiet march down the high street, not a full-blown brawl on the tarmac."

"I'm glad," said Alice. "Not about the brawl, but I was afraid you'd be bored. Must have felt like old times."

"Hello you two." Roddy was walking across the gangway. "Just wanted to make sure you were alright. We lost you and ... Dear girl, you've been fighting again." He rested a hand on the lounger beside Alice's head. "How many times have I told you!" He winked.

Alice squeezed out a wry smile. "You should see the other girl."

"I can see that you've been well attended too. No broken bones I hope."

"No, just cuts and bruises, luckily. I was rescued by a policeman otherwise it could have been a lot worse. How did you get on?"

"We caused havoc and stuck two fingers up at the council. Job well done, I'd say. Though the best bit is that you've kicked the Augustus John story off the *Courier*'s front page."

Alice jerked upright. "Oh, that is good news. There must be a lot of coverage of the demo."

"Finn Kinnaman was there taking pictures, really good ones too. There's a ton of them on the *Courier*'s website."

"There were lots of arrests, so they have stories about those as well," said Roddy. "Including dear Julia Marsh. And I didn't think she was capable of a mischievous thought." He patted the sun lounger. "I won't keep you, I just popped in to check you got back alright."

Alice stretched her arms high, raised and lowered her shoulders, hoping to relieve the tension tightening her muscles. She looked at Joe, so steady and purposeful.

"How do you do it, Joe?"

"What's that?" He sat on the director's chair.

"Stay so calm, while everything around you is spiralling out of control?"

"When I'm taking pictures, I just focus on the job I'm doing. And try to stay out of the way."

"Don't you ever feel the urge to jump in and take sides, especially when someone small gets pummelled by someone bigger?"

"I did when I first started and I've got the scars to prove it." He rubbed the white line down his cheek. "In a war zone, you see lots of nasty things. But it's not my fight, I'm just an observer. People don't appreciate you interfering. I learnt that the hard way."

For a moment, Alice wondered whether observing rather than acting was an option for her too.

She eased herself out of the lounger. "I'm going down to clean up."

In the cabin, she stared at her reflection. A lump was

growing underneath the cut on her forehead, whilst a dark shadow formed beneath her eye.

She rubbed her arm, pushing up her t-shirt sleeve to reveal a collection of darkening bruises. She ached all over and her legs felt wobbly, so she lay down on the bed.

The centenary exhibition, she decided, was beyond saving. How did she always manage to make such a mess of things? In the space of just a few days a dead body had practically bobbed up in front of her, a prize drawing had been stolen on her shift, probably gone forever. *Beach* was, well, wherever Edward Hacker had hidden it. And Duncan was furious with her.

As if that was not enough, she had hacked off the councillors, the gallery's principal funders. Vivien Taylor had not thanked her for the flowers. And Julian de Havilland had seen her getting stuck into the protest against his flagship new shopping centre.

Whatever happened to her nice little curating job? Step up while Jenna's away, Duncan had said. Just gather up a few paintings and stick them on the wall. What could possibly go wrong?

It must be her. Chaos hid around every corner waiting to jump out at her when she was least expecting it. Or maybe she just wasn't suited to curating. Should she give it up and do something else?

Maybe Roddy was right, perhaps it was time to settle down. Joe wanted her to move in with him and she knew he wanted a family. She could stay at home and play with babies all day. Leave the real work to the grown-ups.

Alice glanced around the cabin and over to her incident board, where her eye caught the postcard of Augustus John's girl. It was times like this when she missed her father the most. How she envied her girlfriends as they recounted their fathers' advice on everything from boyfriends, to moving out and moving on. Sometimes, she could barely listen.

In heavier moments, the envy was too much and she railed against her father, who had so casually walked out on his family – and on her. She wondered whether he had done the same with his second family, as she assumed he had another wife and more children. Knowing that he might have done so did not make her feel any better.

Alice got up and unpinned the postcard. The girl's face faded away and in its place was an outline of her father's features. She gazed into the blank hooded eyes.

"Are you ever coming back, Dad?"

She chucked the postcard on the coffee table, and the very movement seemed to replenish her energy. She swiped up the postcard again and pinned it back on the board, thumping in the pin with her fist. She strode around the cabin, feeling her aches ease away and her limbs grow stronger. She stood in front of the incident board, legs astride, and titled her chin.

"It would be silly to give up the opportunity I've waited so long for," she said to the girl. "Especially after everything I've been through. I think I deserve this chance.

I can make the centenary exhibition the best show the gallery has ever had. And I'm damn well going to do it."

Chapter 27

The police station's waiting room was cramped and stifling, one corner fan having little impact on its sweaty occupants. Alice sat beside a tattooed man, whose manspreading legs pushed her into the obese teenage girl on her other side. She rubbed clammy palms together, and learnt from a poster on the wall how to prevent pick-pockets.

Alice should have given a statement before now, but she had been deliberating whether to tell them about Stefan Erickson's visit. The gallery's alarm system would record that it had been disengaged that evening and the police would know that now. Alice assumed they would think it was one of the staff, but she could not know whether they suspected her.

Withholding information from the police was risky, but she calculated it was preferable to exposing the undiscovered Augustus John artwork. If that was made public, she would be hounded for keeping the news to herself, then castigated for losing the drawing.

She had fixed on a story that was true, if incomplete, and she had just given her prepared statement to two police officers. However, any hope of finding out what the police knew of Stefan's visit evaporated quickly. The officers didn't know anything about anything. All questions had to be put to DI Salisbury.

And that was going to be weird.

The last time Alice saw Nathan Salisbury, apart from the day after the break-in, he was sitting in his mother's living room on the puce floral sofa Alice hated. And she was explaining how their long-distance relationship could never work. His new job with the Manchester force demanded long hours and a wheelbarrow-full of emotional tribulation, while she still had another year of college left. They hardly saw each other as it was and when they did, they were both exhausted.

It was a hard decision, and for some time afterwards Alice agonised over whether she had done the right thing. After the split, she often wondered how Nathan was getting on. Once, she even called him, leaving a drunken message on his voicemail and regretting it the following morning as she nursed her hangover. It was not until she met Joe that Nathan's memory faded away. Until now.

"You wanted to see me?" Nathan said, a double row of dark eyelashes sweeping radiant grey eyes. "Come on through to the interview room."

As she followed him along the corridor, she took in the broad shoulders, the swagger – confident without being showy – and the polite "Sir" uttered by everyone he passed. He entered a small room and invited Alice to take a seat. It was quieter than the waiting room, but no less stuffy. The only concession to visitors was a jug of tepid water and a stack of plastic cups. Alice helped herself.

Nathan Salisbury lowered his athletic body into the chair opposite, his navy jacket sleeve riding up enough to reveal gold cufflinks on his blue shirt.

"It's good to see you, Alice. I hope you don't mind me calling you Alice, this is an official meeting after all?" She shook her head. "Good. So, how can I help you?"

She looked at his lean, tanned face.

She wanted to say, "When did you get so hot? And you've been working out, too." She glanced at his left hand. "And you're available." But when she sat up straight and cleared her throat, what came out was: "As you know, I'm curating the centenary exhibition at Gregory's House." Assured, not boastful … "So, you can imagine that I'm very upset about the theft of my paintings, especially the Augustus John drawing." A little pompous, maybe? "And I wanted to see how your investigation was going. And to see if I could help."

Nathan's passive expression remained intact. He put down his pen, lining it up alongside a notebook.

"I appreciate your offer." His sonorous voice was calm and even. "And you *can* help, by giving us the fullest and most truthful account of your day the drawing went missing. Tell us every little detail, even if you don't think it's important. Would you do that for me, Alice?"

It dawned on Alice that he must have asked the two plods what she'd said. And that he didn't believe her.

Alice looked out the window behind him, following a squirrel as it bounded along a muscular branch.

"I was thinking more about art expertise. We have lots of contacts in the art world. People who buy and sell paintings, dealers, people like that. I thought we could give you some advice. You know, likely suspects, that sort of thing."

"You're right that we need some art expertise." Nathan smiled. "So, I'm bringing a specialist into the investigation. She's recovered valuable artworks before, so she knows her way around the art world."

So he already had it covered.

"As it happens, I know the best man. In fact, he specialises in Augustus John and his era, so he'd be perfect. I know he'd make himself available if I asked him."

"If we find ourselves in need of any extra expertise, we'll know where to go." He scanned her face, eyes narrowing as if he was searching for something. "I need to ask, Alice: Where were you that evening?"

Thunder clapped in her head and her throat clammed. She gripped both sides of the chair, willed herself to stay calm.

"I spent the evening with friends. Dinner at Marjorie Cavendish's house."

Nathan just stared.

"And your specialist, Nathan, er, DI Nath— DI Salisbury? Does she have any likely suspects? Or do you?"

Nathan placed his palms on the table and moved them together until his fingertips touched. A beam of light from the window picked out just a trace of moisture across his temples. Nathan frowned and Alice averted her eyes, looking back at the squirrel outside.

That, she thought, is one serious police face.

"We're just gathering information, which is why we need a full account from you. After that, I'm confident we'll have a credible lead. We'll be ably assisted by our art specialist and if we require any further assistance, we will seek appropriate advice." His face softened. "I realise this must be difficult for you Alice, but I hope that helps relieve your anxieties."

"Absolutely. But you will let us know when you have a suspect? Just so we're prepared at the gallery."

"Duncan Jones will be briefed as and when appropriate. Do you have any other questions?"

"Yes, I do. The dead man in the river. Jason Marley? What can you tell me about him?"

Nathan clenched his jaw and glanced over Alice's head. He tipped his head to one side and was just about to speak when the door opened and a voice said, "Phone call, boss."

"Thanks Riley, just coming." Nathan jumped up and walked around the table, resting a hand on the back of Alice's chair so she had to look up at him. "It would be good to catch up, and I'd like to hear about your exhibition. How about a drink next week?" He patted the chair and smiled. And a chorus of doves fluttered around her head.

A few minutes later, Alice was floating along Sam's Lane. Nathan had done really well for himself. He deserved it. And it would be lovely to see him again.

She was looking forward to that drink.

She ran across *Daisy*'s gangway and jumped onto the deck.

It was a pity Nathan wasn't more helpful on the suspects. Still, as a detective inspector he could hardly blurt out confidential information. And there was nothing stopping her conducting her own enquiries.

Alice could use the centenary exhibition as cover and question the lenders, local art collectors and dealers she knew. She had her own incident room set up, with her own list of suspects. Now all she needed to do was to find some evidence.

Chapter 28

In *Daisy*'s cabin, Alice fired up her laptop and settled down on the bean bag to investigate her three prime suspects for the Augustus John theft.

First, Edward Hacker. His blog on the Hacker, Stanley & Dole website was filled with his fundraising activities. Last month he had run a mini marathon, and had posted a picture of himself handing the money raised to the rep of a local charity. Absent from his blog, though, was any reference to the council or its art collection.

Alice went back to the council's list of borrowers. HSD had borrowed an artwork every June for the past eleven years and others at random times, a total of sixteen in all.

If Edward Hacker had chosen the paintings himself, it displayed an eclectic taste in art. She wondered why he had chosen those particular works.

Perhaps there was a clue in the paintings themselves … Vivien Taylor had said she could see the council's collection, so she would do just that.

She couldn't afford to wait for Monica Streatham to get back from holiday. A call to the town hall resulted in another conversation with Helen Yardley, who invited Alice to view the collection any time before five.

She bit the head off a green jelly baby. Julian de Havilland was next. Like Edward Hacker, he did not show an interest in art, but neither had he spent his spare time running marathons. However, he had a lot to say about the proposed shopping centre and even more about the opposition to it, much of it involving Jason Marley.

Though she learnt more about her suspects, none of the material took Alice any closer to the Augustus John drawing.

She ate the jelly baby's body and turned her attention reluctantly to Stefan Erickson, the last name on her shortlist of potential suspects. His name went into the search box. As the list of results came up, a piece from a Stockholm newspaper turned her mouth dry.

Stefan had been investigated for stealing a painting from a wealthy art collector in the city. He was arrested, and questioned for two days, but released when police were unable to find enough evidence to charge him. The article was dated 1997, so she calculated that Stefan would have been about eighteen years old. Perhaps it had been a teenage prank, from which he must have learnt a hard lesson, as she had never heard a hint of impropriety against him. However, a large glug of water did little to alleviate her parched mouth.

Not having the heart to research her friend further, she went up on deck where she found Roddy and Joe standing over bits of plastic and metal which lay strewn over *Daisy*'s deck.

"What's this?"

"Joe is fixing my dinghy's outboard." Roddy was sitting on the lounger while Joe wiped a piece of metal with an oily rag. "So I can whizz up to town on the river instead of walking."

"Gosh, Joe, that's brilliant."

Joe said, "How did you get on with the police?"

"Really well. It was all good." She hoped that sounded convincing. "Roddy, would you mind speaking to Lady Graydon today? I want to see if we can borrow her Picasso for the exhibition, instead of the family portrait she originally promised. I thought she might be more receptive to you asking her than me."

"You don't have my charm, it's true. I will extract the Picasso for you."

"Thank you. I'm off to a meeting now, so I'll see you both later."

As the town hall came into view, Alice's stomach somersaulted. She dreaded seeing Vivien Taylor.

The entrance lobby was packed with wedding guests waiting to file into the Grand Library. Alice mingled until Helen Yardley spirited her away and into the basement.

"It's all very straightforward," said Helen. "The collection starts over there and runs down these aisles. Here, I've brought you a list of the paintings, they're ordered numerically. If you see anything you like, let me know. I'll have to leave you to it, I'm really busy." And with that she left.

Alice relaxed. She welcomed the opportunity to nose away without anyone peering over her shoulder.

She unfolded her list of lenders, where she had marked the paintings that Edward Hacker and HSD had borrowed. She would start with those.

The collection was neatly ordered in racks and clearly numbered. Alice tracked along a line of units until she reached number twenty-two. A watercolour by a local artist, it had been borrowed by HSD for five weeks in 2014.

Alice held the frame and eased the painting out of its slot. An agreeable enough landscape, portraying a section of the river by Narebridge, painted by a noted nineteenth-century artist. A respectable choice for a firm of solicitors.

Number twenty-nine was an oil landscape, trees and fields, which could have been anywhere in the country. So far, so ordinary. As were the next fourteen artworks that HSD had accessed from the collection over the previous eight years.

Alice swished the list back and forth, sighing. This group of unremarkable artworks told her nothing about Edward Hacker or why he might have stolen the Augustus John drawing.

In hindsight, the visit was probably a long shot. He could have picked the works for any number of reasons that had nothing to do with personal taste.

Still, she wanted to see the Gwen John, so it would not be a wasted journey. She was keen to display the two John siblings' works alongside each other in a future exhibition. Now that, she told herself, would be quite a draw.

The Gwen John was listed as number fifty-seven. At the allocated space, Alice pulled down the painting: a portrait of a seventeenth-century family by an unfamiliar artist. She put the family back and lifted down the pieces from either side, but the Gwen John was not there either.

Alice skipped back to the beginning and checked the first compartment for another piece on her list. Yes, it held the correct painting. As did the next few that she tried.

Number nine was an oil painting of a wary-looking stag. It had been correctly listed, so Alice slid it back into its compartment. However, the painting stalled before it was the whole way in, leaving one edge protruding. She pushed it harder but it would not go any further.

Reaching into the unit, she felt a large hard-backed envelope and lifted it out. As she did so, a piece of paper fluttered out and down to the floor. She bent to pick it up. It was a receipt from a company called Art in Your Home.

"Alice." Helen Yardley was calling from the door. Alice shoved the receipt into her pocket and slid the painting back in its space. "We're closing now, you'll have to leave so I can lock up. How did you get on?"

"I didn't get all the way round, but thanks anyway."

"Perhaps you can come again when Monica's back from holiday."

As she entered the entrance lobby, Vivien Taylor was heading towards her across an emptying floor. Alice stopped and went to offer a greeting, but the councillor was talking on her mobile and thundered straight past without acknowledgement. Her heels clicked along the corridor until they faded away.

In the market square, she sat by the fountain and pulled out the Art in Your Home receipt. It was for a 'reproduction' of one oil painting – *The Stag*, by Charles Popper.

Number nine on the council's art collection list was *The Stag*. Meaning, Alice assumed, that the piece in the town hall was the reproduction.

Somebody had taken the painting, had it copied and put the copy in the town hall, keeping the original for themselves.

Alice took out her list of borrowers. Number nine, Charles Popper's *The Stag*, was last borrowed in April 2015. By Julian de Havilland.

Chapter 29

ALICE PACED AROUND HER incident room, throwing virtual darts at de Havilland's picture on the board. How many other paintings had he taken? And where were they now?

Alice wrote the questions on a blank card, added it to the incident board and fell back on the bean bag.

She had already elevated Julian de Havilland in her own mind to prime suspect.

How had he managed to get away with such a racket without anyone noticing? Surely Monica Streatham, as the keeper of the collection, must have known … How had she not suspected anything untoward? After all a copy, even a good one, was still a copy. Perhaps Monica was in on it too?

Julian de Havilland had to have found a home for the original paintings somewhere. Locally? Surely not, but she could ask the various lenders about any new paintings they had acquired when she visited them. If she could ferret out information about unusual dealings, it could lead to the recovery of the Augustus John.

And then there was Jason Marley. He had to be the link between Beach and the shopping centre. But how?

Her phone beeped and she got up to answer it.

"Hey, how are you?" It was Claudia. "Just wanted to check that you survived your demo ordeal. I hear you got duffed up."

"I'm fine now, thanks. It's not something I'm planning on doing again any time soon, though."

"You've probably seen that we're running the demo as our main story and that we've already mentioned you were treated at the scene. I wanted to run your side of the story as a follow-up piece. Why you were there, your impressions of the event and in particular, your treatment by the police."

"Why? Was that an issue? I thought they were really helpful."

"There are different views on that. Some people think the police were a bit heavy-handed. There were lots of arrests and there's a feeling that's because the protest was right outside the town hall."

Alice had no intention of talking about her experience to anyone, least of all a journalist. Her picture on the front page of the *Courier*, she was fairly sure, would send Duncan into counselling for the rest of his life. Still, she was keen to keep Claudia on side. If she did agree, perhaps she could get something out of it.

She knelt on the sofa and picked at a piece of loose thread from a cushion.

"Tell you what, Claudia, I'll do you a swapsie. I'll talk to you about the protest, if you tell me about Jason Marley's judicial review of the Dunn Road shopping centre development. How does that sound?"

"Good. We should meet for a proper chat. Are you free now?"

"… and the next thing I knew, I was in an ambulance."

Claudia sipped her water and put the glass down on *Daisy*'s deck. "Thanks, Alice, I appreciate you telling me your story. I know it's not easy to relive traumatic events."

Alice gave a wry smile. "Well, now that's over, come down to the saloon and I'll show you my Mary Potter painting."

Before Claudia arrived, Alice had closed the door to the cabin, not wanting to give the journalist a glimpse of her incident board, and a free story.

"I love the shape of that jug," said Claudia. "I've only seen Potter's landscapes before, but I much prefer this."

"Me too, and I only found it by chance, at a furniture auction in Norfolk. Joe was looking for a dining table and I saw this poking out from behind a dresser. It wasn't even one of the lots. So, I made them an offer and they took it. I don't think they realised what they had."

"Well, let's hope you got a genuine Potter. I got fobbed off with a forgery recently and that was from a respectable London gallery."

"The art world is riddled with stories like that. One time, I was researching a Jean-Baptiste-Camille Carot work I had in an exhibition and discovered that of the 2,500 paintings he produced, 7,800 of them were in America! He's got to be the most forged painter in the world. Tell me this. You must have lots of good stories about forgeries and other shenanigans in the art world. Have you published any of them?"

"If only! I have loads, but our editor is risk-averse, so he won't touch them with a barge pole."

Alice perched on the arm of the sofa. "Oh, do tell."

Claudia settled at the opposite end. "I once met someone who knew Tom Keating. She had one of Tom's John Constable lookalikes."

"No way."

"Yes. Amazingly, he'd given it to her as a birthday present, can you imagine?"

"I bet she was looking at holiday homes in the Caribbean after that."

"That's what I'd be doing. But I think Tess had more than a little crush on Tom and she would never have sold it." Claudia winked. "Anyway, she showed me the techniques Tom used to produce a really good fake."

"Isn't it all about using materials of the right age, matching colours exactly, providing a provenance authenticated by an expert?"

"All those for sure, but also how to put a genuine-looking signature onto a fake painting."

"You know how to do that?"

"I wanted to write a tongue-in-cheek piece about how to spot a fake, using Tess's painting. Tom had been dead for years by then; besides, he wrote a book himself on his fakes, so what was the harm?"

"And your boss vetoed it?"

Claudia nodded.

"I sympathise, I've got one of those too."

The two women laughed.

"Well, this has been fun, we should have a proper drink soon. Before I go, I'll tell you all about Jason Marley's judicial review."

After Claudia had gone, Alice wrote the key points about

Jason's application for judicial review on a blank index card and pinned it on her incident board under 'Carrie Developments'.

"Mission accomplished!" Roddy's voice boomed from the hatch door as he lumbered down the companionway. "We've done it."

"Brilliant. We're getting Lady Graydon's Picasso for the exhibition."

"Don't be ridiculous! She's not lending one of her most precious paintings to some troublemaker who gets beaten up at a protest. No, we've fixed the motor on my boat."

"You mean I have," said Joe behind him.

"Joe helped a bit, but if I hadn't handed him the tools in the right order, we'd have been there all day."

"Yeah, I'm sure. It's a pity about the Picasso. Still, we have a chance to put that right on Monday, Roddy, as you and I are having lunch with Sean Cummings."

"There is nothing good in that man's house, and by the way, I am not eating in his bordello."

Joe looked up from the fridge, a beer in his hand. "Bordello?"

"Don't worry, Joe, Roddy's exaggerating, it's not a real bordello."

"But Sean Cummings is a real bore! However, I'll go for the free lunch. Now, I need a lie down after today's exertions." A weary wave and he disappeared up the hatch steps.

Joe surveyed the incident board, a clouded look on his face. He took Alice's arm and gently pulled her towards him.

"Is this wise, Alice? You could leave all this stuff to the police, you know."

"So I've been told. But the John drawing disappeared on my shift. I'm pretty sure I didn't set the alarm when I left the gallery with Stefan. That means I lost the drawing, so it's on me to recover it."

"Even if you did forget to set the alarm, you're not responsible for the theft and you're definitely not responsible for Jason Marley's death. I don't know why you're pursuing that, too."

Alice had not told him about the 'JM' letter. She knew he would only worry about her.

"I know, it's just something I have to do. I don't expect you to understand, but please don't try to stop me."

Joe held her gaze for a moment, then gave a small nod. He kissed her forehead.

"Thank you. Your support means a lot to me."

"If there's anything I can do to help, just ask."

Alice put her arms around his waist and rested her head against his shoulder. She closed her eyes and her body followed the flex of his muscles as he rubbed her back and swayed from side to side. This should be the right moment to tell him how she felt about him. And a few days ago, she might have done so. But after meeting Nathan, well …

Chapter 30

On Monday morning, Alice lay on the bed underneath the open window and allowed the cool river breeze to caress her skin. Outside, a pair of ducks heckled each other. A low whoosh, like the hiss of hot iron on silk, marked the arrival of a third duck to break up the argument.

The other side of the bed was unoccupied. Joe must have left ages ago.

A text from Joe told her to wake up. Then: '*I'm meeting Finn Kinnaman for a drink at The Bull later. Come and join us?*'

She texted back, '*Sure.*' She still hadn't seen the photos Finn took at Vivien Taylor's party and she wanted to use some of them in the exhibition catalogue.

Alice got up and dressed.

The phone buzzed again and Alice beamed when Nathan's name popped up.

'*Flat out so can't make tonight. But are you still on for that drink this week?*'

What was the harm? It was only a drink.

'*Absolutely. Looking forward,*' she replied.

Alice noticed shadows under Julia Marsh's eyes as she set down two glasses of sparkling water on the table in her courtyard.

"How are you feeling?"

"I'm fine, I wasn't at the police station as long as some of the others." She dropped a slice of lemon into her glass. "It was fun though wasn't it? Typical of Richard Smith to liven things up by lying in the road."

"So that bit wasn't planned?"

"Oh, no. We agreed to march calmly down the high street, across the bridge and convene for speeches by the cricket ground. But, all that went out the window once Richard started his lie-in protest. And of course the police arrived."

"It's a pity it ended that way." Alice took off her sunglasses and put them on the table.

"Ooh, that's a nice shade of purple!"

"I know. At least the swelling's gone down, though." Alice tapped around her eye. "There was something I wanted to ask you, Julia. At the demo, you said that Jason Marley told you he knew all about Carrie. Do you know what he meant by that?"

"Only that he applied for a judicial review of the council's decision to grant planning and award the contract to a developer. He was confident of winning the case as he knew about this 'Carrie'. That isn't very helpful, but it's all I know."

"Did you know that the company that won the contract is called Carrie Developments?"

"No, I didn't," Julia played with a red ball earring. "I assumed Carrie was a person, but that makes more sense."

"Did Jason give you anything to read? A report or his notes, perhaps?"

"Only the leaflet that I gave you the last time you were here. To be honest, I didn't really understand the review bit."

"I was wondering where he got his information from. Is there someone else in the group that Jason consulted?"

"I don't know. There was a woman he said had helped him put the review document together. I don't know who she was, a girlfriend I assumed."

"He didn't mention a name?"

"If he did, I don't recall it I'm afraid."

"Don't worry, but if you do remember, would you let me know please?"

"Of course. By the way, I heard back from Courtney Slow. He said he would love to come to the gallery and talk about his work. He'll send through some dates."

But Alice was thinking about Jason Marley. A sound legal case and a mysterious girlfriend? Jason Marley had been an interesting man.

Sean Cummings skipped across the polished hallway floor and ushered Alice into the dining room. The burgundy curtains were open, the burgundy walls were lush, there were tassels hanging from the chandelier.

Roddy was right. There was something of the night about this room, even in broad daylight.

"We'll do a tour of my paintings after lunch, but I wanted to show you my latest acquisition first."

Sean stood beside a sculpture. "And, here she is. What do you think?" He gazed at Alice with Bambi brown eyes, hands on hips, a pink-striped shirt stretching across his narrow chest.

Alice contemplated the piece, leaning her head to one side while she searched for the right words. She looked for something that spoke to her, and what she saw was a sludge-coloured heap of … well, just a heap, really.

"It's interesting. Where did you acquire it, may I ask?"

"My dealer in Paris. It's by an exciting young sculptor called Bobo Hassan. He sent me some photos of the piece and I loved it, so I made an offer immediately." His eyes rolled and he flicked his left hand from side to side. "But I can't decide where to put it. We've been in this house a year and I still haven't got used to the space, it has a different vibe to our last home. Jeffrey hates the sculpture and wants it in the drawing room, which we hardly ever use it. But what is the point of having this lovely sculpture where nobody ever sees it?"

Alice was with Jeffrey.

"Yes, I can appreciate the problem."

Sean's housekeeper announced that lunch was served in the garden.

"*Sous le soleil,* I thought," said Sean. "It's too hot to eat indoors."

Roddy was watching a pair of alpacas munching grass in a paddock at the bottom of the garden. He joined them as they stepped onto a large patio dotted with artisan shrubs in stainless steel pots.

"Make yourselves comfortable," said Sean. "I'll get some wine. Red or white?"

"White for me, please," said Alice.

"Red please."

Sean disappeared into the house and when he was out of earshot, Roddy leaned over. "So, what do you think?"

"He's wearing orange jeans."

"I did warn you. But I mean, what do you think of that revolting sculpture? I think Bobo saw a dodo coming."

Alice laughed. "You're not even exaggerating, for once."

"Here we are." Sean appeared carrying a silver tray with three glasses. "These are my very own wines. Jeffrey bought me some rows in a French vineyard for my birthday five years ago and this batch is the best yet. White for you Alice – it's nice and chilled. Cheers everyone. Here's to good art and good taste."

"That's very good wine, Sean, congratulations," said Alice.

"The red is fine, too," said Roddy.

"Another vineyard, but that's very kind of you both."

Sean blushed, which Alice found adorable.

"Roddy said you might do me the honour of picking an artwork from my collection for your exhibition."

After seeing the sculpture, Alice wasn't so sure. "I'd love to," she said cheerfully, "if that's alright with you."

"It would be my pleasure. I'm delighted when other people get to see one of my artworks. I've acquired a few more pieces since I spoke to Jenna Farling and you'll see those too. Though you can't have Bobo's sculpture, I couldn't bear to part with it so soon."

Alice avoided looking at Roddy.

"That's a shame. Never mind."

"Just one small thing, Alice, as we're talking about the exhibition. I did just want to mention security…"

Alice had expected the question and was glad that she had prepared an answer.

"We are currently assessing our already robust security arrangements and we'll put in place whatever new systems we need to. On police advice."

At least she hoped that's what Duncan was doing.

"That's very reassuring, but I had to check, you do understand?" Sean stared down his Roman nose and Alice nodded. "We can't stop determined thieves, Alice, but we can make it difficult for them. Do start eating."

Alice dived into a beautifully presented chicken salad, helping herself to fresh bread from a basket in the centre of the table.

A car came down the driveway at the side of the house and pulled up at a garage near the patio.

"That's Lucas, my nephew," said Sean. "He borrowed a friend's new car and took it for a spin. A Porsche, I believe."

"It's a Cayman GTS convertible."

Sean held his chicken filled fork in mid-air. "You clever girl! How did you know?"

"Walker Hampton has one and I went for a ride in it the other day."

"Funny, it's the very same car." Sean put the fork down. "Walker bragged that he'd taken a beautiful woman out for a spin when he dropped it off earlier. So that was you – how interesting."

"There's another man who would find that interesting, too," said Roddy.

Alice bent further over her plate and studied her salad. The fork slipped from her clammy hand and clattered onto the plate.

"The new paintings you bought recently, Sean, did you get them from your Parisian dealer too?"

"Only one of them, the others came from different sources, mostly London this time."

"Is there anyone locally you buy from? Any friends who are fellow collectors?"

"Between you and me, Alice," Sean said with a pained expression, "there's nobody around here with any taste."

Alice put a napkin over her mouth and stifled a snort.

"With the exception of Walker Hampton, of course. But he doesn't deal like he used to. The last artwork I bought from him was an Eric Ravilious woodcut, and that must have been fifteen years ago."

"Oh, do you still have it?" said Alice. "I love his work."

Afterwards, Alice tripped along the road with Roddy, the Eric Ravilious woodcut tucked under her arm.

"Don't look so pleased with yourself," said Roddy. "It was pure luck we found the Ravilious amongst all that tat."

"And a woodcut too, the only one we'll have in the exhibition. If Walker hadn't convinced Sean to buy it, we probably wouldn't have it at all."

"Talking of Hampton, what were you doing careering around the countryside with him in his new sports car?"

"He asked me something similar about you. And, frankly, I think you can both mind your own business and stop interrogating me about what I do."

Roddy shrugged and they walked on in silence.

Alice usually treated Roddy's interest in her relationship with Joe as an annoying joke. She thought his commitment comments old-fashioned, even inappropriate. Whilst she realised he was only looking out for her, sometimes it felt as though he was trying to be her father. She wondered what her father would have said in the same situation. Would he have tried to push her into moving in with Joe? Would he have even liked him? The thought reminded her of Julia Marsh's remark earlier about Jason Marley.

"Tell me, Roddy. Do you know if Jason Marley had a partner, or a girlfriend?"

"He had a woman he kept locked up in his attic, who he let out to cook his dinner and write his protest leaflets."

"Did he or didn't he?"

"He did and almost exactly as I've described. They used to eat together and she helped him with his protest movement. That's all I know."

"What was her name?"

"I don't know."

"Did you ever meet her?"

"No. Though, I suppose she would have gone to his funeral yesterday. I wish now that I'd gone too."

Alice considered who else would have attended. Neither Livvie nor Julia Marsh had gone. But there was one person she knew had. And she could give him a call and ask him about Jason's girlfriend. Walker Hampton.

Chapter 31

IN THE END, ALICE put off calling Walker and settled down to work instead. Much as she enjoyed his flirtatious attentions he wasn't, to put it frankly, her thing.

'*We are unable to help you with your request. Thank you for your interest.*' Alice had received the same message from every source she tried, and the people who owned and ran Carrie Developments remained elusive.

Directors of companies registered in the British Virgin Islands were protected by the territory's stringent anonymity laws and were not subject to public scrutiny. Instead, they were listed on a register held by the Registrar of Corporate Affairs. Without it, Alice could not know who headed up the organisation planning to build the shopping centre on Dunn Road.

If Jason Marley knew all about Carrie, she reasoned, then he must have known who the directors were. Was that why he started a legal process to overturn the council's decision?

But where and how did he get the information? His mysterious girlfriend?

Alice took a break on *Daisy*'s deck. Along the barge's side, pots of basil and rosemary were tinged with brown.

She bent down to tend them, their fragrance punching the air as they slurped from the watering can. The smell brought a whine to Alice's stomach. It was not long since lunch, but wealthy Sean Cummings had served up paupers' portions.

Alice had to find a way to break through the British Virgin Islands' anonymity barrier. She paced around the cabin searching for inspiration. Her eyes fell on the memory stick from Freddie Garfield. She picked it up and held it in her hand.

She might have the perfect use for it. All she had to do now was get to Hacker, Stanley & Dole before it closed.

Toby was on duty again, but this time in the waiting room, stacking magazines into neat piles. He looked up at the clock as Alice raced through the front door and gave a weary greeting as she approached.

"Could I have a quick word with Edward Hacker please?"

"He's left for the day. Can I take a message?"

"Oh, that's a nuisance. I told him I would stop by at this time."

"I'm sorry, but he's not here. What's it about?"

"The portrait of William Hacker in Edward's office, we were talking about it when I was here the other day. He said I could use it in my exhibition catalogue. I don't suppose I could just pop in and take a quick photo?"

Toby frowned and threw a copy of *Country Life* on the top of the pile.

"It will only take a couple of minutes. I'll be finished before five, promise."

Toby brightened and waved her through.

Alice marched passed empty desks and into Edward Hacker's office. At the door she turned around and looked for Toby, but he was hidden behind a dividing screen. She entered the office and pushed the door shut.

She took out her phone and clicked a few shots of the Hacker portrait. A couple of steps closer and she took another shot. She walked behind Edward Hacker's desk and glanced over its surface. Folders, a container of pens, double decker trays stuffed with bound documents, and a really old desktop computer.

Profits, she thought, in the wallet, not in the office equipment.

Voices wafted through the door. She waited until they faded away, then she pulled the memory stick out of her pocket and plugged it into the computer. The screen woke up and flashed a picture of Edward Hacker standing in a field, the middle of a six man line-up. He was wearing a green tweed jacket and waistcoat, with a matching flat cap. A broken shotgun was tucked under his left arm and a couple of pheasants hung from his right hand.

Alice went to work, her heart beating fast. Two minutes later, she slipped the memory stick back in her pocket and left.

"Thank you, Toby. I've got everything I need. Have a good evening."

Alice closed Hacker, Stanley & Dole's front door behind her and headed for The Bull.

Chapter 32

GLASSES CHINKED, CHATTER DRONED and green music played underneath. Alice sat beside Joe in The Bull's courtyard as he related a hair-raising Somalian adventure story. She swigged cool beer from a bottle and fingered the memory stick in her pocket. Finn Kinnaman laughed at Joe's punchline.

"And how was lunch at the bordello?" said Joe.

"As it happens, it went fantastically well. We got to see Sean's new sculpture, which Roddy thought was a pile of camel dung."

"That good, huh?"

"He was right, though, it was horrible."

"Is he lending something?" said Finn.

"Yes, though not that sculpture, thank God, he lent a lovely woodcut instead. We found it completely by chance, under a dust cover in a bedroom he's decorating."

"I know that feeling," said Finn. "I've been redecorating Mum's shop and I have to cover everything every time. Mum swears she always finds something she hasn't seen for ages when she takes the covers off."

"Meant to say, I love the pale green," said Alice. "Love your mum's clothes, come to think of it. By the way, I'd like to see your pictures of Vivien Taylor's party."

"Sure, I'll send them over. Fine place she has there."

"Isn't it amazing? Joe, you should gate-crash her next party, so you can have a look."

"I'm not sure I'd go to the trouble. Besides, I've seen it already, the outside at any rate. I kayaked up that way last summer. Saw the studio too, the one her husband uses."

Alice felt her cheeks heat as she remembered her encounter with Walker and their near-miss kiss.

"Any progress on recovering Vivien's drawing?"

"Sadly not. At least, DI Salisbury didn't tell me anything when I spoke to him yesterday."

Now her cheeks were really burning. Nathan had barely been out of her mind since their meeting, as she raked through happy memories of their time together. And there were many. It was a gentle, easy relationship, with no fights.

Even at the time, she knew the distance between them would not be a problem. It would only be for a year anyway. When Alice's degree finished, she would move to Manchester too. There was a gallery there she was keen to apply to.

Instead, she broke off the relationship. Looking back now, she could not put her finger on why. No affairs, no smelly socks left on the floor, no raised voices; Nathan had been everything she could have asked for in a boyfriend. So, what had scared her off?

Perhaps Nathan Salisbury had made the mistake of being perfect. Or was it just her?

Joe seemed to be raking over his own memories. "Do you miss covering hard news, Finn? You've shot some notorious criminals before."

"I'm happy shooting privileged people enjoying their privileges, thanks. I'm enjoying the quiet life. A spot of fishing, a round of golf, a friendly local pub. I'm happy in Great Wheaton. How about you? Do you miss the sound of gunfire at night?"

"No. I'm leaving all the excitement to Alice."

"Good evening."

Alice's heart thumped as she recognised the voice. She stalled and steadied herself before looking into Walker Hampton's smiling face. Her eyes darted around him, but she could not see Vivien.

"Are you here to see the band?"

"Yes, it's one of Joe's recommendations." Introductions were made and the men shook hands.

"From your accent, Joe, I'd say you'd know The Perrystones well."

"They're from Galway, my home town. It's grand they're playing here now."

Alice squirmed under Walker's gaze. She moved her hand towards Joe's, but stopped before it reached his arm.

"Well, I'll leave you to it," said Walker. "I hope you all enjoy the show."

Joe looked over at Alice. "Everything alright?"

"Fine."

"I'm sorry I'm late," said Claudia. She kissed Finn's cheek, while Alice gave Joe's arm a squeeze. "Was that Walker Hampton I just saw? Not the sort of place I'd expect to see him."

"He came to hear the band, I suppose," said Alice.

"Not his sort of band either, I would have thought. I wonder if something else has attracted his attention …"

So she must knew about Alice's visit to Walker's studio. They all did, probably.

"What's today's column, Claudia?"

"I'm filling in for someone else today, Joe. A piece on an assault last night – outside here actually."

"Anything serious?"

"Just some young drunks picking fights with each other. No one was seriously hurt."

A woman knocked Finn as she walked behind him and he spilt beer over his hand. He pulled a blue handkerchief from his pocket and wiped away the liquid.

"What have you heard on the Augustus John drawing?"

"Nothing new."

The Perrystones started up, and Alice settled down to watch the set. She had first heard the band when Joe took her on a music crawl through Galway. They ate mussels straight from the bay, washed down with several pints of the black stuff, and watched a succession of Celtic bands perform in the pubs along Quay Street. She loved the weave of strings, voices, and whistles. She loved the tempo and whooped along with the rest of the audience.

Her foot tapped, her head nodded. Another round of beers. The crowd clapped. She knew this one and sang along. More beer.

The band took a break. Claudia wanted a smoke, so Alice accompanied her through the crowd and onto the street.

"By the way, I almost forgot to tell you," said Claudia. "Jason Marley. After we talked about him yesterday, I thought I'd ask the police about their investigation into his death. The post mortem concluded that Jason did drown. But that was after he sustained injuries consistent with being hit by a car. They think he fell into the river after a hit and run. They're treating his death as murder."

Chapter 33

DAZZLING RAYS STUNG ALICE'S eyes the next morning as she emerged from *Daisy*'s saloon, and she retreated down the companionway to collect her sunglasses.

It had been a long night. After The Perrystones, Claudia had left to work on her article and Alice had gone on to another bar with Joe and Finn. One beer later and she was done, so the men walked her home before disappearing into the night. Alice lay down on her bed, still wearing her silver Vans, and succumbed.

Leaning against *Daisy*'s side, she looked along Sam's Lane to where the ponies stood at the gate of Farrell's field. She whistled and Patches looked up, ears pricked.

Alice had loved to ride as a child.

Her pocket vibrated. A text from Walker Hampton.

'*Hope you enjoyed the band. Lunch?*'

She didn't really have time for Walker, but he did go to Jason Marley's funeral, so he should know who else attended. Jason's girlfriend, perhaps …

'*1 pm at* The Bull?'

'*Look forward to it.*'

Alice mulled over her conversation with Claudia the

previous evening. She wrote the word '*Murder*' on an index card and pinned it below Jason's picture on the incident board.

Jason Marley had been mown down on a quiet street in Great Wheaton. On purpose. And when he should have been meeting her. Who could have done such a thing? And why? She pondered the list of suspects on the incident board she had already identified for the theft. Julian de Havilland, Edward Hacker, Stefan Erickson. Was one of them also a murderer?

Julian de Havilland had an obvious motive – Jason had opposed his shopping centre development. But resorting to murder seemed extreme.

She dialled Nathan Salisbury's number.

"Good morning Alice."

She smiled at his voice.

"It's about Jason Marley's murder. I wanted to know whether you had any suspects?"

"I don't usually discuss suspects, at least not at such an early stage in my inquiry, so I can't answer that question."

"I get that. It's just that I saw him that morning, you know, in the river, right outside the gallery, so …"

"I completely understand, Alice. Mr Marley's death must have caused you some distress; a crime like that is unsettling at the best of times. But I can assure you we have everything in hand. We've carried out several interviews already and we've investigated car repair shops, along with other leads. If it would help, I'm happy to meet up with you and you can ask me as many questions as you like."

"I'd like that."

Alice ended the call, closed her eyes and sank into the

bean bag. Her fluttering stomach confirmed how good it would be to see Nathan.

When she opened her eyes, she saw the memory stick lying on the coffee table. She picked it up, plugged it into her laptop and uploaded every file that included the word 'Carrie' from Hacker's computer.

There were a great many.

The folders were numbered, save for one entitled 'Misc correspondence'. It was a good place to start. She opened it up and found a number of letters between Hacker and Dennis Grant, CEO of Carrie Developments.

Alice selected one of Edward Hacker's letters written on HSD headed paper, copied it and deleted the contents, leaving the headers intact. Then she created an online email address that included Hacker's initials and the name of the firm. On the now blank headed paper, she addressed a letter to the Registrar of Corporate Affairs in the British Virgin Islands. She requested a copy of the register of directors of all companies in the territory. Using Edward Hacker's name, she asked the register to be sent to her at the new email address. As an agent for Carrie Developments, a company registered in the territory, Edward Hacker was entitled to the information. She pressed Send.

She tried one of the other folders but was asked for a password. She tried several others, with the same result.

Her technical skills certainly did not extend to accessing password-protected files, and she yanked the stick out of the laptop and chucked it onto the coffee table.

She did not look up when she heard the double knock on the saloon window, she knew Livvie would be crossing the gangway to the deck by now.

"Morning!" Livvie popped her head round the cabin door. "What the—"

"I know, it's my incident board."

"It's like some kind of TV drama. Pictures of suspects, pieces of coloured string connecting things together, a coffee table filled with … crap." Livvie laughed. "It looks very professional."

"I thought I'd get some information through the exhibition lenders that will help me hunt down the artworks," said Alice. "Perhaps throw some light on Jason Marley's murder, too. Did you bring the cuttings book?"

"Yep." Livvie laid a scrapbook on the sofa. "I can't believe that someone deliberately killed Jason. Are you sure Claudia Rowan got that right?"

"I got it confirmed by Nathan Salisbury too, so there's no mistake. Someone ran Jason down, then sped off. The assumption is that the force knocked him into the river. God, poor guy."

"And the police haven't traced the car?"

"I don't think so, though Nathan did say the police have spoken to car repair shops and—"

Alice felt suddenly weak and she grabbed the back of the sofa.

Livvie caught her arm. "Hey, what happened? Are you okay?"

"Walker. He said his car was in the garage to fix a prang."

"And you think Walker Hampton killed Jason? What would he gain from that?"

Alice held up both hands. "Good question, we need to think logically. Walker and Jason have been friends since childhood and Walker supported Jason's opposition to the Dunn Road development. So, there would be no reason for him to kill him." Alice breathed a deep sigh and released her grip on the sofa. "Phew, that's a relief."

"Why is it such a relief that Walker Hampton is not a murderer?"

"Because I'm having lunch with him."

Livvie rolled her eyes. "You're impossible. Just make sure your gorgeous man doesn't find out." Livvie took a step towards the door. "Listen, I've got to get back to the café. If you need any help with any of that" – she pointed to the incident board – "just ask. I want Jason's killer nailed as much as you do."

Alice flicked through the cuttings book. Neatly trimmed articles from the *Courier* and other publications recorded Jason's protest against the Dunn Road shopping centre. It began in 2012, when Carrie Developments and rival companies put forward tenders for a retail and leisure centre on the site. Jason attended the first council meeting to discuss the issue and spoke "with passion", according to the *Courier*, against the plans.

He spoke at council meetings whenever the Dunn Road development was on the agenda, or even when it was not. A regular presence at the 'Have your Say' slot, his views were stated concisely and consistently at every opportunity.

In the event, it had made no difference – the council went ahead regardless. But Jason had made a nuisance of himself and at the end of the day, perhaps that was all he could have done.

Alice was impressed with Jason's record of dissent. He disagreed with the council and had taken it on, with a persistent programme of calculated action against it. Marches, speeches, leaflets, letters to newspapers, interviews. All recorded in the cuttings book. He had achieved something important, done something that mattered. Alice felt butterflies in her stomach. Pride, and perhaps a little envy.

As she flicked through the book, one story jumped off the page. Jason had been arrested. That was not the story – he was arrested many times. But this time, he had shouted his protest during a council meeting and would not shut up. He was asked to leave the chamber and when he refused he was forcibly removed and subsequently arrested for creating a public nuisance.

The meeting was held to award Carrie Developments the contract. They waited until Jason was ejected, then Julian de Havilland asked for a named vote. Instead of the usual "Hands up and say aye!" type of vote, councillors were called by name and had to state whether they were for or against the award. They all agreed bar one – Councillor Felicity Gault.

Could Felicity Gault, Alice wondered, be the woman who gave Jason information? It would make sense. As a councillor, she would know what was going on. She might have passed Jason confidential information which he then used for his judicial review application.

Julian de Havilland had asked for the named vote. Did he want people to know that Felicity Gault voted against Carrie Developments? Why would it matter? All the other councillors voted in favour, so Felicity's dissent made no difference to the outcome.

Perhaps Julian had wanted to embarrass her. Strange, though, given that they were in the same political party. Alice would never understand politicians …

It was time Alice found out more about Julian de Havilland. A chat with Felicity Gault might help, so she gave her a call. Alice explained why she wanted to meet her and as Felicity was spending the day at home, she invited Alice over.

But first, there was lunch with Walker.

Chapter 34

Walker had been urbane and fun over lunch, but Alice had learned nothing more about Jason Marley. From what she could ascertain, Walker had spent most of Jason's funeral in the pub and could barely name any of the attendees.

A fifteen minute walk from The Bull, to the east side of Great Wheaton, brought Alice to Earle Road and a row of Victorian terraced houses. At the end of the line, Felicity Gault's front door was opened by a chirpy, blonde girl who directed Alice to her grandmother in the garden.

The women sat in Felicity's petite, colourful garden on wicker chairs with flamingo-patterned cushions. A magpie pecked at a bone, watched by a couple of King Charles Spaniels lying on the grass nearby.

"I'm only too happy to talk about Julian de Havilland. In fact, I'm surprised nobody has asked me about him before. What do you want to know?" Intelligent blue eyes looked out from a pale, creased face framed by shoulder-length grey hair.

"Several things, but first of all, Carrie Developments. As I mentioned to you on the phone, I saw you voted against the company getting the Dunn Road development contract and I wondered why that was?"

"As councillors on the steering committee we were given a report on the five companies that tendered for the contract. Only two of them met the criteria, so they went through to the second round. I agreed with the assessment. There was a meeting to decide which of the two contractors to appoint. You read the public report on both companies, but the councillors were given another, more detailed report."

Felicity turned over a sheet of paper on her lap. "This is the front page of the first report and you can see that Carrie Developments and Zettus Construction were the two recommended companies. Here is the front page of the second report and the recommended companies are now Carrie Developments and *Caramel Stone*."

Alice took the pages from Felicity.

"At first, I thought it was a mistake and queried it with the officer who'd produced the reports. But then I got a phone call from Julian de Havilland saying there was no mistake. Zettus Construction had withdrawn, so Caramel Stone had been promoted, as it were, to give councillors a choice in the second round of the tender process."

"But Caramel Stone hadn't met the criteria."

"Exactly." Felicity leant forward. "I asked him what the point of having selection criteria was, if he was going to ignore it. But he was in no mood for a debate. He said that's what he'd decided and he expected me to vote for Carrie Developments, as they were the best option."

"Isn't that against some rule? Coercion or something."

"Politics isn't the nicest business, which is why I got out of it in the end." Felicity put the rest of her papers on the ground beside her chair. "Though I was surprised at Julian's behaviour. He was usually so polite and mild-mannered. It was a bit heavy-handed of him to say the least."

"But why did you vote against Carrie Developments when they were the best option?"

"Well that was the point, Alice, I didn't think they were. In the first report Carrie and Zettus Construction's applications were more or less even on technical aspects. But Zettus was cheaper, would finish quicker and was more considerate of residents. To me, they were the best option."

"So why was Julian so keen on Carrie Developments?"

"I don't know, he just made it clear they were his preferred option. Anyway, then we were told that, unusually, the two companies would give a presentation to councillors on their bids. Caramel Stone's representative gave a thin presentation – it seemed to me like he had only been told about it minutes earlier and was making it up on the hoof."

"And the Carrie rep gave a better pitch?"

The spaniels growled at each other over the bone. Felicity got up and threw it into a bin.

"Hardly. Oh, he was full of himself, a cocky, unpleasant little man. But he didn't have a grip on his brief and he couldn't answer any of my questions."

"What was he in the organisation?"

"I didn't get his title. David something. He was intimidating and looked like he was ex-military. Perhaps he was brought in to scare us into voting for Carrie Developments." Felicity's tinkling laugh invited Alice to join in.

"So, you voted against Carrie Developments at the meeting. What happened after that?"

"Nothing. I expected Julian to tell me off for not doing what I'd been told, but he didn't say a word. Then a couple of days later I got a call from Jason Marley asking if I would meet him." Felicity smiled. "Anyway, I was going on holiday the next day, so we agreed to talk when I got back. However, I changed my mind, so we didn't end up meeting after all."

"Why the change of heart?"

Felicity looked into her lap. When she looked up, her eyes were welling. "I promised my husband I wouldn't talk about this again, but it was a long time ago and now that Jason's dead I don't suppose it matters anymore." She sighed. "When I got back from holiday, two envelopes had been posted by hand through my letterbox. They both contained abusive and threatening messages, warning me against meeting Jason Marley."

Alice leant forward, ready to catch Felicity's next words as soon as they dropped.

"I was on my own when I opened them, and at first I thought that someone might be in the house. I was terrified, so rigid with fear that I was still sitting in the same position when my husband got home. We called the police and they took the letters away. Then Derry and I agreed we would forget about it and not mention it again."

"Did you ever find out who had sent the letters?"

"No. The police didn't either, though I'm not convinced they tried very hard. They were a bit fed up with Jason by that stage."

Alice couldn't help wondering what she, all alone on *Daisy*, would have done in the same situation.

"You must have been scared witless. I admire you for carrying on at the council, it must have been difficult for you."

"I didn't carry on. There was an election five months later and I didn't stand again. My career in public life came to an ignominious end, something I'm not proud of."

"It doesn't have to end like that." Alice patted Felicity's arm. "Jason's murder is unsolved. I'm going to find out what Carrie Developments and Julian de Havilland have in common. I've also got two missing paintings and I think Julian may be connected to that too. I would be very grateful for any assistance you can give me."

Felicity consulted her lap again, then looked at Alice with wide eyes.

"Why not? Nobody warned me not to talk to you."

Flecks of white sparkled through a sprawling tree as the late afternoon sun moved behind it. Alice pondered Felicity's story of coercion and bullying at the council as she walked to the river, and Roddy's barge.

Alice did not doubt Felicity's story. But who would have sent her the letters? Julian de Havilland? Or someone at Carrie Developments? They stood to miss out on the contract if the councillors voted against – but the letters were sent after the contract was awarded, so what was the point, other than to scare an old lady?

The sender must have been so terrified of what Jason Marley had to tell Felicity Gault, that they warned her off meeting him. But what had he known? And had it cost him his life?

Who better to ask than Nathan Salisbury.

Chapter 35

"When I suggested you shouldn't do anything silly, I meant things like flirting with your biggest funder's husband."

Roddy flicked his paintbrush, splattering spots of green paint onto Alice's arm. She brushed them away, turning them into thin streaks. She pulled herself out of Roddy's deckchair, crossed the deck and settled into a rickety director's chair.

It occurred to her that Roddy might have something to say about that little drink she had had with Nathan Salisbury. Unconsciously, she touched the spot on her cheek where Nathan had kissed it, and smiled.

"Dear girl, please come back to me." Roddy stood over her, paintbrush pointing at her head.

"Just thinking about something. Anyway, I wasn't flirting with Walker and I don't think he was flirting with me."

"Well, now you're just being annoying. Hampton isn't capable of not flirting, he even gave me a look-over once." Roddy smiled at the memory. "Though we were both very drunk at the time."

"Okay, he may have flirted a little, but he's really not my type. Anyway, he and Vivien have separate bedrooms."

"Of course, they do. What's the point of having a huge house if you can't have your own room?"

Roddy mixed yellow with green and dabbed the paint onto a half-formed tree.

"And Walker has all those lovely paintings in his room, so he can enjoy them by himself. Anyway, I met him because I wanted to ask him about Jason Marley, seeing as they knew each other so well."

"And what did he say?"

"Nothing I didn't already know. He just wanted to talk about the Augustus John drawing. Understandable I suppose – who had seen it at the gallery, that sort of thing. It didn't sound like Vivien had told him much."

"So, he lunched you to prise information about the drawing from you. How interesting! It wouldn't surprise me if Hampton had stolen the thing himself."

Alice swung her sunglasses to and fro. "You are joking, of course."

"Not really, Hampton is a collector with taste and knowledge. He has lots of shady contacts – he was a banker after all – so he could easily have stolen the drawing and sold it on to a discreet buyer. It's probably overseas now, never to be seen again."

"But why would he do it? He doesn't need the money and if he got caught he'd go to prison."

"It's sport to him, he needs some excitement." Roddy picked up another brush and teased the green blobs into leaves.

"He has a lovely life. He's rich, he travels and he's got a fantastic studio for painting. What more could he want?"

"Dear girl, the bedroom arrangements tell you everything you need to know about the Hampton–Taylor relationship.

They are friends and colleagues, but it is a marriage of convenience, for both of them." Roddy lifted the brush from the canvas and looked away.

There was a long silence, then Alice said, "Are you thinking about Elisabeth?"

Roddy laid down the brush, picked up a dirty rag and wiped his hands. "I was thinking about her paintings. My conversations with your lenders have reignited a desire to find one of them. Before, I thought it would be too painful to live with Elisabeth's work. But I always loved her paintings and now I want to have one."

"I can understand that. I've held onto the Augustus John postcard my father gave me because I felt it brought him closer." She got up, walked over to the barge's side and looked over the river.

Suddenly, Alice spun around. "I could help you find one of her paintings, if you want me to? I'm already asking people about the Augustus John drawing, so I can ask about Elisabeth's work too. Do you have any idea who she sold to?"

"No, I never asked her about her clients. Besides, it was years ago, her paintings could be anywhere." He attempted a smile. "It's sweet of you, Alice, but don't worry. Besides, you'd probably take it as an invitation for more flirting with Walker Hampton!"

"I am not flirting with him, he's flirting with me. Though, I suppose I could ask him …" She laughed.

"Don't even think about it. I know it seems I'm interfering, but you should be wary of Hampton. He's a hard-nosed, self-interested man. He uses people, then spits them out when he's finished with them." Roddy closed the paint box and fastened it with a metal clip.

"Besides, you should pay more attention to his wife. By the way, what is the latest on her drawing?"

"There's no news. Nathan Salisbury is bringing in a specialist from London, so hopefully that will speed things along. In the meantime, I'll carry on speaking to the lenders – I still think they're more likely to know where the drawing went than some woman from London."

"Agreed. And what of *Beach*? Did you get anywhere with that?"

"No. Edward Hacker admitted he had borrowed it, but he won't say where it is now."

"It sounds like you've got everything covered. DI Salisbury can put his feet up."

Alice half-frowned, half smiled. "At least, you'll be pleased to know I'm doing something for Joe. I'm cooking a fancy dinner tonight. And before you make some sarcastic remark—"

"I think you mean some witty remark."

"… some witty remark about my cooking, I've done something sensible for a change. I've bought it from Livvie, so all I have to do is heat it up. That does count as cooking doesn't it?"

"As far as I'm concerned, there's no other kind!"

Alice pulled open *Daisy*'s hatch door and sped through to the cabin, dumping her bag on the sofa as she flew passed. She threw off her clothes and skipped into the bathroom.

After a refreshing shower, Alice retrieved her white jeans from the back of the chair in the corner of the cabin. She took Livvie's dinner from the fridge and walked round the bend in the river to Joe's apartment.

The view from Joe's balcony was completely different to the one from *Daisy*'s deck, despite being only a few hundred metres along the water. Near the bridge, summer stallholders, making the most of the long, warm evenings, sold drinks and snacks. Their squawks and shouts reached Alice two floors up. On the grassy banks opposite, picnickers squeezed into prime waterside spots. One man was chilling a bottle of wine in the river, one end of string tied around the neck of the bottle, the other to the leg of his folding chair.

"The cricket club has a firework display tonight, so we'll get a good view from here." Joe rested both arms on the balcony railing. "Or we could wander over there if you like."

"Okay. I could do with a walk after that dinner."

"It's about time you learnt how to cook, I reckon." Joe put a hand on Alice's back. "I could teach you if you like."

"I may well take you up on that."

She finished her wine and twirled the stem in her fingers. Dinner had been a success. Alice was pleased she had bought it rather than wrestle with Joe's kitchen and her lack of cooking skills. She leant against Joe and he put an arm around her shoulder.

"By the way," he said. "I've put Finn's pictures on the computer for you, so you can see them on my big screen."

"Oh good, thanks for that. Can we see them now?"

They sat side by side at Joe's desk, and he loaded the images.

"It looks like you all had a good time," he said.

"Vivien Taylor certainly knows how to throw a party. There were waiters everywhere doling out glasses of very good champagne."

"Rafferty had had a few by the look of him."

Alice smiled at a picture of Roddy, open-mouthed, in full flow, eyebrows and glass raised. "He really enjoyed himself, he doesn't go to many parties these days."

"Did he manage to get any material for your catalogue in between the drinks?"

"Surprisingly, yes. Well, not surprising that he got some lovely stories, but that he remembered them and even wrote them down. He gave me sheets of handwritten notes the next day, like a schoolboy handing in his homework."

"You did right giving him that job I reckon, it's doing him good. Will you use these pictures in the catalogue too?"

"Possibly only the ones of Vivien and the Augustus John drawing, though I daren't look at them now. Tempting fate and all that. Pity not to use more of them, though. Gosh, Finn did take a lot of the river."

"He enjoyed the gig. I'd told him there was a good fishing spot just beyond Taylor's house, so he was having a look under the guise of taking pictures. We could run up there ourselves tomorrow. Take the boat out, do some fishing."

"That would be lovely."

Joe's phone rang and he went out onto the balcony.

Alice's eyes switched back to the photos. People came and went, some she recognised, others not. Blushing faces, from Vivien's fine champagne or the sun – or both. Spiritless waiters offering canapes. Vivien flitting around her guests: Roddy, Marjorie, Claudia, Walker.

Walker! So, he had joined the party after all.

Not that he looked in a party mood. He was talking to a man and stabbing a finger right at his face. His body was stiff and he had pulled himself up to his full height, towering over his companion.

Alice recognised the other man as Martin Bradman, one of lenders. She had seen him at the party, even spoken a few words to him.

Alice scanned all the pictures, but there was only one shot of Walker and Martin Bradman together and no others of Walker at all. It was pure luck that Finn had caught it.

Joe's voice came from the balcony. "The fireworks are starting. Want to come out and watch?"

Alice stepped out and put her arm around Joe's waist. He smiled and looped his arm around her shoulder. A burst of red and green shot across the sky, to cries of 'Aahh!' from the crowd below. She snuggled closer to him, resting her cheek in the dent of his shoulder. In the gold and white spray, she pictured the lone figure of Walker Hampton wandering through the empty rooms of his big house. He lingered a moment in her mind, then along with the fireworks, he dissolved into the black sky.

Chapter 36

After a relaxing Sunday, the first thing Alice did on Monday morning was ignore Duncan Jones' email asking for an update on the exhibition. Instead, she sprawled on the bean bag in *Daisy*'s cabin and watched the birds as they crossed and recrossed the network of branches across the river.

The day before, she and Joe had pottered about on the river all day, trying to catch fish. And failing. They had planned to barbeque their catch on the riverbank in the evening, but with nothing biting they had paid a visit to the fishmonger instead. No matter. With fresh bread and chilled wine, they had enjoyed an *el fresco* supper, listening to crickets chirping in the grass as they watched the sun go down.

Alice's laptop slid off her lap onto the floor, wiping the grin from her face. She retrieved it and opened her inbox again.

Interesting. There was a reply from the British Virgin Islands Registrar of Corporate Affairs, with a list of all the companies in the territory, together with their directors.

She scanned down the register until she came to Carrie Developments. There was a short description of the business, given as international construction and project development. Next came the directors and shareholders section – the company stakeholders and the people who pocketed the profits. There was one named director only: Edward Hacker of Hacker, Stanley & Dole.

Alice said the name aloud, as though to make sure. As a solicitor, Hacker would likely be acting on behalf of an unnamed shadow director – a client or clients so keen to mask their identity they had hidden behind yet another layer of anonymity. The brains and money behind Carrie Developments could well lie elsewhere.

Alice scribbled a few words on a piece of paper, added it to her incident board and sat on the edge of the coffee table. Julian de Havilland's line had grown with Felicity Gault's information. Julian, too, was one of Alice's main suspects for the Augustus John theft.

There was only one way to find out what the man was up to. Alice called Julian's office at the town hall and was not surprised when a familiar voice answered the phone.

"This is becoming a habit, Helen."

"How can I help you?" said an unfazed Helen Yardley.

"I'd like to make an appointment to see Councillor Julian de Havilland, please."

"What for?" said Helen, a chill in her voice. "I mean, what is the meeting about?"

"I noticed that he'd borrowed a number of paintings from the council's collection and I wondered what attracted him to those pieces." Alice was stalling, looking at Julian's picture on the incident board. "It's for the exhibition catalogue I'm putting together."

"Councillor de Havilland is not lending a painting to the exhibition, so I'm not sure why you need to speak to him."

"I know he's not personally lending, but the council is. And as he's a senior member of the council, I wanted to capture his thoughts."

"He's very busy at the moment, Alice."

"I thought he would like to be part of the exhibition, seeing as it involves a number of local businesses. The *Courier* is lending a painting, for example. And so is Hacker, Stanley & Dole."

Helen snatched a breath, then dropped silent. "Okay. I'll juggle a few things around and email you a time."

Alice couldn't be sure whether Helen really was going to arrange a meeting, or whether she was trying to fob her off. There was no choice but to wait.

Jason Marley's blank eyes stared out from the board.

"Speak to me, Jason. What happened to you? You were walking along the river, a car hit you, knocking you into the river. Who was driving the car?"

Alice ran a possible sequence through her mind, trying to picture the scene. She looked back at Jason and he looked at her. Witnesses … Had there been any witnesses to Jason's journey, or his appointment with death?

The Coffee Pot was her next stop – she would look for an answer there.

Alice asked Livvie if they could talk privately and the two women slipped through a swing door behind the counter, into Livvie's office.

"Hey, what's up?"

"I've been thinking about witnesses to Jason Marley's death. You catered for one of his meetings at The Shipwreck that evening. As it's just down the road, he must have walked passed your café to get to Silver Street, where he was knocked down. The driver could have been waiting for him outside the pub, then followed him to a quiet spot and run him down. In which case, you might have caught both Jason and the car on your CCTV."

"The police thought that too and they've already asked me for the footage. Fortunately," said Livvie, "I took a copy first."

Livvie fished out a CD from a drawer and slotted it into a laptop on her desk. Alice sat on the only chair, Livvie perched on its arm.

"I went back at ten thirty to collect my plates and Jason had already left; so, let's go back in time and see if we can spot him."

Livvie rewound the footage and stopped at a couple walking arm in arm. Not Jason. Nor was the man with the dog, at ten twenty-two. After them, a group of young chattering women, followed by an equal number of young men with open shirts and wild gestures.

At ten sixteen, a solitary man marched along the footpath. Just four seconds and he was out of shot. Livvie played the footage again, freezing it on the man, centre-frame and at his most visible. Even so, he was side-on to the camera and the image was indistinct – Alice could not make out a clear profile.

"That's him," said Livvie. "I recognise that tattoo on his left arm. See there, the eagle? No mistake."

Livvie let the disc play on and at ten seventeen, a large, dark car came into shot.

"Could that car be following him?" said Alice, pointing at the screen.

"It could be, or it could just be someone driving slowly."

"We can work out how fast it's going." Alice rapped the desktop. "If we time how long it takes the car to travel across the CCTV's span, we can compare it with how long it takes Jason to walk it."

They replayed the footage twice and made a calculation.

"The car was travelling at ten miles an hour and Jason was walking at four," said Alice. "So the car was definitely crawling. We can't be sure it was following Jason, though."

"Let's assume it was. What sort of car is that?"

The women searched the internet for pictures of large saloon cars, running through a variety of models before they hit one that matched the car in the footage.

"I know it's black and white footage but what about the colour? Could it be dark blue? You'd think it would be denser if it was black."

"From the models we've been looking at online, I think we can make a reasonable guess. I'd say it's a midnight blue 5 Series BMW."

Alice froze. There was only one person she knew with a car like that, and his was in the garage being repaired. Walker Hampton.

Chapter 37

Alice stumbled out of The Coffee Pot and onto the busy street – the same street Jason Marley had walked that fateful evening.

A BMW. There were loads of them around the town, in fact there was a 5 Series parked in the road she took to Gregory's House and her meeting with Duncan Jones.

Alice waited for Duncan to finish his phone call. He had still not given his approval for Nicholas Waites' figurines to be shown in the exhibition and Tommy Norton needed to organise plinths.

Duncan started speaking first, before the phone was in its cradle.

"Can you explain why Councillor Taylor wants to talk to me about you and *Beach* and why you've been bothering Councillor de Havilland?" Duncan's thin lips and matching voice spat out the words. "Gregory's House comes under Councillor Taylor's remit, and she has not taken kindly to you asking another councillor to be involved with the centenary exhibition. She'll be here in ten minutes, Alice, and I need a good answer."

Alice pinched the edge of her seat. "She's coming here?"

Duncan nodded.

"Do you want me to be here when she comes?"

"Absolutely not. I want a full explanation now, then I'll meet her by myself."

Alice gave Duncan a filtered account of her attempts to track down *Beach*. It sounded barely believable even to her own ears, but Duncan nodded in agreement.

She seemed to be getting better at this.

"Just over half the exhibition paintings are here in the gallery and several more will be delivered by the end of this week. That includes the MP's painting from the House of Commons collection, which turned out to be easier to move than I thought."

"That's welcome news at least." Duncan's face relaxed a little. "I've seen the artworks downstairs – there are some good pieces."

"I'm still keen on having Nicholas Waites' figurines. They're so beautiful and I'm sure they'll be a crowd pleaser. Is there any leeway on getting a plinth for them?"

"I don't have a budget for it and even if I did, I don't want any more complications. This exhibition has been a nightmare already." He stared out the window and looked as if he would gladly follow his gaze and jump out of it. "What's the status on the catalogue?"

"I have around half the material, but I need to find some more photos. I was thinking of putting in some drawings and other illustrations as well, for variety. What do you think?"

"Sounds fine in principle, though I want to see them before you set the pages. The printing deadline is only four weeks away, so I need to see more progress by the end of this week. And under no circumstances is the deadline to be missed. That catalogue goes on sale on opening night without fail. Is that clear?"

Alice left the gallery the moment the meeting was over, and as she walked towards home she wondered how Duncan was faring with his Taylor encounter.

She turned onto Sam's Lane, slowing as she reached The Coffee Pot. People yabbered in the sunshine and wafts of freshly ground coffee and buttery pastries scented the air. An empty barge was not inviting. Instead, Alice made herself comfortable on the leather sofa.

She watched her friend calm a volatile customer, with just the right words and a smile. Alice surveyed the tables, spotting a couple of her neighbours tucking into Livvie's special toasted paninis. Behind them were two others she recognised – Helen Yardley and Julian de Havilland. Together. The pair were sitting at a small table at the far end of the courtyard, their heads close, in animated conversation.

Alice could think of half a dozen bars and cafés around the town hall. So if they had come down to the river, they must be trying to avoid being seen.

"That's him sorted," said Livvie. "He comes in every week for a moan. What are you staring at?"

"That couple at the end table, how long have they been here?"

"Julian and Helen? They got here about twenty minutes ago."

"You know them?"

"Sure. They've been coming here for years, way before I bought the place. Their father had a boat, which he kept along the bank, just passed *Daisy*. They all used to drop in for breakfast before they went fishing. Julian and Helen carried on coming, even after their father passed away. Said it reminded them of him."

"They're brother and sister?" Alice twisted around and stared at them. "Well, that puts a whole different spin on things. Helen must know all about Carrie Developments too. No wonder she wasn't keen for me to meet Julian."

"Is this part of your investigation into the Dunn Road development?"

Alice repeated her conversation with Felicity Gault.

"And what's more, Edward Hacker of Hacker, Stanley & Dole is sole director of Carrie Developments – I assume for a shadow director."

"Shadow director?"

"Someone who has an agreement with a named director who will do his or her bidding."

"And what does it all mean?" Livvie swished a dishcloth over her shoulder and perched on the sofa's arm.

"Somebody around here owns Carrie Developments and has just landed a fifty million pound contract to build a shopping centre, is what it means. And Julian de Havilland made sure that they, and nobody else, got it."

"Jeez, Alice. That's serious stuff. What are you going to do?" Livvie rested a hand on Alice's knee. "You're not thinking of marching up to Julian de Havilland and demanding an explanation, are you?"

That was exactly what she was thinking of doing …

"I've asked for a meeting with Julian, though I might have a word with Helen in the meantime."

"She's a nice lady. I can't believe she's involved in anything underhand. Her brother, on the other hand …"

Julian got up from the table and headed into the café. Alice picked up a magazine and held it in front of her face. When she heard the door of the gents swing shut, she dashed over to Helen.

"Helen, can I have a quick word?"

Helen paled a little, and peered through the café window.

"I can't talk to you. Not here. I'll contact you about your meeting with Julian."

"Thanks, but I'd like to talk to you as well."

"I can't, Alice. I'll be in touch." Helen wrapped her fingers around her cup. "Please leave, Julian will be back in a minute." Helen's eyes darted from Alice to the window.

"Okay, but will you email me tomorrow please?"

"Yes. Yes, I will."

"Promise?"

"Yes, I promise. Now, go."

Chapter 38

"Hold on a minute, I'll just put my trousers on," Martin Bradman shouted from the other side of his front door.

Alice grimaced and moved back from the doorstep. She pictured Bradman with shirt tails dangling above blanched knees and struggled to suppress a giggle. The door was opened by the tall, wiry man with a thin face and expensively dyed hair who Alice had met at Vivien Taylor's party. She stepped inside the house and was almost knocked out by the smell of aftershave and Brylcreem.

A framed theatre poster for a 1975 production of *The Taming of the Shrew* greeted her in the hallway, the part of Petruchio played by Marty Bradman.

"That's you!" Alice squealed and pointed at the poster. "You were in a West End play? That's amazing."

Martin put up both hands as if in surrender. "Yes. I am a thesp."

Primed for the cue, he sprang to one side of the poster and regaled Alice with the statistics: how many nights of the run, the celebrities who visited backstage, how many after-show parties.

"Oh. My. God. That's so exciting. I've never met a thespian before."

"Well, I'm sure you've heard enough about me." Martin paused, looking like he was waiting for an 'Oh no, I haven't'. "You want to see the painting don't you, so come on through."

Alice followed him into the fabulously untidy living room at the back of the house. Magazines, empty crisps packets and crumpled shirts were piled on every surface.

"Excuse the mess. Tend to live in this room, so I keep everything I need here. Love the views."

The house was tucked into a curve in the river which ran around two sides, and floor-to-ceiling windows framed the scene. A majestic willow tree tossed wispy branches to the ground, where they crept over the bank and into the water.

"It's beautiful." Alice walked over to the window. "And it's so quiet here. You haven't got any near neighbours?"

"Thank the Lord, no. Walker Hampton is my nearest."

"So you know him well?"

"Known Walker since he was a teenager. Looked out for him after his father died. Sound chap, Bertie Hampton." He moved into the centre of the room, clutching his flame-coloured cravat. "Now my dear, you have a choice. This lovely painting here, or that watercolour over there. Which one would you prefer?"

The two paintings were tucked amongst more theatre posters featuring Marty Bradman. Dressed as Captain Hook in one, he leered at Alice, eyebrows twisted, mouth stretched into a snarl. It occurred to Alice that it wasn't a face one would want to meet in the dark.

"Ah, you've seen my Hook. Fine show that one, at Scarborough it was. Very appreciative audience." He stood at the side of the poster and struck a copycat pose. "Walker came up to see the show one night. It was his seventeenth birthday, so I took him to a party afterwards. I went with a blonde, lovely girl, and she fixed Walker up with one of her friends. We arrived, had a glass of champagne, then the girl led Walker away and I didn't see him again for two days!" He laughed a snorting horsey laugh.

"Here's me as Dick Whittington." A three-foot-tall poster featured Marty Bradman wearing tight brown trousers and knee-length boots, topped by a white shirt with enormous balloon sleeves.

"Terrific costume. I had the physique for it, of course. Used to come out the stage door to swarms of fans." He stroked his chin and looked out of the window. "Ah, those were the days."

He picked up a framed photograph from the sideboard and held it out to Alice. "Here's me at the premier. That's the mayor at the front of the group. He threw a marvellous party afterwards. Went with a blonde."

"What other plays have you done?"

"I was a Shakespeare regular. Macbeth, Othello … Romeo, of course. Now it's voiceovers and commercials. Good pay for turning up and reading the lines."

If she closed her eyes, Alice could just hear Martin's rich voice shifting rolls of toilet paper.

As he put the photo back, Alice noticed another – a suited and top-hatted Martin beside a beautiful woman in a floaty white dress.

"That's my wedding day. Got married during *Goldilocks*."

"The lady's not blonde."

Martin contemplated the dark-skinned, dark-haired

woman, seemingly noticing her non-blondness for the first time. "You can't win 'em all!"

The conversation was slipping into mildly unsavoury, if intriguing territory, and Alice needed some answers.

"Did you enjoy Vivien Taylor's party the other day?"

"The old girl knows how to throw a good bash doesn't she? Plenty of good champagne. Had a great time."

"So did I. Though I thought I saw you and Walker having a bit of an argy-bargy?"

"Did you? Don't remember that, though Walker can set off a bit sometimes. We once had an argument about a woman, didn't speak to each other for weeks. She was blonde …"

"Who won the argument?"

"He did, the blighter. Then he went and married her."

"Oh, so you've known Vivien Taylor a long time?"

"That was Walker's first wife. But yes, I met Vivien when she first stepped out with Walker. Charming woman. And very persuasive – she talked me into being a councillor."

"You were a councillor?" Alice almost spat out the words out. She would have been less surprised if Martin had told her that he kept a zebra in his bedroom.

"Yes. 'You won't have to do anything,' she said. 'Just show up, I'll tell you what to say.' Good as her word she was, always gave me my lines. Of course, what she really wanted was my name. Still, it was easy enough fitting the duties around my acting and it was all for a good cause."

"And how long were you a councillor?"

"Twenty years. Just did my mayoral year then gave it up. Long enough run, didn't want to bore everyone."

"You were mayor of Great Wheaton?" This time, there was no disguising her surprise.

"It's *de rigueur*, once you've been a councillor for ten years. That's me as mayor. I've also got one from an anniversary do with some of my predecessors, another one of Vivien's parties. That was a bash, I can tell you. Went with a blonde I'd known for years. Took me three days to recover." Martin sniggered.

"What was the anniversary?"

"The town hall's bicentenary, and there was a civic service to celebrate." He picked through the rest of the photos. "I can't see it here, but it must be around somewhere. I'll dig it out and send it to you if you like. You said you wanted some material for your catalogue, didn't you?"

"Please do, I'd love to see it."

Martin Bradman took centre stage in the room, legs astride, cravat askew, and threw out his arms.

"Now. Paintings! The windswept moors of Yorkshire, or the languid river at Great Wheaton. Alice Haydon, you decide."

Chapter 39

"So, I took the Yorkshire Moors."

Alice showed Roddy a photo of the painting on her mobile. "What did you think of Marty Bradman?"

"He was hilarious, if a bit creepy. I got a run-down of the blondes he'd taken to various parties. Those theatre types really do live on another planet."

"I think he picked up his last blonde from the drag queen bingo. And she wasn't blonde!" Roddy handed back the phone. "Surely we've got all the paintings by now. Feels like we've been at this job for ages."

"Two weeks actually, but we're nearly there. The unticked ones on this list are still to be collected. You pick who you want to see." She tapped the paper. "By the way, how's your own painting coming along?"

"Dear girl, how is an artist to create when he's constantly interrupted by work? It's going slowly since you ask. I can't concentrate when I have to traipse around town collecting artworks." Roddy folded his arms.

Alice frowned. "Okay, don't worry. Look, you carry on with your own painting and I'll deal with the rest of the lenders."

Roddy unfolded his arms and pointed to Alice's incident board.

"On other matters, dare I ask how your investigation is going? I see your incident board has grown since I last saw it."

"I've got lots more information, but I'm no nearer finding any answers. I feel as if it's staring me in the face, but I just can't see it. It's very frustrating."

"Well, if you're nearer the answer than you were before, you'll get to it in good time."

"Let's hope you're right."

After Roddy left, Alice picked a rhubarb and custard sweet from the jar and flopped onto the bean bag. She had hit a blank wall with her investigation into the people behind Carrie Developments, other than knowing they were clients of Hacker, Stanley & Dole.

There were no stars for the exhibition. But the show had to have at least one star piece.

Jenna, she decided, would think her useless if she didn't get something spectacular. And time was running out.

Helen Yardley insisted they meet in Narebridge, worried that someone might see them together in Great Wheaton. It was hot and sticky as Alice drove upriver and even with both windows fully open, the cross-breeze struggled to cool the Defender.

Alice eased into a kerbside space on Narebridge high street and strode to the café Helen had suggested. She found Helen squeezed into a corner seat, the table pulled to her chest, searching eyes peering through her glasses.

"Thank you for coming."

"I'm glad to see you, though I would still like to meet Councillor de Havilland too."

"I know, but you've got me now." Helen attempted a smile. "So, you want to know about the paintings Julian borrowed from the council's collection?"

"Yes. I noticed he'd borrowed several over the last few years. Also …" Alice paused, searching for the words. "When I saw the collection the other day, one of them wasn't the original. And the last person to borrow that work was Julian."

Helen's mouth dropped. She pushed her glasses up her nose and glared at Alice. "What do you mean, not the original?"

"I know it sounds far-fetched, but one of the paintings was a copy. A good one, but a copy."

"What's makes you say that?" Helen fingered a bunch of keys on the table.

"Well this, for a start." Alice handed Helen the Art in Your Home receipt.

Helen turned another shade paler.

"Are you saying that someone is stealing paintings from the council's art collection and replacing them with forgeries?"

"That's what it looks like."

Helen's paleness turned to puzzlement. She was silent for a moment, before a little of her colour returned.

"Actually, that makes sense."

"It does?"

"I can't explain, but it ties in with my own suspicions."

Alice's stomach flipped. "You suspected there was an art thief at the council?"

"Well no, but strange things have been going on over the past few years." Helen peered around the café. "I've been trying to piece them together. But your suspicions about the collection? They do confirm something I already knew."

"Has it got anything to do with Jason Marley's opposition to the Dunn Road development? He knew who was behind Carrie Developments, didn't he?"

"He did." Helen sighed. "He wouldn't tell me who it was, he said the less I knew the better. He worried about me losing my job, or worse. But eventually I convinced him nothing would happen to me. That last night ..." Helen's eyes filled with tears. "That night, he was on his way to see me. He was going to tell me everything. But someone killed him before he got the chance."

Alice too glanced around the café. There were only a couple of occupied tables at the front, but she moved closer to Helen anyway.

"Do you have any idea who it was?"

"I could guess, but we're talking about murder here. I don't want to falsely accuse anyone."

A tear dropped from Helen's chin, and Alice handed her a tissue.

"Jason was your boyfriend, wasn't he?"

Helen nodded. "Jason was kind and generous. He reminded me of my late husband in some ways. Though Bernard would never have had the nerve to defy the council the way Jason did. And in public too." Helen dabbed her eyes. "He didn't want anyone to know about our relationship, especially the councillors, they hated him for what he did."

"I can imagine. Did Julian know about you and Jason?"

"I never told him, but I'm sure he guessed." Helen wiped her face with the tissue and tucked it into her dress pocket. "Jason was right to bring his judicial review and he wasn't going to be deterred, Julian or not. The process to appoint Carrie Developments was flawed, wrong in fact. Jason had the evidence to prove it and I'm sure he'd have won his case."

"But Julian was responsible for the process. And he tried to coerce Felicity Gault into voting for Carrie Developments, even though she knew they weren't the best option. This all took place on Julian's watch, Helen."

"I know it looks bad." Helen tucked in her chin and stared over her glasses. "But Julian didn't have any choice."

Alice straightened up, putting new distance between herself and Helen.

"I understand why you're sticking up for Julian, I know he's your brother."

Helen clutched the table with both hands.

"He is, but that's not the only reason I'm on his side."

"Did someone ask him to make sure Carrie Developments got the contract? Or put pressure on him to do so?"

Helen leaned in close and whispered, "He was told to."

"He was threatened?"

"Shhh. It was made very clear to him that Carrie Developments should get the contract. And this wasn't the first time, oh no. He'd been set up before, during his election campaign."

"You mean the dodgy donation? Someone set Julian up by incorrectly recording the donation and snitching on him to the Electoral Commission."

Helen nodded.

"But the story was only live for a short time, Helen. The *Courier* didn't even run it. He survived, didn't he?"

"He was supposed to survive, Alice, that was the point. The Electoral Commission was smoothed over and the fine was paid for him. But it was only a public survival. Behind the scenes, Julian was in their debt. And it got worse. It destroyed his marriage and if his twins hadn't stood by him as they did, I think he would have broken. And now he has to do as he's told, or he'll be exposed for fraud in public office. He'll be disgraced, maybe even end up in prison."

"George Shaker gave him the donation, right? He's a disgraced businessman himself, so he must be the person behind Carrie Developments, and—"

"Oh no. George Shaker was set up too. He and Julian knew each other well and George just wanted to support a friend. He asked how the donation should be paid and Julian told him the correct and legal way. George did it by the book. He wasn't to know that donations by barred individuals should be declared as such. It was the perfect set-up and there was nothing Julian could do about it."

A waitress cleared a nearby table, loading up her tray with half-eaten cakes and empty coffee cups.

"Why are you telling me all this, Helen?"

"I've worked at GWDC for twenty years. I've loyally supported the administration, councillors of every persuasion, in the expectation that they serve the community to their best ability. But I've come to realise that some of them are only there to serve themselves and they don't care how they do it. Or who pays the price." Helen wiped away another tear. "And Jason paid with his life." She grasped Alice's hand and pulled it towards her. "His killer is still out there and I want him caught. Find him, Alice."

Alice clasped Helen's hand and settled her other hand over the top.

"I will, Helen, I will. But I need to know who's pulling the strings at Carrie Developments. If it's not George Shaker, then who is it?"

"Someone much bigger."

Chapter 40

Someone much bigger. The words rolled around in Alice's head as she walked to the Defender. Whoever Mr X was, he had set up Julian de Havilland, apparently manipulating him at will. He – or she – had put Julian under pressure to award Carrie Developments the Dunn Road shopping centre contact, worth a fortune. But what was his interest in the council's art collection? And *Beach?*

Alice's phone beeped and just as she was pulling it out of her bag, she was bumped by a stocky man jogging along the footpath in the other direction. She swung around, on the verge of yelling, but a pair of bandy legs and a rim of amber curls beneath his peaked cap choked the impulse. Her eyes followed the man until he shot around the corner and disappeared.

It was the man she had seen when she was supposed to meet Jason on the bridge; and here he was again, moments after she had met with Jason's girlfriend. It was no coincidence, surely.

Her hand shook as she unlocked the Defender. She jumped in and sped out of Narebridge. Once on the river road, she slowed down and took a deep breath. She glanced involuntarily in the rear-view mirror, but all she saw was her own wide and frightened eyes.

"Get a hold of yourself, Alice. He obviously lives in the area. Why wouldn't you see him around?"

She wiped the sweat from her forehead and looked out the window. Fields of glowing yellow rape and green pastures, slashed by the grey-blue river, shot by. Two boys in bright orange kayaks raced each other, silver oars sending sparkles of sunlight across the water.

On another balmy evening the previous summer, she and Joe had paddled up this way. Joe had borrowed a rowing boat from a friend and they had glided up the river, soaking in the living landscape. The further they moved away from town, the quieter the waterway became. Their only company were families of ducks and geese and a memorable pair of elegant black swans.

Two miles along, they had stopped for a cold beer at a pub overlooking the river. It was not until the sun began to fade that they realised they had no lights and would have to row back in the dark. The moonless night was so pitch that Alice could barely distinguish the river from its banks. She would have been afraid, but for the reassuring plink of the oars slicing through the water. The river's murmur was calming. It was one of the reasons she so enjoyed living on *Daisy*.

She was so deep in reminiscence that she did not register the jolt at first. But the steering became leaden and the Defender lurched off to the right. Alice clung on to the wheel as it fought to rip itself out of her hands. A wooden fence hurtled towards her. She wrestled with the car, slamming on the brakes. The Defender slowed, but not in time to stop it plunging off the road and into the fence. Its heavy front end broke through the wooden rails and it careered along the grass. Alice hammered on the brakes and the car eventually came to a standstill, leaving her slumped over the wheel.

She lifted her head, blinking away salty tears. She put a hand to her head, but could not feel any bumps, and a check in the mirror revealed no more cuts or bruises than she already had. A flock of sheep had lifted their heads and were staring at her with mild interest, unfazed by the intrusion.

She opened the car door and slid to the ground. Her legs wobbled. She steadied herself and examined the damage. There was only a small dent on the galvanised front bumper, but the back had not escaped so lightly. The driver side wheel guard was buckled and the tyre was in ribbons.

All in all, remarkably little damage.

Alice reached into the glove box and retrieved her insurance documents. Just as she was punching in the number, she heard a shout. A man waved from the roadside, standing in the gap the Defender had made in the fence.

"Hey there!" he yelled across the grass. "Do you need any help?"

"My tyre has blown."

"I'll come over." The man marched through the gap, a black Labrador trotting along beside him.

He reached the car and inspected the ruined tyre.

"That's a blow-out alright. Still, the old Defender landed on her feet." He patted the car's rump. "Do you have a spare?" He raised a questioning jet eyebrow, a contrast to the silver of his closely cropped hair.

"Yes, it's in the back, but you really don't have to do it. I can call the breakdown service."

"It's no problem, it won't take long. If you could take Samson for me please?" He held out the dog's lead. "I'm Victor, by the way."

"Alice."

She was about to protest again, but she was too angry and tired to argue. She opened the back of the Defender and let Victor rummage around collecting tools. He lifted out the heavy tyre with ease, leant it against the car and fitted the jack together. It looked as if he had done the job many times before, so was not in need of any help.

Alice stepped out of the way and stood in the field, holding a stranger's dog while he changed her car tyre.

A surreal end to a bizarre day.

Chapter 41

"A DEAD MAN IN the river, a Mister Big, an increasingly complex incident board, a council with a collection of fakes, an Augustus John drawing on the run …" Roddy pulled his straw hat further over his face and shifted his weight from one foot to the other. "It gets scarier every time I speak to you. I positively fear for my life!"

Alice sat on the sun lounger with one foot on *Daisy*'s rail. "Roddy, I'm serious."

"And that's the problem, Alice. You're taking this far too seriously. Great Wheaton is not the den of thieves you are making it out to be."

"How do you know?"

"Because crime of this nature takes ingenuity and there's nobody in this town with that sort of imagination. The only person I would credit with the right intelligence and cunning is you, dear girl."

"Very funny. Not." Alice swung her other foot onto the rail.

"I mean it, you are the only person I can think of. You have the wherewithal, the knowledge and the contacts to distribute the drawing and the other paintings you say are missing from the council's collection." Roddy paced around the deck, warming to his theme. "And it wouldn't take you five minutes to get a company set up in the British Virgin Islands and make a bid for the Dunn Road development contract. If you put your mind to it, you could be a master criminal."

"Really, I don't know where you got such a mad idea."

"Well, come up with someone else then."

"Hey!" Joe ran along Sam's Lane and across the gangway. He stood on the deck, legs apart, arms outstretched. "You've been shot".

"I'm pretty sure I haven't been shot. But seeing as you said it with such conviction, maybe you can persuade me otherwise." Alice giggled.

"I mean it, Alice. There's a bullet hole in your car. Someone shot at it."

"Come on, Joe. Be serious."

"Come and look for yourself."

The Defender stood battered but proud amongst the other vehicles in the car park. Joe crouched down beside the back wheel on the driver's side. He beckoned Alice and indicated a spot just above the wheel.

"Look at this."

Alice bent close and saw a small, round hole an inch from the edge of the flared wheel arch.

"Someone has taken a shot at it, I'd say. I think a bullet went through the wheel arch trim and hit the tyre, causing the blow-out."

"Really, Joe? I'm having trouble believing that someone just happened to be standing by the road with a gun and decided to take a pop at my car as I went by."

"It seems a tall tale, I admit. But I've seen rifle damage

on military Land Rovers and it looked just like this. I don't want to alarm you, but that's what it looks like."

"You think that someone tried to bump me off?"

"I wouldn't put it quite like that."

"How would you put it?"

"I don't know why it happened, or if it really is a rifle shot, but that's what it looks like. I don't think it could have happened by accident." He put a hand on her shoulder. "Alice, I think someone might have been sending you a message."

"Oh my God, Joe, what's going on? Missing paintings, gunshots, murder, dodgy dealings. I feel like I'm in an episode of *Midsomer Murders*."

"Did you see anyone about at the time?"

"Did I see someone aim at rifle at me in broad daylight? Er, actually no."

"You said a guy changed your tyre."

"Oh yeah, Victor. But he came along after it happened. Besides, there's woodland on the other side of the road at that point. If someone had been in there I would never have seen them."

Joe rapped the Defender's door with his knuckle. "Think carefully, Alice. Did you see anything or anyone unusual earlier in the day?"

Suddenly, Alice's skin felt like ice. The man with the red hair and peaked cap popped into her head.

"Alice. You've gone pale, did you think of something? Do you think you've upset someone with your investigation?"

"I don't know. But if I've really been shot at, I need to find out by whom. And fast."

She thought of Julian de Havilland and Felicity Gault,

of how they had already been scared off. Perhaps she was next …

Back in *Daisy*'s cabin, Roddy handed Alice a mug of tea.

"I—"

"Joe is right, Alice. You've poked the bear and it's woken up. You were lucky and avoided serious harm this time, but you should take this as a warning. And, by the way, I'm being serious."

"I know you are and I appreciate your concern, Roddy. I was in the Defender when it flew off the road, and that was scary enough. Your warning's been noted."

Alice looked from Roddy to Joe. The two men in her life standing shoulder to shoulder, with the same uneasy expressions. Whatever terrible and impulsive decisions she had made in life, she had still managed to find these two lovely men.

"I'll cancel my job in Birmingham," said Joe. "I can stay with you this evening."

"I appreciate the offer, Joe, but you go ahead. I'll be fine."

"It's only a job, it's nothing important. I can get someone to cover."

Alice hesitated, cupping her hands around the china.

"Thank you, Joe, but I'll be okay. *Daisy* is secure once she's locked up properly, and I feel safe here."

Roddy said, "I can sleep over—"

"Absolutely not." She would rather face an intruder than have Roddy snoring on the sofa all night.

"Okay, but I'll sleep in my hammock on deck. So I'll hear if there's anyone about."

Alice nodded.

"Look, could you at least call the police?" said Joe. "Tell them what's happened?"

"Yes," said Roddy. "You should report it."

Alice's stomach skipped at the prospect of speaking to Nathan Salisbury. She wanted to take up his offer to meet again and here was the perfect excuse to contact him.

"Good idea. I'll call Nathan Salisbury."

Joe turned to the window. "Well, it looks like you don't need me then." He swung around and made for the stairs, without looking back. "I've got to go to work."

Alice put her head in her hands. Why couldn't she keep her mouth shut for once in her life?

Roddy said, "Alice, Joe's only trying—"

"Don't."

Roddy held up both hands. He settled himself on the sofa. "Now. What's the latest on the exhibition? It seems like Groundhog Day. Are we actually making any progress?"

Alice smiled, and decided to answer a question with a question.

"How's your own painting going? If you're happy with it, I'd love to have it now, so it's in the bag for the exhibition."

"It's sweet of you, but you have plenty of others to choose from."

"They're not yours! Besides, I thought you'd appreciate the attention."

"Catty! I can't deny I would enjoy being at the centre of a big exhibition again. But I'm struggling with the painting. I'm less confident about it now than I was a couple of days ago."

"I know you'll have your doubts – it wouldn't be you if you didn't – but I'm sure it'll come good for you, Roddy."

Roddy pouted. "On a different matter, what do you propose putting on the front cover of the catalogue?"

"I'm leaving that to Duncan."

"And I take it that we've given up on *Beach*?"

"No, I haven't given up on *Beach*, though I'm figuring in the *Peonies* painting as the council's contribution. But it's strictly Plan B."

"And what about Vivien Taylor? Is she going to offer another work in lieu of her missing Augustus John?"

"I'm definitely leaving that one to Duncan."

Roddy stood up. "I have some errands to run, but I'll be back later. You should bolt the door after me." He put a foot on the bottom step, then turned around. "All nonsense about Jason Marley, the shopping centre and incident boards forgotten?"

"Quite forgotten."

Roddy disappeared through the hatch door. And Alice immediately began planning how she was going to track down Mr Big. The man who nearly killed her.

Chapter 42

DI Nathan Salisbury crouched beside the Defender and ran a hand along the damaged wheel guard. One knee on the ground, he peered under and behind the arch. Satisfied, he stood up, wiping his hands with a handkerchief. He took photos.

"Requires further investigation, that's for sure."

Alice examined his face. His inscrutability was reassuring.

"So, do you think it was a bullet?"

"I'm not an expert, but I've got a friend in the Met's firearms unit and I'll get him to take a look. In the meantime, I'll get it towed to a secure garage, so you'll be without a car for a few days."

They left the car park and wandered along Sam's Lane.

"Now, run through what you did yesterday for me, please. Where did you go and who did you meet?"

Alice was finishing her account just as they reached *Daisy Dawn*.

Nathan patted the barge's side. "I didn't think you were a boating girl. I remember you crying off that boat trip up the Thames."

"It was mid-winter and pouring with rain." Alice laughed. "I didn't think you were that keen yourself."

"The boat didn't look as good in the flesh as it did on the website. But this looks great. It must be a different existence, living on a boat."

"Come on board and have a look."

Nathan strode across the gangway and onto *Daisy*'s deck. Both hands on the side railing, he looked up and down the river.

"What a great view. It's like you're actually part of the scenery. Fantastic."

"I was very lucky to find *Daisy* when I did, I love living here. Now, would you like a drink, Nathan?"

"No thanks, I can't stay long. Though while I am here, I'd like to examine your security. Locks on your doors, alarms, windows."

"You're frightening me, Nathan. What are you suggesting?"

"I'm not suggesting anything. Great Wheaton is a low-crime town, indeed the whole area is particularly low risk. But I do recommend that you take sensible precautions. It's part of our routine now, to get people to recognise the value of personal safety."

Nathan sidled closer, as Alice twiddled with the handle on the hatch door. He smiled and she smiled back. She tried the handle again, the door opened away from her and she stumbled. Nathan caught her elbow and steadied her. She grabbed his arm and caught his familiar scent.

Nathan dropped her arm and stepped back.

Alice felt her cheeks flush and went ahead of him through the hatch door.

"The whole barge was refurbished before I moved in just over a year ago, including new locks and bolts on the hatch door and all the windows. There's an alarm as well, though I must admit I don't use it."

"I would advise that you test it, just to make sure it still works." Nathan inspected the inside of the hatch door. "These locks look solid. Good."

"The owners had *Daisy* fitted out to their own specs. They were planning on taking long trips to France, but then the husband got a job in Singapore and they rented her out while they were away."

Nathan wandered back on deck and stood in the bow. Alice stood beside him, her arm finding his jacket sleeve. It felt good. If she was honest with herself, it felt very good.

As if reading her thoughts, Nathan turned to her, locking his eyes on hers. Her heart sprinted. He moved closer until, just inches away, he tipped her chin towards him and brushed her lips with the lightest of kisses.

She grasped his shoulder, running fingers over his shirt collar, along his neck. He kissed her again and she kissed him back.

Nathan's phone buzzed and they jumped apart. He ignored the call but sent a quick text message.

"I have to go." He took a card from his jacket pocket and handed it to Alice. "That's my mobile number. If you're worried about anything, call me. Anytime."

Alice looked after him as he strode down Sam's Lane. She had broken up with him because he moved away. Now, she wondered what she had been thinking …

Alice took a brisk walk along the river to clear her head. At the bridge, she stood to the side while a noisy line of school children ambled by. Walking on, she crossed the road and followed the path along the edge of a field of waist-high wheat. She stepped up onto the grass verge and ran her fingers over the top of the prickly plant.

Claudia Rowan was still pestering her about the Augustus John theft story she wanted to run. The police had no new leads – it seemed the drawing had vanished into thin air.

She considered giving Claudia a photo of the drawing after all. Even if someone recognised it as an undiscovered Augustus John, while it was missing there was no possibility of getting an authentication. Or, she could tell Claudia about her tyre blow-out and the involvement of the police – if she was interested in running the story, it might bring out a witness or someone with information about the culprit.

As she rounded a bend, a German Shepherd bounded along the path towards her, ducking away at the last moment. The dog rang circles around her, then rolled onto his back.

"Hey Clinton. Nearly got me this time." Alice squatted down, rubbing the dog's stomach while its owner caught up.

"We've been round the field once already and he's still running like a nutter," said Livvie.

"Perhaps he's gone mad in the heat."

"Let's go through the woods, it's cooler."

As they walked beneath the canopy, the temperature plunged and the light dimmed. Alice unrolled her shirt sleeves. Clinton scampered into the undergrowth, disappeared then bounded out again.

"So, how's the incident board shaping up on Jason Marley?"

"Nathan said nothing came from the police appeal for information, so it's stalemate as far as they're concerned. Have you heard anything?"

"Only that anyone who knew Jason is shocked and bewildered. He was very well liked, such an easy-going type. It's hard to believe he had enemies – apart from the council of course. Most of the councillors had no time for him."

"Yes, but they were going ahead with their plans regardless of Jason. He was a nuisance, for sure, but hardly threatening enough for someone to want him dead."

"And they'll soon discover they're not going to get a break just because Jason is gone. The group's going ahead with the judicial review that he started. Julia Marsh is particularly keen, so she's taken a lead."

"That's brave of her. Does she know anything about the process?"

"Not really, but she's getting help from someone who does, apparently. They've got a court hearing next week."

That, thought Alice, will be Helen Yardley.

There was a sharp crack. Alice spun around. Trees, leaves … Nothing more.

"Must be a branch," said Livvie. "It's been so dry they're brittle. I almost got brained by one the other day."

Alice scanned the dense foliage. Other than the low rustle of leaves on a parched oak tree, all was still. Satisfied, she jogged up the path after Livvie.

"Nothing new on the drawing, I take it?" said Livvie.

"Nothing. Most of these lenders buy their stuff from legitimate galleries or dealers. The drawing won't have gone that route. It was probably stolen to order by someone who already had a buyer lined up, possibly outside the country."

"Jeez, Alice. You make it sound like the mafia."

"If that's what happened, then it is organised crime in a way. The *Beach* painting is also missing and I wonder whether that's gone the same way." Alice grabbed a low-hanging branch and ducked underneath.

"What happened to the suspects on your board?"

"Julian de Havilland was my original suspect, but after speaking to Helen, I've ruled him out. Then there's Edward Hacker. I don't think he has the pictures, but I'm not ruling him out completely. I'm pretty sure one of his clients is involved, so Hacker must know more than he's letting on."

"You'll have to find out who his clients are."

"I tried that, but he's very good at keeping his clients confidential."

"And you've got no more leads?"

"Not really. I'm seeing the Averys later. They are serious collectors, quite well known in the local art world. They're last on the list."

They walked deeper into the woods, following Clinton's lead.

"And how's the gorgeous man?" said Livvie.

"Yeah, good."

"You don't sound so sure. Anything wrong?"

"No, no, it's fine." An image of Nathan Salisbury had lingered in Alice's mind, despite her efforts to push it away. She changed the subject. "It's so good to get out during the day. With this role, I can do all my admin in the evenings and spend part of the day doing fun stuff."

"Are you thinking of doing it permanently? Working from home I mean. You could set up your own business from *Daisy*."

"I've thought of that, but I need to concentrate on getting this exhibition out of the way. If I make a success of that, I can put it on my CV and see where we go from there."

Clinton barked and the women spun around. The dog was standing in front of a sprawling bush. He pattered up to the base, sniffed, took a few steps back and barked again. Livvie called him, but he ignored her and carried on barking.

"Just walk on, he'll follow in a minute."

They continued on, and Alice turned and looked back before the path took them out of sight. Clinton hadn't moved, and his bark had notched up an octave.

"It's probably a rabbit, I'll go and get him," said Livvie.

Livvie called Clinton and walked back, Alice following behind. The bush shook as the dog scurried around it, his barking growing fiercer by the second. Livvie made a grab for his collar, but he was off round the back of the bush.

A rabbit shot out of the bush and launched itself into a nearby hole. Clinton was caught on the wrong side of the foliage and raced around, but the rabbit was too quick. The dog sniffed and yelped at the rabbit's front door, but the animal was beyond reach.

A muffled buzzing sound came from behind, and Alice swung around. There was nobody there.

"I could swear that was someone's phone. This wood is really creeping me out."

Livvie was wrestling with Clinton and hadn't heard her. "Once he's got a scent he won't let it go. Damn rabbits everywhere."

As Alice was about to turn away, a streak of blue flashed through the bush's green leaves. Her eyes widened and she craned her neck, trying to see through the foliage. Someone's shirt, perhaps? Her heart skipped a beat.

Clinton pulled free and raced away up the path, Livvie close behind. Soon, Alice was alone amongst the trees. She scoured the undergrowth, bending to look underneath. But all was still and the wearer of the blue shirt was nowhere to be seen.

Chapter 43

MR AND MRS ELLIOTT Avery III lived in a smart house in the smart part of town. They were relative newbies, having arrived from Illinois two years previously, when Mr Avery was transferred to London with his employer, the Bank of Chicago.

"We were looking for a quiet place outside the city and a colleague suggested we look out this way. We came for a drive one Sunday afternoon and stumbled on Great Wheaton. We decided right there and then, we wanted to live here. And we settled in real fine."

Mr 'Call me Eli' Avery puffed his broad chest and opened his expansive arms.

"We've been very happy here. You people made us feel right at home."

"I came from London myself," said Alice, "and I've found people really friendly. It's only been a year, but I already feel like I've been here for ages." Alice glanced at the artworks in the living room. "Did you bring these paintings with you from the States?"

"Yes, but they're just the ones I inherited from my family," said Mrs 'Call me Betty' Avery. "I couldn't leave those behind. But Eli and I wanted to start a new collection, so we gave the rest to our children. We've enjoyed building up another stock of works here. We were going to lend you one of our American artists, but we'd be happy to consider anything else you prefer."

"There are no American artists in the exhibition, so that sounds perfect – and thank you for your generosity."

"Well, see what you make of the painting," said Eli. "We dug out a couple of photos from when we first saw it in the window of a second-hand shop in Tallahassee. If you like it, you can have those for your catalogue."

Eli Avery related the story of how they had bought the piece because they liked it, paying only a few dollars. But after a thorough examination at home, Eli was convinced the unsigned painting was the work of an established twentieth-century American artist. An art historian agreed, so Mr and Mrs Avery started their enviable art collection with an important painting and a lucky find.

"It's in the hall. We'll start there," said Eli.

When Alice saw the painting, it was love at first sight. It was of a nondescript red barn in a clearing, but the light, and the subtlety of the palette, were exquisite.

"It turned out to be a Rockwell," said Eli. "We couldn't believe our luck."

Alice made notes whilst Eli talked, working out a story around the photographs.

"We'll do a tour of the rest now. Let's start in the dining room."

They were as interesting and tasteful as Alice imagined they would be. They were also beautifully framed and hung; the Averys were certainly prepared to put their money into their hobby. Alice thought of the *Peonies* painting from the council's art collection, with its clunky frame. She resolved to convince Duncan to have it reframed if *Beach* didn't turn up.

"We bought this piece locally, saw it at someone's house and loved it."

Alice sighed at an exquisite watercolour of Japanese cherry blossom hanging over a bridge.

"We took it straight off their wall," said Betty. "Put it in the car right there and then."

"Whose painting was it?"

"Walker Hampton's. You must know him, I guess."

"Yes, I know Walker, he has a fabulous collection."

"We were only at his house by chance, would you believe. We were picking up a friend and while she was admiring the garden, we bought this terrific piece."

"Have you bought any other paintings from Walker?"

"No, just this one."

"So where did you go for the rest of your collection? Do you use a local dealer?"

Eli was climbing the stairs.

"No, we don't, though we did buy another painting later on from someone else around here. Someone we met at a dinner party, I can't recall the name. Betty, do you remember who sold us the Remy Blanchard?"

"Gee, Eli, you know how hopeless I am with names. I can barely remember what our grandchildren are called."

"It'll come to me." Eli led Alice into the main bedroom. "We keep our favourite paintings in here."

Alice immediately thought of Walker Hampton.

"We made it real comfy. We often spend the cold evenings tucked up in bed reading and enjoying our artworks." It sounded as if Betty wished it could be winter all the time. If the room's stifling air was anything to go by, it would be toasty in winter.

"Such a beautiful view too, right over the river."

"Sure, it's a great spot. Good for boating."

The three reminisced about sunny summer days lazing about on the water.

As they reached the front door after finishing the tour, Eli Avery remembered who had sold them the Remy Blanchard painting.

Alice dropped her bag on *Daisy*'s deck and took Roddy's proffered glass of wine. The sun was dropping, and the temperature with it, as the two friends clinked glasses.

"While you were hobnobbing with the Averys, I had to endure the Bradman vexation. Unfortunately, I ran into him on Sam's Lane and I couldn't get rid of him. I hope you're suitably grateful."

"I am, thank you, but what was Martin doing here?"

"He brought this over for you." Roddy picked up an envelope from the table beside him. "Said he promised you some photos for the exhibition catalogue."

"He did too. It was sweet of him to bring them over."

"I don't suppose he has much else on, this not being the season for cross-dressing madams."

Alice took the envelope and noticed a bunch of carnations behind the sun lounger. "Did he bring the flowers too?"

"Oh, I forgot. No, they were dropped off by some brusque little man with a Barry Gibb voice. He interrogated me to within an inch of my life, before he was persuaded I would give you the flowers."

Alice fished out a card from amongst the blooms. It read, '*I hope you and the Defender have recovered.*'

"They're from Victor, the man who changed my tyre yesterday. How thoughtful of him."

Roddy snorted.

"What are they like, Martin's photos?" said Alice. "Have you seen them?"

"No. I left them for you."

She opened the envelope and took out the photos. The first one featured Martin Bradman, resplendent in full mayoral regalia of tricorn hat and long black gown, over a shirt with lacy white cuffs. Next was Martin dressed in full Widow Twanky costume from a Christmas 1997 production of *Aladdin*. Alice passed them to Roddy.

"I always wondered why people wanted to be mayors," he said, "but it's obviously so they can dress up." He stood up and slipped on his flip-flops. "I think I need a lie down after that alarming sight. Before I go, do you need me for anything?"

"I'm going to pull all the exhibition catalogue material together, so have you got anything else to go in?"

"No, you have everything."

"Dare I ask how your own painting is coming along? Shall I leave a page free?"

"You may dare, but it comes at your own risk." Roddy picked up his straw hat from the lounger and threw it at Alice. "If I finish it you can have it for the exhibition; if I don't, then you can't. Now don't ask me again."

Alice handed the hat back to Roddy, by way of sealing the deal.

She scanned through the rest of Martin Bradman's photos, all featuring him posing at a variety of mayoral functions. The last photo captured a row of people dressed in similar hats and gowns. The mayors stared into the camera with forced expressions of civic rectitude.

Martin Bradman was in the centre of the group and Alice did not recognise the two people immediately flanking him. But she did know the two at either end of the row. One of them was Vivien Taylor and the other was the person who had sold a painting to Eli and Betty Avery.

Chapter 44

Two missing artworks, one dead man, one shooting, one close encounter in the woods.

Only a couple of weeks before, Alice had wished that her life was more adventurous. She wanted to be senior curator and she would have pushed Jenna Farling over a cliff to get her job. Now that she had it, with all that had happened her chances of keeping the job or getting another one in the art world were diminishing by the day. Things could hardly have gone any worse.

But now she could make up for it. She knew where the missing pieces were. She was not going to wait for the police or their art specialist – she would take matters into her own hands and recover them herself. All she had to do was go and get them.

Alice checked the clock on the kitchen wall. It was nearly midnight and time to go. She changed into black leggings and a black sweatshirt, plaited her hair and pulled on a dark grey beanie. Tossing a few items into a small black backpack, she slipped into a pair of charcoal runners. She slipped out through the hatch door, and was locking up when she heard Livvie's voice on the gangway.

"I've just finished up and I thought I'd come over for a nightcap." Livvie jumped down onto the deck. "Hey, are you going somewhere?"

"Yes, sorry, Livvie, we'll have to chat another time." Alice swung the backpack onto her shoulder.

"In that get up? You look like a burglar. You're not planning to rob a bank are you?"

"Not a bank," said Alice with a wry smile.

"I was joking, but I'm not sure you are. Alice, where are you going and what are you going to do when you get there?"

"Steal back my career." Alice walked over the gangway and onto Sam's Lane.

"I don't know what you're talking about, but whatever it is, Alice Haydon, stop it right now."

"Don't worry Livvie, I know what I'm doing." Alice walked back to her friend and put a hand on her shoulder. "I'll be fine."

"So, you think stealing something back, if that's what you're planning, is going to make things right?" Livvie's voice spiked.

"I don't expect you to understand, but I have to do this my own way."

"Wait, I'll come with you. Just give me a minute to get changed."

"Thanks, but you can't. I mean, there's no need. Look, don't worry, I'll be fine."

Alice turned away and jogged along the path to the far side of Roddy's barge, where a small rubber dinghy lay on the water. Alice eased into the boat and tucked her backpack under the seat. She adjusted the choke and yanked the pull cord. The motor jerked into life and Alice let it run while she untied the rope. She pushed away from the bank and headed upriver.

A thin wedge of moon and scattered stars provided scant light, but Alice knew the way. The motor ran sweetly, so she urged the boat faster along the empty river.

Up ahead, a wooden jetty jutted out into the river. Alice slowed the boat, killed the engine and glided into the bank. She tied the boat to one of the jetty's uprights and clambered onto land. Taking a moment to adjust to solid ground, she secured the backpack over both shoulders and followed a path along the water's edge.

After a few minutes, she veered off the path and into woodland. Tall, dense trees rose up around her, sucking up the natural light. Something touched her shoulder and she jumped. Just the tip of a branch and she smacked it away. A quick smile did nothing to block a pang of panic, but she was not stopping now.

She shook off her fear and pressed on through the woodland, finding a foot-worn path that tracked up a long slope. The path meandered around the trees and when the incline evened out, she walked on.

A sharp crack shot through the air. Alice froze, only her eyes moving from side to side. Nothing in front. Slowly, she turned her head to look behind. Her ears strained, and she heard the whisper of leaves breaking underfoot. On the path ahead. Coming towards her.

She backed away, but the footsteps grew faster and closer. Seeking a hiding place, she stepped off the path and into knee-high undergrowth. She waded through, but thorns tugged at her ankles, slowing her down.

The footsteps were almost upon her. Her heart raced. Though enveloped in darkness, she still feared she would be spotted. There was no time to move any further, so she crouched down, curling herself into a tight ball under the foliage, and waited.

Silence. No more rustling, no footsteps. All was still.

Sweat soaked into Alice's beanie. They must know she was there. Her heartbeat hammered through her body and she thought it must be audible on the other side of the world.

More rustling. Very close now. She fumbled around the ground, found a broken branch and picked it up. The rustling intensified.

Carefully, she parted the leaves and peered out. There was nobody visible, but there was rustling coming from her left. She widened the gap in the bushes and saw a round rump.

She stood up, took a step forward, raised her arm and prepared to strike. As her arm swung through the air, a startled muntjac threw her a frightened glance and bounded off down the path.

Alice leant against a tree, waiting for her beating heart to settle. The branch slipped out of her sweaty hands. She took a deep breath, slipped back onto the path and made her way into a clearing. In the open space beyond the fence at the far side, lay the target.

Chapter 45

The building lay in near darkness, but Alice fumbled her way around it to the back door. She tried the handle on the off chance it had been left unlocked, but no luck. She looked around for a likely hiding place for a spare key, running her hand along the top of the door frame, prising up a stone flag on the ground, but found nothing.

Around the other side of the building, Alice discovered a small window slightly ajar. Reaching inside, she eased up the metal window latch and unfastened the window. Standing on an upturned flowerpot, she pulled it fully open.

Alice pulled her head and shoulders through and after a determined wriggle, the rest of her body followed. She dropped down onto a ceramic sink and then the ground. The cloakroom was also home to a tabby cat, startled awake by the intruder. Alice crouched down to stroke it but it ignored her, stretching out its front paws before closing its eyes again.

Alice opened her backpack and fished out a small torch. She pointed it at the floor, turned it on and followed the light to the door. She opened it a crack and listened.

Hearing only the sound of her own heart beating, she opened the door a little more. Judging it to be safe, she squeezed through.

She played the torch from side to side until the beam picked out a stack of canvases, and she made her way across the room. Wedging the torch between a couple of empty jars on a shelf, she flicked through the artworks until she came to a painting wrapped in brown paper. She lifted it out and laid it on the floor, removing the paper and loosening the bubble wrap underneath.

And there it was. *Beach.*

But it was not what she expected. The image was a crude attempt to capture the sea lapping a beach, something like the work of a child using a painting by numbers kit.

She turned the painting over and ran a finger between the backing board and the frame. They were joined together by framer's tape, which gave slightly to her touch. She placed the painting face down on the floor and took a scalpel from her backpack. With the tip of the knife, she cut down the centre line of the tape along each of the four sides.

Alice eased the backing away from the frame, and between the board and the painting she found a second work; one painting hidden behind another. She swept the torch over the canvas. Even in the that imperfect light, the azure blue of a Mallorcan sea flashed fresh and bright. A fishing village rimming a protected bay, as seen from a restaurant balcony. Alice could almost smell the sea.

It was a humdinger.

"So, you worked it out then," came a voice from behind and above. "Clever girl."

Alice froze and gripped the frame. She looked up and just beyond the pantry door she made out the hazy outline of Marjorie Cavendish.

"I tried to warn you off, but even when your tyre was shot you didn't take any notice." Marjorie's glasses glinted as she moved her head into a shaft of torch light. "Now, put that painting down and move away."

Alice froze to the spot.

"I said move. Now."

"It's not yours, you stole it from the council's collection. And lots more too."

"Yada, yada, nobody's listening. Now move away before I get really annoyed."

Alice put one knee on the ground and straightened up.

"Look Marjorie, we can work something out. I'll take *Beach* back and say it's all been a misunderstanding. I'll say it was my fault. I won't mention your name. Then you can go off and buy other paintings, better ones than this."

"Nobody even noticed the paintings were missing, did they? Besides I replaced that stag one, didn't I?"

"Yes, with a fake."

"Oh, don't be such a snob! There are thousands of fake paintings floating around. One in five artworks in sniffy art galleries like yours is a forgery. But nobody understands that they are works of art in themselves." Marjorie shuffled towards the door. "Besides, people put prints on their walls that are not even produced by hand."

The woman stood firm, legs apart.

"Why *Beach,* anyway? What's so special about this painting?" said Alice.

"Ahh, so you're not as clever as you think you are. I assumed you knew it's by Elisabeth Moreno, Roddy's girlfriend. I discovered her when I visited him in Mallorca. She was such a talented artist and I bought one of her beautiful paintings, selling it on for a hefty profit. So, I bought more over time, finding keen buyers with more cash."

"In other words, you created a secondary market for Elisabeth's work and artificially pushed up the price. Very clever."

In the fuzzy light, Marjorie's body appeared to have spread across the doorway.

"I spent my evenings sucking up to Roger's boorish acquaintances, talking up Elisabeth's work and getting them to pay top money. Despite her being an almost unknown artist. I created a market for her work. She was nobody until I made her."

Alice had never seen Elisabeth's work before. She had lived and died in Mallorca, but one of her paintings had ended up here in Great Wheaton, hidden in Marjorie Cavendish's pantry.

"And then she died and there were no more paintings for you to sell," said Alice. "That is, until you found this one in the council's collection. You took it, so you could carry on making money out of her."

"What's wrong with that? People still make millions out of John Constable and he's been dead for two hundred years."

Alice looked at *Beach*, specks of sunlit patches breaking the sea.

"They're doing it legally. You stole this painting because you felt like it."

"If you think that everyone in the art world is honourable, then you're a naïve, silly girl. Dealers exploit artists and sellers all the time, to make money for themselves.

And with paintings they know are fakes. At least Elisabeth's paintings are genuine."

Alice scrunched her nose. "But why did you do it?"

"Because I could." Marjorie drew closer to Alice, fluffy pink slippers emerging through the gloom. "And I said the same thing to Jason Marley when he asked me why I'd set up Carrie Developments and made myself a pile out of the Dunn Road development. Because I could. There, I've said it again."

Alice flinched. "Jason found out you were the director behind Carrie Developments. So he did know all about Carrie, just as Julia Marsh said. And then you got rid of him."

"Exactly. Just as I'm going to get rid of you." Marjorie blinked behind her glasses and gave a crooked smile. "By the way, how did you know it was me?"

"I worked it out through Delilah."

"My dog?" Marjorie spluttered.

"Yes. That nice man Victor who changed my tyre – he had another black Labrador, called Samson. You said that Delilah had a twin and I figured that Samson must be Delilah's twin, the one you said you gave to your handyman. Samson and Delilah."

"Well done."

"But it was the voice that confirmed it. I had heard your handyman's high voice when I had dinner at your home. But I didn't make the connection till Roddy mentioned that Victor, the man who brought me flowers, had a 'Barry Gibb' voice. I thought it had to be the same man."

Marjorie put both hands in her dressing gown pockets.

"And Victor – David Victor – is your handyman. The man who fixed your hose pipe and shot my Defender. It seems he does all kinds of dirty work for you."

Marjorie's face, ghoulish in the sub-light, crumpled momentarily and her shoulders rounded.

Alice reached down and grabbed *Beach* in one hand. The action seemed to jolt Marjorie back into life and she stepped backwards into the kitchen.

"Right, talking over. Last chance, pretty girl. Put the painting down."

"No."

"Okay, you asked for it."

Alice was holding Marjorie's stony eyes, so she did not see the older woman pull a hand out of her pocket. It was not until Marjorie held her arm out in front of her, that Alice saw the gun. Pointing straight at her.

"Put the painting down, Alice," she said, with a voice like ice.

Alice's world paused, like a movie stuck on a frame. Then, as if someone had thrown a switch and started the movie again, she knew what to do.

"Hand it over!" shouted Marjorie.

"You want *Beach*? Okay, here it is."

Alice flung the painting at Marjorie. It clipped the unsuspecting woman on her shoulder, flew on and fell to the kitchen floor. Marjorie yelped and dropped the gun, sending it across the floor and out of sight. She staggered back, clutching her shoulder. She trod on the painting, tottered over to one side and into a wooden chair. She tumbled down, reaching out with one hand to cushion her fall.

Alice darted out of the pantry and reached for the gun, her fingers catching the cold metal. But Marjorie was quicker. Alice felt Marjorie's hand on her back, forcing her down on her knees. The gun slid out of reach.

Moving quickly for a large woman, Marjorie bent down and snatched the weapon.

Alice grabbed her calf, receiving a couple of heavy blows to her shoulder in return. Marjorie fell to the ground again and kicked out at Alice, sending her onto her back. The gun was near. Alice snatched at it, but found only air. She snatched again, but Marjorie scrambled over her and got there first. She grabbed the gun and stood over the prostrate Alice.

"This time it really is goodbye, pretty girl."

The crack of gunshot was the last sound Alice heard, before she plunged down into a well of darkness.

Chapter 46

"Alice," said a voice tinged with panic. "Alice. Wake up."

In the floaty world between sleep and wakefulness, Alice struggled to place the familiar voice. Until a sharp pain bolted through her head, bringing her back to reality. The pain seeped across her temples and down the right side of her face.

"Alice, can you hear me?" said the soft Irish voice.

There was no mistaking it this time. She prised her eyes open.

"Joe!"

Alice lifted a hand towards him, but a searing pain from her right shoulder prevented her moving any further.

"Crapola, that hurts!" Warm liquid trickled down her arm.

"It will hurt alright, you've been shot." Joe placed Alice's hand on her stomach. "Hold still a minute, while I fetch something to stop the bleeding."

She lifted her hand to her face, and it came back smeared in blood. She tried to lift her head, but it was too painful.

"What happened? How did you get here?"

"I came back early from my job, worried that I'd left you by yourself. I got to *Daisy Dawn* in time to see you take off in Roddy's dinghy. Livvie said you were on your way to rob someone, so I followed you." He pressed a tea towel into her shoulder. "I missed your conversation with Marjorie, but as she was pointing a gun at you, I guess you said something to hack her off."

Alice gritted her teeth and snorted a half-laugh.

"Fortunately, she didn't hear me come in, so I gave her a good whack with a saucepan. She still pulled the trigger, but the bullet just grazed your shoulder. It looks fairly superficial – you should be fine."

"Where is Marjorie now?"

"Over there, keeping the furniture company."

Marjorie was sitting on the floor. Her hands were tied behind her back and around a table leg, feet bound together.

"You won't get away with this, Alice Haydon. I have powerful friends."

"Yada, yada, Marjorie."

Alice looked back at Joe, watching as he concentrated on the job in hand.

The only time she literally needed someone to save her life, and who was there?

"Joe."

He ran a finger down her nose and Alice could not stop the tears rolling over her cheeks.

Chapter 47

Alice lay back on the sun lounger, watching her friends. Roddy stood at *Daisy*'s side, his floppy straw hat low over his face. Joe was on the director's chair, finishing off a bacon sandwich fresh from The Coffee Pot. Livvie poured coffee and handed round steaming mugs.

A rowing crew powered along the river, sending the swan family scurrying for shelter. Alice, one arm in a sling, rubbed her other shoulder, while contemplating a new collection of bruises on her leg.

"Good morning."

Nathan Salisbury breezed over the gangway and onto the deck. He crouched down beside Alice and squeezed her arm. "I'm glad to see you're up and in pretty good shape, all things considered."

"If Joe hadn't arrived when he did. Well …"

Nathan shot Joe a guarded look.

"He did arrive, lucky for you – and that's all you need to remember."

Roddy ambled over to Alice's side and rested a hand on top of the lounger.

"Well, DI Salisbury, we are waiting with bated breath. Has she confessed?"

"Mrs Cavendish will have difficulty maintaining her innocence with the evidence we have against her. Thanks to you, Alice, and your ingenuity in following the trail to her home."

"Well," said Roddy. "Let's hear it Haydon, how did you find out that Marjorie was stealing from the council's art collection?"

Alice looked at their expectant faces and a rush of adrenaline coursed through her body. For what seemed like the first time ever, she held the floor.

"Well, it was looking for *Beach* that started it. I came across Edward Hacker and that led me to Carrie Developments and the Dunn Road shopping development. I wanted to know who was behind the organisation, especially when I realised that it may have had something to do with Jason Marley's death. As I followed the leads, Edward Hacker's name and company kept coming up. I thought that one of his clients had to be behind it, so I dug deeper."

"By downloading Hacker's files and impersonating him," said Nathan. "Which, given your valuable contribution to our investigation, I suppose I can forget."

"Then what?" prompted Livvie.

"I saw Marjorie in one of Martin Bradman's photos. She had been a councillor years ago. So, I went back over the documents Freddie Garfield gave me and found that Marjorie had chaired the council's business committee. She knew the Dunn Road site had been identified for the shopping centre, so I guessed she must have she set up Carrie Developments and bought the land. Then she leased it back to the council at an exorbitant rate."

"And when she left the council, Julian de Havilland did her dirty work for her?" said Roddy.

"Yes, ultimately, but under duress from Marjorie's partner in crime – Vivien Taylor, who chaired the same business committee on which Marjorie and Julian served. Vivien and Marjorie already knew each other and I can't imagine Vivien took much persuading to join Carrie Developments as a shadow director."

The sun was dazzling from directly overhead and Alice's head started to ache. She reached under the lounger for a baseball cap.

"Helen Yardley said it was when Julian was given oversight of the Dunn Road project that he was set up by Marjorie and Vivien. It was Vivien who falsely recorded George Shaker's election donation and tipped off the Electoral Commission. Julian was under the two women's control and he felt he couldn't do anything other than follow their instructions."

"I didn't think I'd ever say poor Julian, but poor Julian…" Livvie said.

"After that, it was all too easy for the Cavendish and Taylor partnership."

"But how did Marjorie know you were on to her?"

"When Jason Marley confronted her, she knew her involvement with Carrie Developments was no longer a secret. Edward Hacker told her I had been to his office and she put two and two together. So she had David Victor keep an eye on me."

"That's who was following you around?" said Joe.

"No, he got his ex-army pal, the red-haired man I saw a couple of times, to follow me and keep Victor informed about what I was doing."

"So, Victor knew that you were driving back from Narebridge on your own and he waited for you so that—"

"So that he could take a shot," Alice continued. "But he was only aiming to scare me. Or at least that's what Marjorie told me."

"And the companies getting council contracts were also owned by Marjorie and Vivien, which is why I could never get any of the work," said Livvie.

"We're looking into the council's tender processes," said Nathan. "So, we would like a statement from you, Miss Manners. And you too," he said to Alice. "We wouldn't have got to Mrs Cavendish so quickly without you. But the next time you decide to confront an armed criminal on your own, Alice, please tell me first." He smiled and touched his forehead with his index finger. "I have to go, but I'll see you soon."

Alice watched him make his way across the gangway. If she had told him about her suspicions sooner, she might not have been shot. But then, she wouldn't have been saved by Joe …

Joe crossed the deck. "The Augustus John drawing wasn't there, was it?" he said. "What are you going to do about that?"

Alice rubbed his arm. "Don't worry, I'm not going to do anything. I'll leave that to Nathan and his art specialist."

"But you won't have it for your exhibition."

"But you will have a new Roddy Rafferty work."

"Roddy, you'll finish your painting for us?"

"If it's shown beside Elisabeth's *Beach,* I will. We always promised ourselves we'd do a joint exhibition, but we never did."

"That's a lovely idea, Roddy. Consider it done."

Alice and Roddy clinked glasses of Rioja in *Daisy*'s cabin and toasted the incident board.

"You have to admit, Roddy, it did its job."

"It certainly did and you, dear girl, pulled it off. I'm very proud of you." Roddy put his glass on the coffee table. "And what about *Beach*? What will happen to it now?"

"It will go on display as part of the centenary exhibition and then it'll go back to the town hall. It's a beautiful painting, Roddy. Elisabeth was a very talented artist."

"She was indeed. She—" Roddy choked as tears flowed down his cheeks.

Alice handed him a tissue. He wiped his eyes and looked out of the window. When he turned back, the tears were still streaming, but he let them come.

"Elisabeth and her work are the only things that can make me cry." He grinned through the tears. "But I'm over the moon about seeing one of her paintings again."

Alice's heart purred. "I'm going to get you that painting, Roddy, and then you'll have something of Elisabeth's. I'll ask Julian de Havilland to give it to you. That's if you want it."

"I would love nothing more. Do you really think Julian will let it go?"

"Well, we got Marjorie Cavendish off his back, so I think he owes us, don't you?"

Chapter 48

On a warm September evening, Gregory's House was heaving. The building buzzed: visitors, lenders, critics and funders mingling amongst the exhibits.

A bashful Nicholas Waites, flanked by his children, stood beside his late wife's figurines, describing the story behind their creation. When Duncan Jones had finally seen them, he had been moved by the clay children and the little dog with its red and yellow ball, and had agreed to their inclusion in the show.

Alice found Roddy in the downstairs gallery, at the centre of an enthralled crowd, regaling them with Mallorcan tales of *Beach,* wine and a talented artist called Elisabeth Moreno. He was wearing the borrowed cream linen suit he had worn for Vivien Taylor's unveiling party; though this time the shirt struggled to contain his puffed chest.

Duncan Jones was also having difficulty containing his excitement, downing a glass of champagne in just a few gulps.

"*Beach* is such a lovely piece, thank goodness it's finally on the wall of a public art gallery where it belongs."

"Well, isn't it a good job that someone pursued it and didn't just take a painting of pink peonies instead?"

Alice put a hand on her hip and Duncan had the decency to looked chagrined.

"Yes, it is thanks to you that it's here at all. Even though you did disobey all my instructions. Which I will ignore. This time. By the way, that early Rafferty is a revelation. And to think we had it right here in our own basement and didn't know it."

"Duncan, it never occurred to me that Nicholas Waites would lend anything other than an average landscape, so I didn't even bother unwrapping it. Though he did tell me his wife had bought it in Mallorca and had exquisite taste, so I guess I should have picked up on that clue!"

"Now that Jenna's left for Hong Kong to join her husband, you are going to stay on as senior curator, aren't you Alice? Permanently, I mean."

"I'll think about it."

Alice ambled up the stairs, soaking up compliments on the exhibition. She made her way to the Ann Gregory room and her favourite piece of the show. The Frida Kahlo was a burst of joy. As she looked at it, she fell in love with it all over again.

"Do you see anything you fancy?"

Walker Hampton leaned against the wall, chocolate eyes twinkling. He was wearing a clean shirt, ironed too, teamed with navy chinos and proper shoes.

"Déjà vu. Thank you for sending this, Walker. It's a beautiful piece, I love it to bits."

"I hoped so, that's why I picked it out for you."

"I'm glad you're here for the opening, I wasn't sure you'd make it."

"Well, the wife's in prison and there was nothing on TV, so I thought I'd mozzie over and see what was going on."

Walker rubbed his chin and grinned. Alice searched his face and for the first time, noticed frost in his eyes.

"It took me a while," she said, "to work out that Marjorie and Vivien were in that racket together. I have to ask, Walker. The paintings they stole from the council's collection – are any of them at your house?"

"If only. Anything would be better than Vivien's appalling assortment of so-called artworks."

"It seems that Marjorie was the brains behind the outfit, the art thefts as well as Carrie Developments, so at least Vivien didn't plan any of their schemes."

"Dear Vivien is a doer, not a thinker. She would never have come up with such an ingenious plan on her own."

"And it was ingenious. Why would anyone suspect a pair of genteel ladies, diligently devoting themselves to public service? If it hadn't been for Jason Marley's death, I'm not sure I would have found them out either."

"Full marks for tenacity. If it had been me, I would have been put off after being shot the first time. How is the wound by the way?"

Alice rubbed her shoulder. "It's healed perfectly, thanks." She moved toward him. "The police have drawn a blank with your Augustus John drawing, Walker. I'm so sorry. It's such a beautiful piece. I would love to see it again."

"And one day you will – if you happen to be passing my bedroom." He winked, his face suddenly alive, and he beamed a very broad grin indeed.

"Walker, you didn't? Oh, you devil!" Walker stepped away and Alice watched him as he faded into the crowd, still smiling.

Alice wandered through the gallery, into the garden and down to the river's edge. The last of the sun's rays sparkled on the surface and melted into the dark water beneath. Coloured beams from fairy lights strung from branch to branch, danced across the river, broken by the swan family as it glided along. Summer was fading and balmy evenings would surely become fewer as the autumn chill set in. In the background, happy chatter from the guests rose and fell in time with the string quartet.

"What are you doing out here by yourself? I thought you'd be inside lapping up the compliments." Joe draped his arm across her shoulder. "Not still thinking about it all are you?"

"Not so much, but yes. I don't know how Vivien and Marjorie came up with such devious schemes to get rich at everyone else's expense."

"When it comes to enriching themselves, some people never run out of ideas."

"But I don't understand how they had the nerve. Lying and cheating so coolly."

"Some people get themselves into positions of power just to take advantage of them. Unfortunately, people around them sometimes half-know what's happening, but are afraid to say anything. So they just carry on getting away with it."

She clinched her hands over his arm.

"And what about you? Are you going to get power crazy now that you've made senior curator?"

"You'd better believe it!"

Alice turned and circled her arms around Joe's waist. He held her tight and she leant into him.

It occurred to Alice, for the first time, how much Joe had been through too.

She untangled herself and reached into her dress pocket for the postcard of Augustus John's girl. She whispered her thanks to the girl one last time, then flung the postcard into the river.

"What are you doing?" Joe rushed to the edge, peering into the water. "I'll fetch something to fish it out."

"Leave it, I don't need it anymore. I kept it because it was the only thing I had of my dad's and I thought, somehow, it would bring him back to me. But I've accepted that he's gone forever. The postcard is just a painful reminder that he's not here for me. I wonder, looking back, whether he ever really was … Anyway, now it's time to let him go."

She looked into Joe's eyes. "Thank you, Joe."

"What for?"

"For being you and for being here."

Joe eyes sparkled, Alice flung her arms around his neck and kissed him.

"Joe?"

"Yes, Alice."

"If the offer to move in with you is still open, I'd like to take it up please. I'd love to live with you. Hundred percent."

"Well, seeing as you ask so nicely, I would love to live with you, too."

"I promise to be tidy and I'll try to cook dinner sometimes. I know I'm a terrible cook, but you can teach me a few things."

Joe threw back his head and laughed. He hugged Alice closer.

"Good, because that was my plan!"

And she pushed him in the river.

IF YOU LIKED PAINT a Murder, you can follow Alice Haydon's adventures in the 2nd book of the series. *Sculpt a Murder* is coming soon.

If you enjoyed the book, please consider writing a review and let other cozy mystery fans know what you thought about the book. Review on Amazon at: www.amazon.co.uk

Follow Lily Ashton at www.lilyashton.com